Maybe One Day

Ashlyn Harmon

Moonwake Books, LLC

Published by Moonwake Books, LLC

Book Cover by Yummy Book Covers

Edited by Earley Editing, LLC

To anyone who feels like they're chasing an impossible dream.
I see you. Keep going. You've got this.

This book contains many discussions about mental health and anxiety. These discussions handle topics like feelings of inadequacy, self-image, and overall anxiety.

Glossary

Here is a quick reference guide for all the swimming terminology used within this book.

- **Event:** A race of any given distance. (i.e. the 200 meter freestyle, the 200 meter individual medley, etc.)

- **Heat:** The preliminary sessions in the morning of a meet are composed of heats. When there are too many swimmers to compete in an event at the same time, it's broken into heats based on seed times posted by each swimmer.

- **Heat Sheets:** A listing of every swimmers seed times in the events at a meet. These times are submitted by coaches weeks in advance and are used at the meet to tell spectators what the order of events is, who is competing, and gives a general timeframe for the session.

- **Individual Medley (IM):** All four strokes together in one race. Order is butterfly, backstroke, breaststroke, freestyle. Equal distance must be swam in each stroke.

- **Olympic Trials:** A sanctioned long course meet held the year of the Olympic games to determine which swimmers will represent the USA on the team. A total of 52 athletes are named to the team, 26 men and 26 women.

- **Psych Sheets:** A list released prior to the start of the meet, ranking each athlete entered in each event by their seed times.

- **Seed time:** The time a swimmer uses for entrance to a meet. It's what determines their lane and heat in each particular event.

- **Underwaters:** Unequipped swimming beneath the surface of the water, typically seen after the swimmer leaves the blocks and after they push off the wall at turns.

Chapter 1

THEN

June 2021
Omaha, NE

I was about to get my heart broken.

Sliding out of the driver's seat of my Jeep, I squinted up at the Riverview Convention Center, the sun reflecting off the glass facing. All around me, people were clamoring toward the entrance, eager for the week-long monumental meet to get underway. Over the next several days, the stakes would be raised as hundreds of athletes competed for the fifty-two spots available on the 2021 Olympic Swim Team.

This wasn't the first time I'd stood in this parking lot for this meet, but it was different this time around. For one thing, this was the last meet *Adair Swim* would be attending. After this, our blog was hanging up its metaphorical goggles while my best friend and I moved on to whatever came next in life. For another, Bryce Clark was somewhere in there, and he was going to break my heart.

This building held so many amazing memories for me; it was almost blasphemous to tarnish it with what was to come. But I couldn't do this anymore.

I couldn't keep pretending we can have more, be more.

To my right, my passenger door closed with a thud as Mia Sheridan stared up at the building. The wind whipped strands of her dark hair across her pale cheeks, her lips set in a grim frown.

The sport of swimming formed our friendship. It fueled our dreams and challenged us to do something crazy. Since 2012, we had been semi-successfully running the blog, meeting, and interviewing Olympians, and doing the one thing we never really thought we could do. The goodbye we were staring down was as bittersweet as we always knew it would be. This couldn't last forever.

Mia turned to meet my gaze, a small smile tugging at the corners of her lips. "Ready to do this, Josie?"

My answer was a resounding "I don't know, but probably not" as I wrung my hands together. But I couldn't say that, could I? "I'm as ready as I ever will be."

Seeming to accept my non-answer, Mia didn't say anything else until we crossed the parking lot to follow the crowd to the entrance that was decked in larger-than-life photos of some of the most well-known athletes. I couldn't stop myself from scanning the portraits for Bryce. Even from where we stood waiting to cross the street, I found his grinning face plastered over one of the many doors security wasn't ushering people through.

I couldn't look away.

"We're not here in any official media capacity," Mia reminded me, tone low. "We get to decide who we talk to."

If only it were that easy. If only I could flip a switch and stop caring about him, ignoring his presence when the world constantly tried to remind me we were both here. If I could do that, it never would have gotten this far. I wouldn't be an anxious mess, anticipating the moment I'd have to face the only man who's ever had the potential to ruin me.

"Look, Jos, you're in control here," Mia continued. "The two of you have barely spoken in the last year and, with the pandemic, it's been even longer since you've seen one another. You can walk away from this."

I glanced over at her, frowning. "You know I can't. I've tried many times. At least, if I talk to him, I might have a shot at getting answers and some closure."

She didn't look at all convinced as the light changed, and we started crossing. "I know, but I also know the hold this guy has on you. The last thing I want is for you to jump back into bed with him the second he flashes you his half-smile that seems to be your Achilles heel."

I wanted to pretend I wasn't that easy, but we both knew it would be a lie. To me, it always felt like that look was reserved for me, convincing me there was something more between us.

Whatever this was between us had been going on for over five years and, no matter how many times I swore it wouldn't happen again, we always came back together. We didn't see each other often, but when we did, a magnetic current seemed to draw us together until we were stumbling through the door of a hotel room, unable to part from one another for even a breath.

From the very first moment I laid eyes on him, it was inevitable.

Yet, for him, our connection was never anything real. Not in the same way it was real for me.

The deafening silence that had settled between us in the last year of uncertainty was undeniable proof. The minute he didn't know when—or even if—he'd see me again, he had no reason to reach out.

Knowing all that, I should be able to take Mia's advice. I should be able to take my broken heart and go, but I couldn't.

As Mia and I got in line to go through security, I frowned at her. "I need to hear it from him. I need him to tell me it's over, whatever it was. That there's nothing to salvage, and I've been ridiculous this whole time."

She looked at me with pure sympathy, handing her bag over to a security guard. I didn't get what the point of a clear bag was if they still looked at everything inside. "He has told you, several times. You knew what this whole thing was. I warned you to be careful. He was up front with you from the beginning."

A guard waved her through before I had the chance to respond. Then it was my turn to hand over my bag and I was forced to mull over what she had said. From the moment we met, Bryce had told me he wasn't in the market for a serious relationship. He was focused on his career, but when a friends-with-benefits situation fell into my lap, I jumped at the chance to have him any way I could. A naïve part of me hoped he'd change his mind along the way, so I ignored the warnings from Mia and everyone else around me. Including Bryce himself.

Once I was waved through, I joined Mia again. "I know I let this get away from me, and I know how it makes me look, but things happened between us in the middle. Things you don't know about."

"This has nothing to do with how you look, Josie. This has everything to do with the fact Bryce-fucking-Clark is about to break my best friend's heart and I'm just supposed to stand by and watch it happen."

I stared at her, thinking back to a conversation the two of us had years ago, back when Bryce and I barely knew one another.

"Mia, you and I both know this man was always going to break my heart. It's been breaking since the moment I decided to sleep with him—probably even longer."

Mia's pale green eyes flashed with anger. "And that is why I think you should avoid him! Don't give him the chance to hurt you more than he already has."

I met her gaze, hoping the weird communication we shared whenever we looked at each other was working today. I needed her to understand what I couldn't say out loud, especially not here, where I can already smell the chlorine seeping into every crack and crevice of this building. "And you know I can't do that."

The tension in her shoulders dropped, and she nodded. "I do, but I'm not letting you do this alone. I don't care if he is an Olympian. I'll still kick him in the balls if I need to."

Laughing, I nodded in agreement as I took a second to enjoy the mental image that evoked. It was no secret among our small group of friends that Bryce was a little afraid of Mia, which was exactly how she wanted it to be. She was prickly, but she didn't give a shit about what people thought of her, and she was fiercely protective of the people she loved. Getting on her bad side was a mistake, and my impending heartbreak at his hands has had Bryce toeing that line since the day we met.

"All right," Mia declared, clearly ready for a change in topic. "We have a couple of minutes before we should head up and find our seats for prelims. Should we stop at the merchandise booths and take a quick look around?"

Grateful for the distraction, I dropped my hands from their twisting.

There was already a slight chill in the air—a reminder that no one could ever be prepared for what the indoor temperature would be like at one of these meets.

"Yeah, I might need to get a pullover."

"Of course." Mia laughed, linking her arm through mine to lead me away from the mass of people. "You wouldn't be you if you didn't."

Grinning, I stumbled at her excitement before falling into step with her. It was the first genuine grin I'd had all morning, and it was there solely because I knew I'd be okay if I had Mia by my side.

⁓ ⁓

As we took our seats poolside, the smell of chlorine became over-powering. Coaches and athletes crowded the deck below, the pool already packed with athletes warming up. The tension was palpable as I scanned the faces of nervous swimmers in search of someone I knew. While the seats were less crowded during the morning session, there was still quite a bit to take in.

The atmosphere of surrounding a morning session differs com-pletely from the one that will come later tonight. Instead of loud voices filling packed seats, the sparsely occupied arena is humming with the din of droning voices, parents and loved ones waiting to watch their athlete compete. Jittery parents with arms crossed stand at the barricades, biting nails as their eyes follow their children as they warm up. Calm, collected coaches walk along the length of the pool, stopwatches in hand and whistles around their necks.

Warmups are the easy part. The part that's controllable, and every single person here is in their element.

Every single person on that deck had a dream they were chasing. Every single person in the stands had someone they were cheering on. The idea exhilarated me, but today it made me feel sick to my stomach.

Despite the uncertainty of where I stood with Bryce, I wanted to see him get a gold medal. I wanted to see him head to Tokyo for his second games. I also had a sinking feeling this would be his last shot. At twenty-six, he was getting a little old to be chasing a gold medal. It wasn't impossible, not by a longshot, but this was typically when everyone waited for the inevitable retirement announcement.

"Honestly, these seats are a lot better than I thought they'd be," Mia commented. She was also rapidly scanning the deck. "I hate picking seats without knowing what the setup will be."

"They're great," I agreed. "We should have no problem seeing everything."

Our seats were a couple of rows back from the deck, putting us in clear view of anyone who knew us. Which was more intentional when I picked the seats over two years ago. Now it just made anxiety crawl up my throat, hoping nothing would happen with the two of us in such a public area.

"Speaking of seeing everything," Mia said with a laugh, standing from her seat. "Carter, hey!"

I looked up to find Bryce's best friend, Carter Abrams, coming toward us, and stood to greet him as well. Clearly, he hadn't gotten into the pool yet, as he wore a pair of gray sweats low on his hips, a black T-shirt, and a baseball cap over his messy brown hair. The grin on his face brightened as he stepped around the barricade to come hug us.

"Hey, guys," he greeted, separating from Mia before he pulled me into a tight hug.

I savored the hug from Carter, who'd become a good friend. I knew if things with Bryce went the way I expected them to, I'd lose him, too. They'd been best friends their whole lives, only separating after college. When it came down to it, I knew whose side Carter would choose, but I didn't fault him for it.

"I didn't expect to see you here," he said. "I know a bunch of people relinquished their tickets when they had to push the date back."

"We thought about it when we were given the option, but decided against it. This is going to be our last meet. We wanted to make sure we could come," Mia explained. Carter's gaze drifted to me before snapping back on her. "We'd already paid for the tickets and, if I didn't feel safe traveling, Josie still lives in Omaha, so she'd use them."

Carter nodded as his blue eyes flickered in my direction again. "So, the rumor's true then? *Adair Swim* is shutting down?"

"It's time." I shrugged, allowing my gaze to wander across the pool deck.

I felt the prickling sensation of being watched. The eyes on me felt all too familiar. Finding the person they belonged to took me seconds. Bryce Clark stood across the deck, talking to his coach, but his attention kept shifting to us. He was wearing a blue brief, his cap, and goggles dangled from his hand. The smattering of tattoos he had on his chest were on full display, including the prominent Olympic rings on his right side, near his ribs. A second after I noticed him, his gray eyes met mine across the pool and I froze.

The stupid, hopelessly romantic part of me hoped our normal routine would follow. He'd give me that half-smile and I would know, at least in some capacity, that we were okay.

That didn't happen, though. He looked at me like I was a stranger. His gaze briefly met Carter's before returning to me with a blank look on his face. He held my stare for a few moments before dropping it completely, focusing back on his coach.

"What the hell was that?" Mia looked murderous. Not wanting to have this conversation here, I shrugged, but she wasn't having that. "Don't act all nonchalant, Joslyn Martin! He acted like he was looking through you, not at you."

"I—I should start warming up," Carter announced, taking a step back. "We'll catch up later in the week. Sound good?"

Mia continued to stare at me, so I gave him a small smile in confirmation. As soon as he'd gotten out of earshot, I turned to my own best friend. "Don't make a big deal out of nothing, Mia. Maybe he didn't see me?"

"Oh, please," she scoffed. "The two of you find each other like some freaky fairy tale characters or something. He knew exactly who he was looking at."

Commenting on that seemed dangerous. Commenting on that seemed like it would lead to me having to admit I was a little in love with Bryce, despite knowing it was the last thing I should have let myself do. Commenting on that seemed like an utter disaster.

"You're talking to him, right?" Mia sat back down. I followed her lead, pretending to be engrossed in the heat sheets in my lap. "Please tell me you're talking to him."

I picked at an invisible strand on my pants, avoiding her gaze. "Weren't you the one who told me I didn't have to? You said I could avoid him and let it fade naturally."

"That's not how feelings work, Josie. Now I think you deserve the chance to tell him to go to hell."

I wasn't going to tell him that. Mia would, but I could never.

But I wasn't going to seek him out. I never wanted him to think I was some obsessive woman who was desperate enough to do anything to have an Olympian on her arm. He'd made it clear where we stood. So, I didn't push. I let him take things the way he wanted them to go.

I knew that was part of the problem, but I couldn't go back and fix it. It was true what they said about hindsight.

"I'll talk to him," I promised her. "But to end things. To tell him it's over."

"Good. He doesn't deserve another piece of you."

I knew he didn't, but he already had so many pieces of me I was worried I'd never be whole again. I'd been preparing for this moment since I first met Bryce Clark, but now that it was here, I knew I could never be ready for this heartbreak.

Chapter 2

NOW

April 2023

Omaha, NE

"I might have just met your future husband, Joslyn!"

I'm not even fazed when my colleague, Sarah, approaches my desk on Monday morning. The start of the week meant new associates starting at Hunt & Sloan Consulting firm, and that meant Sarah would spend the morning scoping out the new hires to figure out who is suitable for her single friends.

This isn't the first time Sarah has approached me with a claim to have found my soulmate, nor do I think this will be the last. Nothing came from these interactions, except for one relationship that lasted a few months. Yet, I never stopped secretly hoping one of them would stick and turn into something real.

"Ah, another Prince Charming." I grin, glancing up from my computer. "All right, lay it on me. What makes this one special?"

Her grin brightens as she begins ticking each pro on her finger. "He's your age, no ring, tall—like, *really* tall—well built, and damn good-looking."

Sarah likes to list shallow things and never tell me any of the potential cons. She let me find those out on my own, usually in one awkward date in the heart of downtown Omaha.

"And what makes this one different from the last four?" While the question comes out sarcastically, I've already locked my computer and am pushing away from my desk. "Give me something to work with here."

"Because I already know the two of you have something in common—he was a swimmer!"

I bit back an annoyed sigh at the way she used the sport I love—the one that had been such a huge part of my life—as a bargaining chip to get me interested in a man neither one of us knew anything about. For years, Mia and I fought against judgmental comments that claimed we started Adair Swimming because of the attractive men and not because of our obsession with the sport. Any friendships or relationships we formed with athletes happened organically, but that didn't stop rumors from circulating.

"Maybe you guys know each other."

I roll my eyes. "You know that's not how it works, right? People who are involved in the sport don't automatically know each other."

"Well, yeah, obviously," she huffed, leading me down a long hallway. "But wouldn't it be romantic if you did? He said he swam in college and through most of his twenties."

Picture-perfect meet cutes never happen in real life, though. "Well, swimming in college narrows it down. Mia and I primarily dealt with pros and Division 1 athletes. Do you know where he went to school?"

She waves me off. "It doesn't matter. You'll meet him soon enough and you can ask."

She turns to lead me toward the sales department. Hunt & Sloan develops software programs to teach businesses how to better run their day-to-day operations, including employee satisfaction, hiring, general human resources, and budgeting. As a content editor, my job is to help make those programs sound good in written media. Though the creative in me never seems to get along with the analytical men who inhabit this side of the building.

I groan. "He's in sales, really?" We both have to know how this is going to go. "Sarah, this isn't going to work out."

"Okay, yes, most of the guys who work over here are jerks, but that doesn't mean they all are." She swipes her badge to unlock the door, holding it open for me. "You shouldn't be so jaded, Joslyn. Besides, you might know him, remember?"

Although I laugh, I know there is a small part of her that isn't quite able to wrap her mind around the fact I probably don't know him. She might not know the full context of the swimming part of my life, but the little she did know has always confused her. She fit the exact stereotype Mia and I tried to prove wrong—the sport exists outside the Olympics, and it exists outside of a few big names.

"Here comes the moment of truth." She grins at me from over her shoulder. "That's him ahead, with the dark blond hair."

Following her line of sight, I slow to a stop as I take in the man standing about a head taller than almost everyone else surrounding his desk. Though his back is turned to me, and he is dressed in a well-tailored suit that fits him perfectly, I could recognize the body of a swimmer anywhere. Tall, broad shoulders, lean frame—more annoying, there is something familiar about him.

Then he laughs at something one of the other surrounding men says and the sound is like a sucker punch to the gut. I will—for the rest of my life—know that laugh anywhere.

Bryce Clark is less than ten feet in front of me.

"Bryce," Sarah calls in a sing-song voice, oblivious to the internal crisis I am having. "I have someone I want you to meet."

At the sound of his name, he turns to face us, an easy grin etched across his handsome features. The same strong jaw, the light stubble I'm not used to seeing, and the warm blue-gray eyes I used to get lost in. His hair is the only part of him that's different; instead of messy dark blond waves, he's carefully styled it.

Still, it is like staring at the ghost of someone I never thought I'd see again. What is he doing here? Not just at my company, but in Omaha.

I don't know how, but I manage to regain my composure enough to continue toward him. As soon as I am within reach of him, though, I am hit with the faint, lingering scent of chlorine. My head is flooded with memories we'd shared over the years. After years without smelling chlorine regularly, it seems my memories will now only attribute the scent to him. Despite the countless times the smell can be linked to moments he had nothing to do with.

Funny how the brain and heart work like that.

His gray eyes move from Sarah to me, then his wide, open grin drops into a polite smile. Almost like he doesn't recognize me, but I know him well enough to know when he wears a façade. It hasn't even been a full two years since we last saw one another. He knows exactly who I am. And I am not about to let him pretend any differently.

When I allowed myself the luxury of imagining this moment, no matter how preposterous it seemed, I always thought I'd be the one to stare blankly, feigning indifference. Proving he didn't break me, and I didn't need him.

This, though, is him pretending not to be uncomfortable or bothered. I've seen this look on him more than once. But I refuse to let him steal this moment from me.

If anyone understands how long a second is, how much can happen in that amount of time, it's us. In swimming, the difference between winning a medal or going home empty-handed can come down to hundredths of a second. For ten long, awkward seconds, we stare at one another. The longer I hold his gaze, the more I can see his cocky confidence deteriorating right before my eyes. He is as unsure about how to react to my presence as I am to his.

Good. I want my existence to throw him off the same way his had done to me for years. I want his ego and confidence to sway because of me. He deserves it. Especially after he single-handedly made me question my place in a sport I loved. Bryce Clark made me feel like an outsider in a world we both shared. Now, a petty part of me is ready to give him the same experience in his new one.

Sarah is frowning beside me, looking between us like she's trying to figure out what's happening. "I feel like I'm missing something here, Joslyn."

Bryce arches a brow at the use of my full name.

When I realize he isn't going to be the one to break the silence, I take another tenth of a second to gather what little bit of fuck-you-for-hurting-me confidence I have left and offer a tight smile. "Turns out, Bryce and I do know one another."

Not sensing the growing tension between us, her eyes grow comically wide. "Oh, my god! That's amazing."

"Don't get too excited," I advise, giving our audience a pointed look.

Realizing they've been caught listening in, everyone scatters back to their desks, immediately beginning to act busy, a sure sign they are still listening. Meanwhile, Bryce remains quiet.

Sarah's practically bouncing on her heels beside me as she focuses on my ex . . . Well, on Bryce. "Why didn't you tell me you knew Joslyn?"

Having the question directed at him seems to snap him out of his daze. He gives a shrug, eyes drifting back to me. "You never told me her last name. Besides, she's always been Josie to me."

I cross my arms over my chest. "Ah, so you do remember me. I use my full name at work."

His smile is steady. "Gotcha. It's good to see you, Josie."

The sincerity radiating in his eyes softens my sharp edges ever so slightly. As much as it pains me to admit it, I missed him more than I should've. "Yeah, you too."

Sarah's gaze bounces between us like she's watching an intense tennis match. "You more than just know one another. I'm sensing some serious history here."

God, if she only knew the half of it.

"We know one another through swimming," Bryce explains. His gaze keeps shifting back to me, though. Like he can't believe I'm standing here, and he's worried I'll disappear if he looks away for too long. "We became friends. Good friends, actually."

Friends. The word brings a flood of memories—him cornering me against a wall, the smell of chlorine encompassing me before he captures my lips with his; the two of us laughing as the rising sun eases through a gap in the curtains in the hotel room we'd rented out in downtown Indianapolis; and the look in his eyes the last time we saw each other, when he so perfectly broke my heart. "Friends" doesn't even begin to cover what transpired between us. The word doesn't do it justice and, more than anything else, it enrages me.

"Were we? Because I'm not sure that's the term I'd use to describe whatever happened between us. You made it clear we weren't friends. We weren't anything at all."

Bryce ducks his head, a faint blush coating his cheeks as he becomes fascinated by his shoes. "I probably deserve that."

"Probably?"

The emphasis I put on that one word earns the attention of everyone around us again. No one is pretending to be engrossed in work anymore. They have a reason to pay attention now. I'm making a scene. And I'm suddenly very aware of the audience we have as I start losing the battle against the angry tears stinging the corners of my eyes.

Taking a deep, shaky breath, I plaster on the fakest smile I can muster. Since things between Bryce and me ended, I've come to master pretending everything is okay. "Look, I have a meeting I need to finish preparing for. Bryce, it was lovely to see you again. Best of luck with your journey here at Hunt & Sloan. Hopefully, you can stay out of my way, and we can go another couple of years without speaking."

"Josie, come on," he pleads, eyes darting to the people surrounding us.

I nod, biting the inside of my cheek. Of course, he's trying to build a reputation here. Reliving the past doesn't fit into that. Maybe that's always come before me.

"Please don't be like that," he finally mutters. "We should talk about what happened."

My smile stays locked in place. "No, I don't think so. I tried talking to you about this so many times, but you wrote me off. Now it's my chance to return the favor."

I turn on my heel, walking away before he has the chance to say anything. As I start back toward my desk, I'm determined not to look back. I'm the one walking away this time, and I'm tired of looking back.

I can hear Sarah behind me, trying to catch up after apologizing on my behalf, but I'm not slowing down. Not until I know I'm out of his line of sight.

"Joslyn." Sarah spoke as soon as she's close enough to grasp my arm, pulling me to a stop. When I turn to face her, her worry is evident. "What was that back there? He watched you leave like you'd kicked his puppy."

I sigh, shaking my head to clear the thoughts muddled with pain and anger. "Look, Sarah, I don't want to talk about it. I appreciate you trying to help me find someone, but after this, I need you to back off a bit."

She drops my arm. "I didn't know that was going to happen, Joslyn!"

"I know," I assure her quickly, not wanting her to think this was her fault. "That back there was a whole mess of heartbreak and feelings I'm not ready to relive right now. Or ever. I need some space right now."

She looks skeptical, but relents. "Okay. If I'd known how it'd go, I wouldn't have introduced you."

"It's better I found out this way." The idea of randomly bumping into him in the hall or elevator makes my heart seize.

"You know, you might have to work with him occasionally, right? There's overlap between your departments."

"I'll face that when it comes. In the meantime, I just want us to stay on our own sides and pretend the other doesn't exist."

Her brow arches. "And do you think you can do it?"

I know I can't, but I'm not about to tell her that. I know there's no way to stop myself from thinking of him, or feeling on edge with him close by, but I can't let his presence distract me. Is this my dream job? Not by a long shot. But it is far from a bad career, and the money is good. It's where I need to be right now. "It won't be a problem, but I do need to prep for my meeting."

I can tell she isn't convinced, but she doesn't push the subject further. "Okay, I'll let you get back to work. We'll do lunch later this week, right?"

Lunch is her way of fishing for information about what happened between Bryce and me, but I'm not about to give it to her. That story is between a group of people who meant everything to me. While Sarah's the person I'm closest to at work, we aren't friends outside of this building. After I lost Bryce and gave up the blog, everyone except Mia seemed to follow. So now I kept my circle small.

"Sure," I promise her. "Have a good day, Sarah."

With nothing left to say, the two of us part with a quick wave. As I move through the winding corridors, taking the long way back to my desk, I pull my phone out and dial Mia's number. Since she's also likely at work, I get sent to voicemail.

"Hey," I say, leaning back against a wall as I heard the familiar beep. "Call me when you get off tonight. Bryce Clark just came waltzing back into my life. To answer your unasked question—no, I'm not okay."

Chapter 3

THen

June 2021
Omaha, NE

I found it nearly impossible to focus on the rest of the morning session. No matter how hard I fought against it, my mind kept drifting back to him. I began to prepare for our inevitable conversation mentally and emotionally. There were so many ways it could go.

And Bryce had already looked right through me.

I knew it was the furthest thing from a healthy coping mechanism. Preparing for the worst wasn't something I could control, but it gave me a false confidence that I could be prepared for anything. And if I was prepared for anything, maybe it wouldn't hurt as bad.

Before I knew it, prelims were over, and the arena was emptying around us. Neither Mia nor I had spoken much during the morning session, and that remained true as we gathered our stuff and followed the crowd out.

Once we'd been swallowed up by the crowd, Mia broke the silence. "You seem to be lost in your own little world. Do you even know how he swam this morning? Or do you—"

"He came in second in his heat, has the third fastest time going into finals tonight," I rattled off. Everything else was a little hazy, but

I knew that much. "He'll hate his time, I'm sure, but it was a solid swim, and he has more in the tank for tonight."

"I'm impressed. I'm not sure I would have been able to focus much on anything. Especially with him and how he's acting."

"I did the best I could." I brushed her comment off like it was nothing, but my chest tightened. "I'm sure I'll be able to focus on the whole meet once I've talked to him."

"Hey, you don't have to explain anything to me, or make any sort of promises, Jos. You have every right to be distracted. As your best friend, though, I want to know what the plan of action is. Would you rather talk to him the first chance you get or later in the week?"

I frowned as we stepped off the escalator, heading toward the main lobby. "Honestly, I don't know. I feel like I should wait. I'm not worried about his placement, but it's not a sure thing he'll make the team tonight. This is his signature event, Mia. I shouldn't be distracting him with something like this."

For most of Bryce's events, the only person guaranteed a spot on the team was the first place finisher. If there were enough spots on the team open at the end, the second place finisher would be added to the roster, but it wasn't always promised. Especially this early into the meet.

"No, Jos." Mia frowned, shaking her head. "You're protecting him and sacrificing your own peace of mind to do so. Which is not okay. I understand how conflicted you feel, because I want to see all our friends do well, including him, but you can't put yourself through hell to keep him in the right headspace."

I let out a frustrated sigh. "I don't want to be the reason he doesn't make the team."

"Whether he makes the team is not on you," she stressed. "Bryce is a grown adult. If he didn't want to have a confrontation with you here, then he should have answered your texts or calls, or reached out on his own. He knows you live here and that you'd likely be here. If he doesn't make the team after you talk to him, the only person he can blame is himself."

The tightness in my chest worsened as we moved into the crowded lobby. All around us, people were either trying to get to the exit, to the merchandise area, or lingering around the athlete's entrance to see who came wandering out.

"What am I supposed to do, then?" I asked Mia. "Do you want me to text him, demand I meet him before finals tonight?"

Grabbing my arm, Mia pulled me off to the side so we could stop long enough to talk. My back was to the hustle and bustle of the crowd, making me focus solely on her. "Of course not. All I'm saying is you should take whatever opportunity you get to talk to him."

She made a good point. Why was I driving myself crazy over a man who hadn't respected me enough to reply to a damn text message in the last two years? I had given so much of myself to him, and I deserved to take some of it back. To be the one in control of this whole mess for once.

Mia inhaled sharply, brown eyes staring at something over my head. "Looks like your opportunity has arrived," she stated before I could turn to see what she was looking at.

My blood ran cold, but I turned toward the athlete's entrance, my eyes locking on a familiar figure standing just inside the door, talking to a swimmer I didn't recognize. Back in his gray sweatpants and T-shirt, Bryce was on his way out.

My gaze glanced around at the people still lingering around, either waiting for loved ones or for a chance to see their favorite swimmer. The lobby was more public than I wanted, but if he made the choice to not reply to my texts, this was the only opportunity I had. Besides, a part of me wanted to catch him off guard a little bit. I didn't want to give him time to plan whatever statement he wanted to give, like our conversation was an interview.

My gut was telling me it was now or never.

"Are you seizing the moment, Josie?"

I glanced back at my best friend, my heart already punching against my chest as the adrenaline kicked in. Swallowing against the lump forming in my throat, I nodded.

Mia gave my arm an encouraging squeeze. "If you need me, I'll be right here."

Unable to find my voice, I nodded again, and she released my arm. Suddenly feeling unstable on my own feet, I focused all my attention on making my way to the barrier they had set up to offer some protection for the athletes. Resting my hand against the cool metal was grounding, and I was able to take some deep breaths.

I waited and watched as Bryce finished his conversation, standing in a spot that ensured I'd be the first thing he saw when he went to leave. A couple of kids were lingering further down the barricade, giving me strange looks. I glanced back at Mia, who offered me another reassuring smile. When I looked back, Bryce was walking toward me.

I swallowed against the lump in my throat. Here we go.

Three very distinct emotions flashed through his eyes—delight, surprise, and uncertainty—before his expression morphed into indifference. It was the same look he used when talking to media personnel he wasn't fond of. I'd seen it more than a few times, but never directed at me. Until now.

When he reached me, the two of us stood frozen with only a metal barrier between us. I had never felt further away from him. If this was any other meet, he'd give me a smirk and tell me what hotel he was staying at, or we'd make plans to grab lunch with friends between sessions.

But this was not every other meet. This was the end of everything.

Somehow, I managed to be the one to find my voice first. "I think we need to talk."

He gave a casual shrug, stuffing his hands in the pockets of his sweats. He glanced at Mia over the top of my head before focusing back on me. "I heard you're not doing media this time around, but sure, we can talk."

"What does that matter?" I frowned. "I want to talk to you, not do an interview."

He blinked. "I don't know what you think we need to talk about; I heard you and Mia are done. The blog is shutting down."

Which means Carter wasn't the only one who knew. And since neither one of us had specifically told anyone, it had to come from the post Mia had put up on the blog the day she left for Omaha, talking about bidding farewell to this. He never gave me the chance to tell him myself.

"Well, yeah, Bryce. We've been at this a long time, and we've spent a lot of money on it with little payout. We can't sustain it forever. It's time to move on with our lives."

His indifference stayed in place, a façade I wasn't going to break through. Not this time. "Cool. I guess this is it, then."

My eyebrows shot up, mouth gaping open slightly. "W-what? No! It doesn't have to be, Bryce. You and I can—"

"We can what, Josie?" he snapped back. "Make this work or some bullshit like that?"

And there it was. The first cracks were splintering their way across my heart. "I don't—"

"There is no you and me, Josie," he cut me off, voice low to ensure no one else could hear him. "We fucked a few times, nothing more. That's the end of it. There's no 'us' to save or whatever you were going to say."

I had no idea how this was turning out so much worse than I imagined. I didn't expect him to make it this personal. I found myself wanting the two of us to get back on the same page. "Bryce, come on. You know, it was never that simple. We were friends."

We were much more than that. Or, at least, to me we were. But now I was doubting everything I knew.

Bryce looked amused, which hurt my splintered heart more. I never would have guessed he was capable of being this cruel. "Yeah, sure we were. Whatever you say. Have a nice life, Josie."

Dumbfounded, I blankly stared at his back as he walked along the barricade, greeting the group of kids. I stood frozen as he signed a few caps and kickboards, chatting it up with them. Like he hadn't shattered me into a million pieces and left me to gather them back up.

An arm wrapped around my shoulder as Mia pulled me to her side. I sank against her. "I always thought he had too much audacity."

Groaning, I rested my head against her shoulder, needing the comfort to keep the tears at bay. "So, you heard it all?"

"No, I was too far away to hear it. I'm great at reading lips, though. He's still right there, Jos. Say the word and I'll go punch him in his handsome face."

I fought back the urge to grin. "I can't afford to bail you out of jail."

"And I would do terribly in jail," Mia mused. "He's not worth it, but you are. You know I've got your back, right?"

"I know." I looked away from Bryce, stepping out of Mia's hold so I could turn to her. "That's the funny thing about getting your heart broken, no matter how much you've prepared yourself for it, it'll always hurt worse than you expect."

The fire was back in her eyes as her expression darkened, looking at him over my shoulder. "Josie . . ."

"I'm fine." Uncertain eyes locked on me again. "I will be fine. I did what I needed to do, and it sucked. Now, I want to get out of here and never look back."

For the millionth time during our friendship, I was reminded why she was the best of the best. She didn't offer any words of wisdom; she didn't say "I told you so" even though she had every right to. Instead, she linked her arm through mine, told me to hold my head high, and marched me straight past him. I didn't know how I managed it, but I kept my chin up and my eyes focused straight ahead.

With Mia—who flipped him off—by my side, I managed to exit Riverview Convention Center and make it all the way back to my Jeep before I needed to stop. Once we did, I turned to her, and let my tears fall.

She pulled me into the tightest hug.

For the remainder of the week, Bryce and I avoided one another like the plague. Never once speaking. As the meet went on, I couldn't help but feel more and more uncomfortable with each passing day. I didn't know what he'd told his friends, but the sympathetic look Carter gave me on the third day was a sign he'd said something. None of our mutual friends spoke to us, signaling sides had been chosen. Their reaction angered Mia more, blaming Bryce Clark for the way I lost some of my love for the sport.

Because saying goodbye to the blog didn't mean goodbye to the sport. But now it might.

He made the team in the 400 IM that night, though. He surprised everyone, including himself, by touching the wall first. As he pulled himself from the water, I could see how much he was hurting; after years of dedicating everything to this sport, the exhaustion was becoming evident.

It was the only event he made the team in.

A month later, he claimed gold in Tokyo. Despite everything, Mia and I were on a video call screaming our hearts out during his race. When he could barely walk across the deck for his interview, the medal he'd claim soon after almost didn't matter. Mia and I watched while on the phone, both of us commenting on how tired he looked. How much that one race seemed to age him. How over it all he seemed to be.

So, we waited for the retirement posts.

He didn't retire after Tokyo, though. At least not right away. He made it another year, going to the World Championships and finishing well there, too. Even so, his heart wasn't in it. The younger athletes were catching up to him and his program kept getting shorter and shorter.

About a month after the World Championship, he quietly announced his retirement on social media, stating he wasn't feeling as confident in his ability to recover from a shoulder injury he'd been fighting since 2019.

I hadn't even known he was injured.

Once he'd officially retired, he seemed to disappear. This wasn't uncommon for a lot of swimmers after they walked away from the sport, wanting the space and peace to figure out what came next. Still, it was weird how a chapter of my life seemed to end without really ending after that post.

It was the end of an era for both of us, but I was ready to move on without him.

Chapter 4

NOW

April 2023

Omaha, NE

As soon as five o'clock hits, my phone lights up with a picture of Mia.

Grinning, I accept the call, cradling the phone between my ear and shoulder as I pack my bag. "Why am I not surprised you called the second I was off?"

"Because we've been best friends for almost a decade, obviously," she replies. "I would have called and texted until you answered, but I knew you had a meeting this afternoon. Now, you've kept me in suspense for too long. Tell me everything!"

Sighing, I lean against my desk, unable to wait to have this conversation here. "He works here now."

"As in, Bryce works for your company and is just visiting the Omaha office, or he works for your company and lives in Omaha now?"

"The second one. He literally works across the building from me, same floor, and everything."

"What the fuck?" Her shock isn't at all surprising. Neither one of us could have anticipated him moving to Omaha, Nebraska.

"My sentiments exactly," I dryly reply. "Sarah insisted she had someone I needed to meet, and I got the biggest shock of my life."

Mia groans, the sound echoing in my ear. "You need to stop letting her do this, Josie. She should mind her own business. Especially after Paul, who was ready to marry you by the second date and have babies by the third. She doesn't know what you want."

"Oh, this was the last straw. I'm not letting her anywhere near my love life again. Imagine the way it felt to see him standing there, Mia."

"I'm sorry, Jos," she says. "Tell me everything, so we can figure out a plan."

Naturally, I do just that. I tell her every detail I can remember because she's the only person in my life who will understand what I went through this morning. She was there for it all, and is more than aware of what he's capable of doing to me. I recount how my heart clenched when my eyes landed on his, and about the butterflies in the pit of my stomach.

And I tell her how mad I was with myself for reacting that way because he hurt me more than anyone. It's not fair that he still has that effect on me. I admit how I thought I was over him, but seeing him again made me question that.

And Mia listens. She listens as I pour every drop of information—listens as I pick at the emotional scabs I thought had healed long ago. She doesn't interrupt or give me advice I never asked for. She keeps quiet until I run out of things to say almost twenty minutes later.

"Out of every place he could get a job with a business degree—out of every place in Omaha he could work for. How is it he ends up there?"

Obviously, this is the first question she asks. We are both interested in the way fate and coincidences play out in our lives. We'd sit on the phone for hours, wine-drunk as we do tarot readings and talk about the universe. She's the one I went to when I need to pick things apart.

"If you figure it out, let me know," I tell her. "He never struck me as the kind of guy who'd willingly move to the Midwest, especially not Nebraska."

She makes a sound in agreement. "Well, obviously, there's nothing we can do about it now. He's here. Remember, he's the outsider this time, Josie, not you. You do not have to back down to him and you don't have to let him have any sort of control. Or another piece of you. The two of you can coexist on that huge corporate campus."

Having her say what I've been telling myself all day gives me a slight boost in my confidence. I've got this. I'm in control of what comes next. "If our paths have to cross, there's no reason we shouldn't be able to handle it professionally."

"Exactly. You've got this, girl."

We chat as I finish packing my bag, catching up on our days besides the drama mine started off with. Eventually, she lets me go, and I'm left with the realization that I've been in the office a half hour later than I need to be. I was anxious to get home, take my bra off, and sink into my couch with a rom-com.

When I step onto the elevator, the tension I'd been carrying since seeing Bryce finally fades. I got through the day without too much distraction. After talking it through with Mia, I feel confident I can survive this. Closing my eyes with a sigh, I remind myself that I can be the bigger person.

"Hold the door!"

My eyes shoot open.

The politeness engrained in every midwestern person has me reaching to stop the doors before I recognize the voice. A second later, Bryce Clark slides through the doors into the world's slowest elevator. Fucking fantastic.

"Josie," he greets with a nod, leaning against the opposite wall as the doors slide closed at what felt like a glacial pace. "Did you have a good rest of your day?"

Scoffing, I pull out my phone to focus on anything but him. I merely start flipping through my apps, but I cling to the screen like my life depends on it. And maybe it does, since my heart feels like it's ready to launch out of my chest. "Are you seriously going to try to make small talk with me right now?"

When he doesn't immediately respond, I glance up to see him gripping the strap of his laptop bag as it stretches over his broad chest—No! The last thing I should be doing is focusing on his physical appearance.

He catches me, though, and his stupid half-smile ticks up the corner of his lips. Suddenly, I'm in my early twenties again and this man is a world of possibilities for me.

He shrugs, maintaining the casual look. "I don't know, I guess. You made it clear you don't want to talk to me."

"Yet, I swear I can hear your voice."

His expression dims at the harsh sarcasm in my tone, and he stands up a bit straighter.

I tilt my head but maintain eye contact. "I don't want to talk to you, Bryce. I have nothing to say to you."

Finally, a melodic chime announces our arrival at the lobby. I will the elevator doors to open faster than they'd closed, desperate to put distance between Bryce and me.

"Well, maybe I have some things I want to say to you."

My gaze darts from the doors back to him. "I think you said more than enough last time we spoke. I don't want to hear whatever it is you want to say. Not now, not ever."

He groans as the doors slide open. "Seriously, Josie?"

I fight the urge to run. Instead, I force myself to take a normal step out of the elevator and make for the front door. I bid goodnight to the security guard as I pass his desk. The moment I'm out in the Omaha sunshine, a breath of relief escapes me. The sliding doors close behind me. He hadn't followed me.

This time, I'm the one who walked away. After the last time, I'd made a promise to myself that if our paths ever crossed again, I'd be the one who walked away.

And I'm not about to let him come back into my life with that cocky arrogance, demanding I listen when he's finally ready to talk.

I'd given him many chances.

Now that I'm facing it, I know I can't look back. More than anything, I want to see if he's standing there—shocked in the same way I had been three years ago. But if I want to survive this, survive him, I have to keep. There is nothing to go back to.

Chapter 5

NOW

April 2023
Omaha, NE

I go almost a week without interacting with Bryce.

A couple times, we'd see each other across a room or be in the same elevator, but those forced exchanges remained professional, never leading to anything more. I'm grateful he's taking the hint this time. Part of me worried he'd let details of our past slip to someone in the office, but so far, only some are aware we know each other. Nothing more, nothing less.

Mia demands daily updates, wanting details as simple as what he ate for lunch. Which is a bit ridiculous, but I know she's just being protective.

Sarah has somewhat listened to my request. She still attempts to insert herself into my nonexistent love life by introducing me to people or suggesting guys I should give another shot. She's attempted to broach the topic of Bryce, but I'm far from ready to share that side of myself with her, so I keep quiet.

By the time Friday morning rolls around, I'm sitting at my desk with a red pen in hand, reading through a stack of promotional content we'd be presenting to a potential client in the hopes of selling them our onboarding package. It's a personalized package that will be part of a much larger pitch due to be presented in a couple of weeks. Everything about it needs to be perfect, meaning I've been reading the same documents several times over.

A throat clears behind me as I strike through a paragraph that is, mostly, grammatically incoherent. The sound nearly makes me jump out of my skin, causing the red line to be much darker than I intended because of my pressure on the pen.

A deep laugh echoes behind me, sending shivers down my spine and making me tense up. "Still the jumpiest person alive, I see."

I school my features into a look of indifference before turning to face him. I'm still not used to seeing Bryce in corporate attire—but he always looked hot as hell. Today he's wearing immaculate black pants and a light-blue button down with the sleeves already rolled up to his forearms. A to-go coffee cup is in his hand.

The look on his face is something I'm less familiar with. He looks almost bashful.

Still, I'm determined not to let this man get to me, so I turn my eyes back to the documents at hand. "What can I help you with?"

He holds out the coffee like some kind of peace offering. Even from here, I can smell the rich mocha mixed with espresso and know he'd gotten this on his way into the office. "I brought you a coffee. Caffè mochas are still your favorite, right?"

I know what he's doing, because it's the same thing he's done for years. Whenever I'd gotten annoyed with him, he'd sneak me a coffee from the spread offered to athletes, coaches, and other officials. It hadn't been amazing coffee, but it'd be better than whatever was being sold at the concession stand.

I consider telling him I no longer drink the caffeinated beverage, but he'd see right through me. Besides, the warm chocolate smell is too enticing, and I have a strict rule about never turning down a free coffee. So, I set aside my papers and take it from him, mumbling a quick thanks.

I take a small sip of the chocolaty espresso goodness and almost melt in my seat. When the familiar taste rolls across my tongue, I realize I know this coffee. A local café in the Old Market makes it—the same café I venture to on days when I want to get out of the office or even work on my writing. It's been my favorite since finding the café when I started at Hunt & Sloan; a fact I'm sure he doesn't know.

"Glad to see some things haven't changed." His amused voice brings me down from the caffeine cloud I'm floating on. "I stopped at a place near my apartment and took a chance your go-to order was the same."

Still trying to wrap my head around the kind gesture, I glance up, and find him looking at me with a soft smile. There's no hint of an ulterior motive. He isn't trying to get me to talk; he's just being thoughtful. The side of him I'm lucky enough to see glimpses of. It is, without a doubt, the side of him I miss the absolute most.

I have no choice but to accept the olive branch, offering a grin in return. "Thank you. This was very sweet of you, but you didn't have to."

He waves my gratitude off. Another thing he used to do after gifting me coffee. "It's not that big of a deal. I figured you were loaded with just as much work as I am with this pitch coming up. Honestly, I didn't expect to be involved in something like this so quickly."

"I'm not surprised they pulled you in," I admit, having seen similar instances before. "They put you in the deep end right away to see how well you can swim. It's not all on you, though. You have a team to back you up."

He smirks. "Lucky for them, I'm an excellent swimmer. I've got the Olympic medals and everything to prove it." He chuckles when I roll my eyes. "Still, I feel like I don't have enough experience to do something like this yet."

"It'll come."

Although I say it, I'm not sure how much I believe it. I can't see Bryce doing something like this. Yes, he'd studied business, but convincing people to spend thousands of dollars on programs their businesses don't necessarily need, nor ever utilize often enough to get a return on their investment, isn't what I'd picture him doing. Yeah, our services might be good, and they can help people be successful, but they're not needed the way we pretend they are. I can't see Bryce selling something so . . . shallow.

"You think so?"

"Oh, sure." I nod. "Before you know it, it'll be second nature. You'll be able to tell everyone how our way of thinking revolutionizes the way companies hire, manage their teams, and see their profit margins expand."

He arches an eyebrow. "That sounded like it came straight out of a company handbook."

I smirk back. "If you read the company handbook, you'd know it did. I swear they have it on every third page."

"Yeah, you caught me." He laughs. Then his gray eyes glance over my head to the papers and my open laptop on my desk before looking back at me. "So, what is it you do here?"

"I'm a content editor. It's our job to make sure our products and the information we're putting out there are perfect and irresistible. My team and I basically make your job easier."

His brows furrow, a frown settling across his features. "I thought you wanted to be a writer."

The comment is like having a bucket of cold water dropped on me. Not only does it point out I'm not following my dream, but it's also a reminder of how well we know each other. After spending nights snuggled under blankets and talking about what our futures might hold, we know a lot about each other. Back then, we could always talk to each other, except for when it mattered.

"I mean, technically I do a lot of writing in this job," I reply, trying to get the frown off his face. "You should see some of the paragraphs that come across my desk."

He meets my gaze again, clearly unimpressed. "That's not writing, Josie. You're rewriting something someone else wrote. You wanted to write a book."

My stomach clenches at the thought of the barely touched manuscript sitting on my desktop at home—the one I continue to swear I'll go back to, but keep coming up with excuses as to why it doesn't happen. The dream he's referencing is so close I can almost taste it, tell myself it'd be mine someday, knowing the reality I'm living will keep me from it for as long as possible.

I don't feel like being reminded of that right now.

"Well, I also wanted to run a successful website covering the exciting world of professional swimming." I laugh, but he doesn't budge, just crosses his arms over his chest, biceps threatening the integrity of his shirt. "I still write, Bryce. This is just something to pay the bills until the book is published."

He doesn't look convinced, but he doesn't press the subject. "I guess that makes sense. I have a meeting soon, so I should probably head back over to my desk."

Although I miss moments like this, where we just talk, I know I can't let on to it. "Yeah, of course. I have a lot to do this morning, too. Thanks again for the coffee. I do appreciate it."

He smiles—a real, breathtaking smile that has goosebumps running up my arms. "You're welcome, Josie. Does this mean you don't hate me anymore?"

My own grin falters as the word "hate" hits my ears. Hate Bryce? While it is something I often wished I could have brought myself to do, I was never successful in getting there. Even now. I need him to know that. "I could never hate you, Bryce. No matter how badly I wanted to."

"I don't know if that's an insult or a compliment."

I consider the question for a moment. "It just means I don't hate you. It also means I'm not sure how to like you again yet."

He ducks his head, taking a step back, almost like he wants to distance himself from me. "Makes sense. I guess I'll just have to keep bringing you coffee until you figure out how to like me again. You're forgetting I know your weaknesses, Josie Martin."

We both know it won't be that easy. Things aren't like they were a few years ago; he can't just bring me coffee and magically fix everything. However, we both know it's a good way to start.

"I look forward to it." I feel my heart swoop to the pit of my stomach. "Have a good day, Bryce."

I expect the cocky confidence to come back in that moment, but it doesn't. His smile is a genuinely happy one. "You too, Josie."

With that, he turns to walk back the way he came, leaving me with a feeling I know all too well. I experienced the same sensation back in 2015 when I first laid eyes on him. Intuition told me he was going to end up impacting my life more than I would expect. Bryce is creeping back into my life. That feeling is back, and I'm not sure if I'm ready to deal with what that's going to mean now.

⁓⁓⁓

The morning passes quickly, as it usually does when I'm engrossed in huge projects. By the time I finally look at the clock, I realize I've worked right past my normal lunch time. As if the reminder of time had sent a signal to my stomach, it let out a low growl.

Deciding it's time for a well-deserved break, I log off my computer and gather my stuff before heading toward the elevators, where I find Bryce waiting. Looking down at his phone, he's too distracted to notice me approaching. I consider heading for the stairs to avoid facing another interaction with him. But I don't know if I want to. Maybe it's my turn to extend an olive branch.

A teasing grin stretches across my face as I move to stand beside him. "Don't you look all sorts of official." My smile grows when he jumps. Once he recovers, the confusion is evident on his face. "Standing here in dress pants and a button down, waiting for the elevator while you check your messages. I never thought I'd see corporate Bryce Clark."

He tugs at his collar, which has two buttons undone. "Yeah, the Bryce Clark you know is still getting used to this new version of himself, too."

This morning, I'd been too blind by how good I thought he looked to notice how uncomfortable he looks. Not that I'm surprised. Bryce went from a job that required him to wear sweats or next to nothing, to one with stiff button downs and starchy fabrics in boring, appropriate colors. While he looks no less attractive, I find myself missing the joggers and soft sweatshirts.

"Besides, I wasn't checking my messages for work. I was texting Carter. He's in Australia with his ex-boyfriend, and he's been sending me pictures of all the adorable and terrifying animals they've seen."

Carter's face flashes in my mind, making my smile brighten. A second later, though, the rest of Bryce's statement catches up with me. "Ex-boyfriend? He's on a trip with his ex?"

Bryce laughs. "They booked the trip before they broke up, nonrefundable; and you know how Carter is. He's literally the only person who can say 'we can still be friends' and mean it."

Carter is one of the nicest, sweetest people I've ever met. He's the type of person who can make a friend anywhere, and he rarely pushes people out of his life. Except for me and Mia. I shook that thought away.

"Does he still do weekly brunch with his ex-girlfriend from his first year of college?"

Bryce chuckles with a nod. "Yes, except now she lives across the country, so it happens over video call."

I giggle, shaking my head as we step into the elevator as the doors slide open. Bryce follows behind me. "He's something else. How is he, though? He's still swimming, right?"

A lot of people had been surprised when Bryce retired, but Carter didn't—they were always a packaged deal. Despite not having his best friend with him as his biggest supporter and competition, Carter has made several comments about wanting to see what else he can do within the sport. Since Bryce's retirement, he's been killing it.

Just because we haven't spoken in two years, doesn't mean I haven't been following his career.

"He's doing good," Bryce says. "He's planning on going to one more Olympics—fingers crossed—and then hanging up his goggles."

"Is it weird? Knowing he's still swimming and you're doing this?" I don't know where the question comes from, but I'm itching to know the answer.

"Doing what? Being an adult?" He laughs at his own joke, but it comes out a little hollow. "I don't know. A little, I guess. I knew I needed to be done. I could barely get out of the pool in Tokyo. My body wasn't bouncing back the way it used to, and I didn't want to be the guy who didn't know when to quit. It was time to quit."

I want to know more, press for the answers I've speculated on for the last two years, but the elevator comes to a stop on the second floor before I have the chance to say anything else.

My eyes widen when I spot Paul standing on the other side. He works on the IT side of things and was the only person Sarah introduced me to that resulted in an actual relationship—despite him asking my opinions on marriage during our second date. Our relationship lasted six months, before I realized the questions posed on the second date were a sign. He was ready for a wife and was looking for the kind of woman I could never be. Though we'd parted amicably, he never failed to ask if I'd reconsider his proposal (yes, he uses that word) every time we run into each other.

As soon as Paul's gaze lands on me, he doesn't so much as spare Bryce a glance as he steps into the elevator, inserting himself between us. "Joslyn, how are you? It's been a while since we've run into each other. You aren't trying to avoid me, right?"

I glance at Bryce out of the corner of my eye, whose eyes are narrowed as he looks between Paul and me. The last thing I want to do was make small talk with another ex-whatever, but I know ignoring him won't be a smart idea either. "Of course not, Paul. I've just been busy. How are you?"

"Oh, good, good," he replies. "Also been busy, which is why I haven't stopped by your desk to persuade you into a date night. We should make that happen soon."

Out of the corner of my eye, I watch Bryce straighten to his full height just as we reach the main floor. "I'm busy, Paul. Besides, we've been through this. We aren't going out anymore."

"Ah, I see," he says, unimpressed with my response. "Perhaps I'll try to catch up with you in a few weeks, when things have calmed down."

Bryce steps past Paul as the door slides open again, but turns to face him as he backs out. Paul looks startled to realize someone else is in the elevator with us. "If you have to talk her into it, you probably shouldn't be asking her out, man." His gray eyes meet mine. "I'll see you later, Josie."

His easy but standoff demeanor has my heart skittering in my chest the way it used to. He knows the effect he has on people. I'd fallen victim to it more than once. Apparently, he still holds the same effect.

Bryce doesn't hang around as I step off the elevator, Paul close behind. He just gives me a slight nod before heading toward the cafeteria. Which means my ex-whatever has left me stranded with my ex-boyfriend.

Ugh, men. I should have worked from home today.

"Josie?" Paul frowns at the nickname, which I never bothered to tell him. Joslyn is printed on my badge, despite me putting Josie down as my preferred name, so I just used it at work. I save the nickname for the people I care about. "No one ever calls you Josie. Do you know him?"

"We've known one another for almost a decade," I admit. "I prefer Josie, so most people in my life call me Josie."

He blinks, as if my answer confuses him. Or like he was worried he's talked to the wrong woman. "I never called you Josie."

I shrug. "Maybe that was part of the problem. Have a nice day, Paul."

When I enter the cafeteria, I find Bryce at the salad bar halfheartedly assembling a bowl as he watches the entryway. He relaxes when his gaze meets mine. Then, the tiniest hint of amusement fills his eyes.

I join him, grabbing a bowl before hissing, "You can't leave me with him!"

He chuckles, flashing me an apologetic grin. As we build our lunches in silence, I can feel his gaze flickering to me every so often.

I reach for the cucumbers. "Just ask me whatever you want to ask me. I feel your judgment from here."

"No judgment," he insists with the shake of his head. "I'm just trying to figure out if you actually dated that asshole."

"Unfortunately, yes," I sigh. "Sarah introduced us."

He lets out a hum. "I'm not surprised by that, or the fact it didn't work out."

I glance over at him, but he's surveying the dressing options like it's the hardest decision he'll tackle all day. "It lasted six months; I'm sure you see why. He wanted a wife, someone who was ready for kids, and I'm not. Plus, there was no chemistry, really."

"I got the impression he was like that. It's none of my business, but is there anyone now?"

I shake my head but hold his gaze. "Not at the moment, no. I'm sure it'll be a matter of time before Sarah has someone she wants me to meet, though."

He snaps the lid closed on his salad, but waits as I add my own dressing. "Well, if that guy is on her track record, I don't think she's doing a very good job of finding someone for you."

"Careful, you're also on her track record." I close my lid, following him over to the line to pay. "Paul was what I needed at the time. She's a good friend and she wants to see me happy."

He says nothing else as our turn comes, and he informs the girl behind the counter he's covering mine as well. As soon as I start to protest, he scans his badge, completing the transaction. "It's a seven-dollar salad, Josie, not a marriage proposal. Besides, if I didn't do it, your ex was about to come over and do it."

"Uh," I say, going rigid as I glance over my shoulder to find Paul watching us, frowning at what he's seeing. I focus back on Bryce with a gulp. "Thank you, I appreciate it."

He waves the thanks off. "There's a table in the corner." My eyes widen, knowing what's about to come as he motions to a table overlooking the river. "Eat lunch with me. You can explain why no one here knows your name."

Laughing, I reluctantly agree. Perhaps it's a bad idea. After all, I can practically hear Mia screaming at me, but it sounds nice. "They know my name, Bryce. Joslyn is my legal name."

"And last I remembered, you hated your name," he argues, sliding into a seat while I take the one across from him. "So, tell me what changed."

"The company printed Joslyn on my badge. I tried to correct people, but no one listened. It just stuck. So, I decided to save Josie for the people who deserved to use it—the ones who really know me and care about me."

His gray eyes lock on me, a rare serious look on his handsome features. "Am I still allowed to use it?"

My breath catches in my throat at the uncertainty in his tone, especially when I can't imagine him calling me Joslyn. I've always been Josie to him, or Jos, and a few times other terms of endearment that remained between us. My heart sinks a little. I never want to be anyone else to him. "Always."

Chapter 6

THEN

June 2018

Columbus, OH

I never thought I'd be this anxious to get off a plane in Ohio—yet here we were.

Usually, I was the person who sat back while other passengers created utter chaos preparing to deplane long before the doors opened. There was nothing more annoying to me than watching the entitlement everyone had the second the seatbelt light went off. The whole thing would go faster if everyone stopped elbowing their way out of seats, only to stand in an uncomfortable position to block the aisle, and attempted to do it in a more organized fashion. But no, everyone had somewhere to be, and their destination was more important than the person beside them.

Although, this time, the people already crowding the aisle were starting to make more sense from where I sat boxed into my window seat.

I wasn't even sure I should be here. Yes, I was excited to see Mia and all our friends, but the reason for the brick in the pit of my stomach was over seeing Bryce. We'd talked periodically throughout the year, even video chatting a few times, but we were avoiding what happened in Indianapolis last year, and he carefully avoided any topic that bordered on getting too real. In the last few weeks, Bryce had stopped responding to my messages in the lead up to us seeing one another again. Normally, I'd say he was focusing on the meet ahead, but I knew the truth. He was putting some distance between us.

It was getting a little old. This guessing game of what kind of mood he'd be in when we finally saw each other. No matter what, it ended the same way, a flash of his smirk and the two of us stumbling through hotel rooms together. Or, at least, that was how it ended ever since the first time two years ago.

How long was I willing to put up with this?

Thankfully, before I could spiral into emotional turmoil, the plane doors opened, and people began filtering out. As the aisle cleared, the couple sitting next to me stood; the man stepping out to grab their bags and offering to do the same with mine. We made small talk as we followed the crowd into the relatively deserted airport before parting ways.

I checked my phone as I made my way to baggage claim, and saw a text message from Mia, who was driving in from North Carolina, informing me she was still about an hour out. I reassured her I was fine waiting and would grab a coffee before switching over to check some other notifications.

I thought through a list of things I could do while I waited. I could start some prep work for before the meet started, but I was feeling the urge to work on something more creative. My anxiety over seeing Bryce—mixed with the anticipation of it—usually gave me a creative boost. Words flowed when I thought of him.

Which was something I was determined not to think about too much.

Whack!

I was so focused on my phone, I didn't realize I was about to run into something solid until it was too late, the collision causing me to lose my footing. The moment I realized the thing I ran into was a person was when their strong hand gripped my upper arm, steadying me before I could land on my butt.

Cheeks flushing with embarrassment, I glanced up, ready to apologize excessively. But the words died on my lips when my gaze locked with a familiar pair of gray eyes. The panic in his eyes told me this run-in wasn't an accident.

I tore my arm from Bryce's grasp, glaring at him. "What the hell is wrong with you? You don't step in front of people who are walking and just stop! I could have fallen."

"But you didn't," he countered. If there was one thing I knew about him, it was the fact he didn't like being called out for the stupid shit he did. Especially in public. "I called your name half a dozen times. What else was I supposed to do to get your attention?"

"Oh, I don't know, tap on my shoulder, grab my hand—literally anything except tripping me in the middle of an airport!"

His cheeks reddened slightly, glancing at the people passing as they gave us strange looks. "Look, I'm sorry, okay? I shouldn't have done that. I should have tried something else."

It was a weak apology; one I wasn't sure I believed. There was also a part of me wondering what he would have done if I'd actually fallen. Would he have laughed at my expense before he helped me up? Or would the apology have been genuine then?

That was the thing about Bryce and me; I was always excited to see him, but the anxiety leading up to it was unnerving. Any time he surprised me, or caught me off guard, a part of me wanted to run the other way and hide. I'd spent the last week wondering what would happen when we got to this point, and I wasn't sure I was ready to face it.

So, I decided I didn't have to face it and shoved past him, continuing toward baggage claim.

"Why are you walking away from me?"

I cursed under my breath as he fell into step beside me, slowing his natural pace to match mine. No matter how quickly I tried to walk away, his six-foot-two frame would catch up with me. "I have to get my bag, Bryce."

"What a coincidence," he replied in an annoyingly cheery tone. "I'm doing the exact same thing. We can walk together."

I rolled my eyes but said nothing as I kept track of the signs overhead, assuring I was going in the right direction. This airport was easy to navigate, but at least it gave me something to do.

"So, what's with the attitude?"

"No attitude," I snapped back. "I'm just amazed at how easy it is for you to decide when I'm worthy of your company and not."

"What? Josie, hold on." His hand wrapped around my arm again, gentler this time, and pulled us to a stop. I refused to look at him, even when he took a step closer, encompassing me in a way that normally made me melt against him. "Where the hell did that come from?"

"Where do you think it came from, Bryce?" I glared up at him. "I mean, honestly, we barely speak to each other throughout the year, then you want to be best friends the second we're in the same city? It's a little exhausting."

His frown deepened. "We're both busy during the year, Josie. You're working; I'm working. We don't see each other often, so of course I want to make the most of it when we're in the same place."

"But only when we're in the same place, right?" A weakness settled in my knees as I feel flushed. "The rest of the time, you couldn't care less. You're living your life, I'm living mine. We would text maybe a handful of times a month, then you went silent this last week."

"I don't know what you want me to say, Josie. You know what the week before a meet looks like for me. I do the same thing all the time. There's not a lot of variety in my day. I don't want to bore you with training updates or meet results. You already keep yourself updated on what's happening. Also, I'm not sure how to do the communication side of things when this isn't anything serious."

There was nothing like having my lack of a status thrown back in my face when I was already feeling humiliated. "Yeah, I get it, Bryce. You're right, we're not friends, or anything more. Thanks for clearing that up for me."

Bryce let out a frustrated groan, but I didn't know if it was directed at himself or me. "You know I didn't mean it like that, Josie! We are friends and I should be a better friend, I know. I'm sorry I kept blowing you off. I had a lot on my plate. You know—"

"I swear, if you tell me your focus is on making the Olympic team, I might not talk to you again this weekend. I know what your priority is, Bryce, and I have done nothing but support you the entire time we've known one another."

He shifted the weight of his backpack higher on his shoulder. "There are a bunch of kids coming up who are just as determined to make the team as me. They're younger and faster."

"And we all know experience plays a huge role in getting on the team," I challenged. "Inexperience can lead to slip-ups."

"So can being overly comfortable. I know it's still two years away, and I shouldn't make it my sole focus, but I want this time to be different, Josie. I'm not taking my eyes off the prize."

"Even if it means letting everyone else slip through the cracks." And by everyone else, I meant me. Much of everyone else in his life had the same focus, the same goal, so it was easier to keep them around. I was the odd factor in the equation, the one he didn't know what to do with. "That's not how I do friendships, Bryce. I will not slip through the cracks until you decide I'm worth your attention again."

When I tugged my arm free, I stood there for a second, giving him a chance to say something before I walked off again. This time, he let me go. The more steps I took, the more tears welled in my eyes, but I refused to cry over a man in an airport. So, I shook it off.

Once I had my bag, I checked the time just to realize I still had at least a half hour before Mia got there. So, I went back to the coffee shop I'd passed, got myself an iced coffee, and set up camp at a table with my notebook. Just like I'd anticipated, my run-in with Bryce had me scribbling ideas destined to break a fictional couple. Half of them would have to go—they were too personal and too Bryce induced, but at least the ideas were flowing.

Still, everything I scribbled got a little too personal, especially when I wrote a line about a girl who was trying to figure out where she fit into the chaotic life of the person she wanted.

Groaning, I dropped my pen before leaning back in my seat, stretching my arms above my head right as Bryce slid into the one across from me.

I scowled. "Go away."

"Who even writes in a notebook anymore?" I slammed my hand on top of the notebook before he could reach for it. He frowned at me. "What? Is it something about me?"

"No, it's ideas that aren't at all connected," I replied, narrowing my eyes even more. "It's rude to read what someone has written without their permission."

His cocky expression dropped to something more apologetic. "I'm sorry. I just . . . I always see you writing, and I want to know what it's about. I'm intrigued."

"You've read my writing, Bryce. I've interviewed you half a dozen times, and I always send the article before it goes live." Maybe he's never actually read a single thing I've written about him.

"Yeah, I read everything you write for Adair, but this is different."

I couldn't focus on the first half of what he'd said. I knew he supported the blog, but to read everything I wrote was a whole other level of support.

"This is the kind of writing you want to do, right?" he questioned. "You want to write books. You think I don't pay attention, Josie, but I do."

To keep my cheeks from heating up at his confession, I took a sip of my coffee before I answered. "Maybe, but you have a funny way of showing it."

Sighing, he stacked his arms on top of each other and leaned across the table. "You're right, I'm usually too wrapped up in myself and it's not fair to you or my other friends. Look, I'm sorry I blew you off this past year, and that I ignored you over the last week. It was stupid and immature. I really have been looking forward to seeing you. Please don't let my idiocy keep you from hanging out with me this weekend."

I stared at him, trying to figure out if he was being sincere or ensuring he said what I wanted to hear. This was a conversation we'd had last summer, after he'd ignored me for a year. We were still finding our footing in whatever it was between us, which meant I was unsure of what was genuine and what was insincere.

I'd gotten good at learning his tells, helping me to distinguish between moments when he's being diplomatic and honest. And this moment was screaming honestly at me. It was in the way he leaned closer, the way he held eye contact, the way his cocky vibe was nowhere to be seen.

Still, I wasn't ready to give in.

"It won't," I assured him. "I've been looking forward to spending time with you, too."

He leaned back in his seat, taking me in. "Great, then what are you doing hanging out in the middle of the airport?"

It astonished me how effortlessly he bounced between shy to confident. "Waiting for Mia." My phone lit up with a message from Mia, telling me she was here. "And she just texted to let me know she's pulling up now."

"Great, I'll walk you out," he offered as I started gathering my stuff. "My ride is about five minutes away, too."

I frowned at him as I zipped up my pen bag, tossing it into my oversized purse. "Wait, why are you still here?"

His cheeks flushed, and he avoided eye contact. "It took forever for them to get our bags unloaded; one guy was about to lose his shit. I'm still not sure what happened. Then I saw you hanging out over here and decided there was no time better than the present for an apology."

I couldn't fight back my grin at what wasn't being said. "You were looking for me."

He tried to play it off with a light chuckle, but there was no escaping this. "I noticed you didn't head right to the exit when you got your bag, and you walked right by me. I wanted to make sure we had an opportunity to talk. I don't know how crazy the rest of the weekend will get."

Worried I'd say something embarrassing, I nodded, and finished gathering my stuff. Silence settled between us as we made toward the exit. It wasn't until the doors were in sight that he finally broke it.

"Are you and Mia going to the pool tonight?"

Tonight mostly consisted of some distance events, and tended not to draw any sort of crowd. It gave us the opportunity to see the venue, get our media passes secured, and see some friends. "Yeah, at least for a while. What about you?"

He nodded. "Coach wants us to get some time in the pool before prelims tomorrow, so I'll be there. Do you have dinner plans?"

There was the annoying flutter of hope again. Hope, especially when Bryce was involved, was a very dangerous thing. "Not that I know of. I'm not sure if Mia's talked to anyone else."

"The two of you should join our group for dinner," he offered. "Carter will be there, plus some of our other mutual friends. I don't think we've decided on a place yet, but it'll be good to hang out with you guys outside of the pool."

I nearly tripped over myself. Normally, when Bryce and I were together outside the pool, it didn't involve a public setting or our friends. Sure, there were people, like Carter, who Mia and I were close enough to do something like this with, but it never happened due to how busy we all were, and the nature of my relationship with Bryce. I didn't want to accept without talking to Mia, though, because this was one of the few times throughout the year we got to see each other.

"That sounds like fun, but I'd want to talk to Mia before agreeing to anything."

"Of course," he said as her car pulled up to the curb in front of us. "You can talk to her and then let me know."

I raised a brow as I motioned toward her SUV. "Or we can run it by her now. See what she has to say."

Bryce glanced over at the car before turning back to me, shifting his weight from one foot to the other. "Yeah, sure, sounds good."

I couldn't hide my amusement at how uncomfortable he looked. "Are you sure about that? You look terrified."

"I'm not terrified," he grumbled, gripping the strap of his bag tighter as he followed me to her car. She was already stepping around the front to greet me and help me with my bag. Bryce let out a quiet groan when her gaze landed on him. "I just don't think she likes me very much. After last summer, something changed in Indianapolis."

There was a part of me that wanted to wave him off, tell him he was wrong, but the trouble started two summers ago, when this friends with benefits thing started between us. It got worse after last summer. Something shifted between her and Bryce. Her iffy view of him had hardened at the World Championship trials. She seemed fine with Carter but was equally stand-offish to Bryce's other close friend, Ronan.

I'd asked her a hundred times about what happened, but all she ever said was she didn't trust him. She worried he'd break my heart and humiliate me. We both knew it was a little too late for my heart to not get involved, so she seemed to be waiting for the inevitable fallout. And made sure Bryce knew she was ready to hate him.

"So, you're not her favorite person in the world," I said, reveling in the chance to tease him. "You're also not her least favorite, which you should consider a win."

"Wait," he called out as I walked ahead to greet her. "What does that mean?"

"Hi, bestie." I hugged Mia with all my might. Bryce hung back and I could feel his apprehension from here. "Bryce is scared of you."

When we parted, she had a mischievous glint in her eyes. "Good, that's how I want it to be." As she moved to open the tailgate, she glanced over at Bryce. "What do you want, Clark? I'm not a car service."

He started the second she addressed him, moving closer to the curb. "Uh, I don't need a ride." She faced him with her arms crossed over her chest, as if to tell him to get to the point. "I made a suggestion to Josie, and she wanted us to talk about it with you."

Mia glanced at me as I moved to lift my bag up to place it next to hers. Normally, I would have expected Bryce to assist me, but he was rooted to his spot on the curb. Which, in all honesty, didn't help his case. "He invited us to dinner tonight, with a group of his friends. Carter included."

"I thought we were going to the pool tonight, at least for a bit."

"We'll be there for a while, too," Bryce explained. "This would be after. I don't know where we're going yet, but it's been a while since we've all hung out. Obviously, most of us swim in the morning, so we won't be out too late."

I bit my lip to keep my laugh in. It sounded like he was trying to convince his mom to let him go out on a school night.

Mia considered the offer for a second. When she glanced at me again, I smiled in the hope to convey I wanted to go. With a sigh, she relented. "Sure, sounds fun. Text Josie the plans once you have them all figured out."

I watch the tension leave Bryce's body. "Yeah, of course." He glanced down at his phone for a second. "My ride is here, so I should go. I'll see you guys tonight."

"Do you want a snack for the drive?"

He looked at Mia, startled. "Do you have snacks in your car?"

She motioned to the box I was already sorting through. "Of course, I do. Grab what you want, then shut the door. I want to see if we can get checked in early."

Mia headed back to the driver's side. As Bryce stepped up next to me, his arm brushed against mine, sending goosebumps along that arm. I handed him one of his favorite kinds of candy as I grabbed a soda for myself. We stepped back so he could hit the button to close the door.

"I swear, she's like a swim mom," I joked, already opening the cap on my soda, and taking a sip. "I told you she doesn't hate you."

He glanced in the window beside us, knowing she was probably watching us through the mirror. "Yeah, but I'm also not her favorite." He stepped back up onto the curb. "Which means I'm going to take my snack, walk away, and see you later tonight."

This was a side of Bryce I rarely got to see. Him with his guard down, and then there was the boyish charm that captivated me. I'd do just about anything to keep it there all the time. "Sounds like a plan."

"I'll text you," he promised, before turning and walking along the curb to his ride.

I watched him go for a second longer before I moved to the passenger seat, sliding in beside Mia. She was watching me closely as I buckled myself in. "What?"

"I thought we were mad at him, because he barely talked to you all year and ignored you the past week or so."

I shrugged because there wasn't much else to say or do. She knew me well enough to understand that Bryce was a weakness of mine. "We talked about it, and he apologized. Us going to dinner tonight doesn't mean I'll jump right back into bed with him."

She gave me a look of disbelief. "Whatever you say, Josie."

Chapter 7

NOW

April 2023

Omaha, NE

In a rare occurrence, I don't have any work to take home with me over the weekend, so I'm free to spend it as I please. Normally, weekends like this will involve me holed up on my couch with a fuzzy blanket while catching up on reading or TV shows. This weekend, though, I'm determined to be more productive with my time and spend it on things that make me happy.

Which is why I find myself walking into my favorite coffee shop in downtown Omaha early Saturday morning, my mother waving me over as soon as she spots me. Her grin is bright as she stands to greet me.

"Hi, sweetie!" I allow her to pull me into a tight hug, the weight of her arms comforting around my shoulders. She kisses my cheek as she pulls away, taking her seat again. "I already got you your favorite."

Sitting on the table was an iced mocha, perfect for the warm weather outside. Dropping my bag into the empty seat, I sink into the one across from her and take the first sip, sighing in relief as the coffee hits my tastebuds. "Thank you."

"We haven't had the chance to do this in a while," she says, fiddling with the napkin under own cup. "I was excited when you texted."

"I'm sorry, Mom. Work has been crazy, life has been a little crazy, and time got away from me."

"You're twenty-nine years old, Joslyn. You don't have to apologize for having a life. Especially when you've given so much of yourself to help us."

I don't like talking about the reason I stayed in Omaha, but it always seems to come up. I don't regret the choices I've made, and I'd make them again, but I don't need to be reminded of them. Nor do I want to be reminded I was nowhere near where I want to be at this point in my life.

I was supposed to be the girl who got out. Yet, I feel like one of the few who stayed. Years have passed at this point, and I'm still living the same life—doing what I'm supposed to do, ignoring what I want to do, and left unsure how to move on.

"How's everything at home?" I have gotten good at changing the subject.

"Oh, we're fine," she replies. "Your father has started researching RVs so we can travel and visit family members next summer."

My gut twists at the mention of their plans once my mother has retired from her job as a school secretary. They get to leave, see bigger and better things, while I'm stuck where I am, where I've always been.

I stayed in Omaha when my father was pushed out of his job, forced into early retirement right after I finished college. My parents weren't ready for the reduced income, to face their debt, and send their child to school. They were faced with an uncertain future, and I felt the need to support them the way they'd supported me.

So, I stayed. I got an entry-level position with Hunt & Sloan and worked my way up to the position as the head of an editing team within a few years. I lived at home longer than I wanted to, helping when, and where I could. Whether it was bills, cleaning, or other maintenance, I was ready, and willing to help.

I give my mom the brightest smile I can muster. "That's exciting! Do you know where you're going to start?"

"We were thinking of heading east, seeing my side of the family, before venturing to the other side. We haven't done much planning, just the very beginning."

The idea of the two of them sequestered into an RV for months almost makes me giggle. While my parents love each other, they never strike me as the kind of couple who can be in such close proximity for so long. I'm already dreading the annoying phone calls I'd get from both.

"How's work, Josie? Has Sarah tried to set you up with anyone else?"

Mom knows all about Sarah's matchmaking, and she doesn't approve. But I have a feeling she'd approve of the most recent one. "She has, actually, but I told her it wouldn't work out."

"Good for you!" She leans forward. "What was wrong with this one?"

"Nothing is wrong with him, per se. I didn't feel like getting my heart broken again." Her gaze snaps up to meet mine. "Bryce Clark is back."

She gasps, her eyes going comically wide. "What? He's here?"

I take a sip of my coffee, trying to suppress my grin. Despite never meeting him, she's been one of his biggest fans. "He lives in Omaha now, and we work together. He's in sales."

"Joslyn! Why didn't you tell me about this? How long have you known?"

"Just two weeks. I've been too busy to tell you. Plus, I wasn't sure what role I wanted him to have in my life. At first, I was content to ignore his presence entirely."

"And now?"

I shift under her gaze, unsure how honest I want to be. There hasn't been anyone serious since Bryce, not even Paul got that close, and my mother is starting to get pushy about me finding someone. If that someone just happened to be the same person she pushed me toward in 2015, even better.

"We're friends, I think. Or, at least, we're working back toward it."

"He's making an effort to get back into your life?" I nod, sipping my coffee. "That sounds great, sweetheart. Whether you've wanted to admit it or not, I know you've missed him."

I'm far from ready to admit that I'm not over him to myself, let alone my mother. Nor am I ready to admit having him close by again was sending me down memory lane and taking a sharp turn into the land of what-if. These feelings are dangerous, and something I need to navigate on my own.

"Enough about me." I grin, needing to change the subject before Mom gets me to open up about things I'm ready to talk about. "Tell me about the plans you have figured out for your trip with Dad!"

She doesn't question the change of subject, but delves straight into the plans they've already worked out. I happily listen, offering suggestions when I have them, and enjoying the quality time with my mom. She and I have always been close, and can read each other like an open book because of it. My mother is one of the few people who understands the weird limbo I'm in.

Once the subject of their retirement trip is exhausted, she asks about my writing and whether I've started searching for a new job. Or even another city to move to. Besides Bryce coming back into my life, nothing has changed in the weeks since we've last talked. That's the reality of my life: stagnant and predictable.

After a couple of hours, it's time to get back to our days. With Mom in need to run some errands, I want to write. Not ready to go back to my apartment and face the silence, I decide to grab another coffee and walk around downtown.

Somehow, I wind up wandering down 10th Street and am approaching the Riverview Convention Center and Stadium. I often pass the glass front building in my day-to-day life and try not to think about the memories contained within it, but that's been harder to do lately.

People crowded the front of the plaza, walking dogs, jogging, or enjoying the sunshine. Staring up at the glass front, the warm sun reflects down on me as everything comes rushing back to me. As it does, I decide not to hide from the memories and focus on whatever subconscious thought brought me here.

I can still hear the crowds cheering, the splash as swimmers take off from their blocks. The chilly air, encompassed by the smell of chlorine, hits me. The memories are from years ago, but standing here now it felt like it had just happened.

What would I say to my younger self? Would I warn her of the unfathomable pain Bryce would cause? Or would I tell her, despite everything, it was worth it, and I'd do it again?

When I finally pull myself from my thoughts, I look around at the surrounding people and, of course, there he is.

The way my gaze naturally falls on him in a crowd doesn't surprise me, even after all this time. Though I am taken aback to find him standing there, hands resting on his hips as he catches his breath, gazing up at the building the same way I have been. Like it holds the secrets to everything that should have been.

The way his dark gray T-shirt clings to the muscles beneath tells me he must be out for a run. Which makes sense, since I know he lives nearby. Still, my heart twists at the thought of him running past this building every day. What thoughts plague him? This was the place where the craziest dream he had came true, not once, but twice. Did any of his memories involve me?

As if feeling my gaze, Bryce's gaze pulls away from the building and lands on me. I suck in a gasp before it can escape, my heart jolting at the intensity in his eyes even from a distance. Then my heart sinks and I offer a shy wave. His face brightens as he closes the distance between us in a few quick strides.

"Hey," I say, "what are you doing out here?"

His grin drops into something a bit more cheeky, flirty even. "You probably won't believe me, but I'm out for a run."

"Ah, so you still hate running," I tease back. "I was beginning to worry I'd ignored this part of you out of my own hatred for running."

He laughs, deep, and warm. I notice a few people flashing lingering gazes his way. That's the kind of person Bryce is—he attracts attention. "Omaha's a great city, but there aren't a lot of pools for me to swim in. Since I live downtown, I run a couple times a week and go to the gym the rest of the days."

For a city that hosted the qualifying meet for the Olympics four times, Omaha isn't a swimming-friendly place. "Yeah, I could have told you that. I haven't swum regularly since college."

Nodding, he squints down at me. "Do you live downtown, too?"

"No, I had coffee with my mom and then decided to walk around before I head home to write. I haven't touched my manuscript in months, so I needed to get the creative energy flowing."

"I'm sure you'll get there," he assures me. "You're a talented writer, Josie."

I bow my head at the compliment. "I'm not sure how I ended up down here, though. I was planning on just wandering around the Old Market."

He glances around the plaza, almost like he has forgotten where we are and what the significance of it is to us. "It kind of sneaks up on you. You don't realize where you are until it's right in front of you, and it's all you can think of. I never set out to run down here, but this is always where I end up."

"When you announced your retirement, you mentioned you hadn't been able to recover from an injury as well as you'd hoped." I can't believe the words tumbling out of my mouth and, by the look of surprise on his face, neither can Bryce. "I didn't even know there was an injury."

He shifts his weight from one foot to the other. Before I can say he doesn't have to respond to my statement, he says, "It happened at the beginning of 2019, and we ended up not seeing each other that year."

"I went to the one in Iowa in March, and you scratched the whole meet," I recall. Back then, I'd thought about how strange it was for him to do something like that, but he'd never replied to any of my messages. "That explains a lot."

"I messed up my shoulder in practice. It wasn't bad enough to require surgery, but it involved a bunch of intensive physical therapy and other treatments. It threw me off my game, and then the world shut down. Dealing with an injury and a global pandemic made my unstable mental health go to shit."

So many loose ends are lining up in my head. The way Bryce had treated me, the way he acted toward the rest of the world. When I'd stepped through the doors of the Riverview Convention Center, part of me wanted to believe we can go back to how things were, before the pandemic, and start over. I guess I never thought about how something like that impacted him.

He'd faded into the background, dealt with his injury in silence, and chose not to bother anyone with what he was going through.

"Whatever you're thinking, Josie, stop." His voice was calm, but firm. "I made sure no one knew. I was the one who didn't respond to you reaching out. I made the choices I made. I don't want you blaming yourself for not seeing it, or whatever else might be going through your head."

I think about what Mia's reaction would be if she could see us now. She always thought he didn't pay attention or know me. He knows me almost as well as she does.

"Is the injury the real reason you retired, or was it something else? It took you a while after all of that."

He frowns at me. "I'm not sure I know what you mean."

"The first time I saw your name on psych sheets after the Olympics, I was shocked." I will forever have the mental image of him struggling across the deck after his race seared into my mind. "Mia and I figured you'd retire after the Olympics."

"Why? Because I couldn't stand up straight and failed to make the final in all my other events?"

My cheeks flush, but he flashes a goofy grin. "Yeah, something like that."

"I was in a lot of pain," he says. "I thought that was going to be the end of it. I left Tokyo thinking I'd never swim professionally again, but I ended up pushing through for another year. I barely made it to World Championships last summer, and I swam like shit once I was there."

"What made you decide you were done?"

"The one-year anniversary of my gold in Tokyo happened while I was at Worlds, and I knew it would never be the same again. And it was a relief." He looks lost in thought as he faces the building again. "I talked to my coaches, some friends, and I quietly stepped back. I was traveling when I announced it, started applying for some jobs and moved here in March."

I've always wondered what that feeling was like. That moment when someone decided to walk away from something they've dedicated their whole life to. Bryce had stared down his dream and decided he'd had enough. I can't imagine the feelings that would come with such a decision. Bryce is one of the few I'd consider close enough to ask. Now that the information is being freely offered to me.

"Looking back, I should have left after Tokyo. I shouldn't have gone one more year," he continues with the same distant look in his eyes. "My body still aches. I think there might have been a part of me holding on for the wrong reasons. I'd accomplished everything I wanted, but I couldn't walk away.

"When I was standing on the podium in Tokyo, I was ecstatic. It sucked that friends and family couldn't be there, but it was the moment I'd been waiting for. It was also bittersweet, because, deep down, I knew I'd never be there again. The flag being raised was me staring at the beginning of the end. I didn't know how to face it."

Tears sting the corner of my eyes as I think back to watching the medal ceremony from my couch—the way I didn't even realize he was already thinking of retiring. As someone on the outside of the sport, it's easy to talk about the comings and goings of various athletes, but I'd hated thinking about when Bryce would be done. Because I never saw him being done.

Retiring from being a professional swimmer, yes. Leaving the sport completely, never.

"You mentioned something about staying for the wrong reasons," I say, needing to get my focus back on the conversation. "What were those?"

He looks down at me, gray eyes squinting against the sun. "I kept looking for you, Josie. From the very first meet, I kept looking for you."

The air feels like it's been sucked out of me. "What?"

Chapter 8

THEN

June 2018

Columbus, OH

Several hours after Mia picked me up from the airport, I found myself sitting at a large table surrounded by a group of rowdy swimmers. Many of them I knew, some I'd barely spoken to, but either way, it was a lot to take in. The numerous conversations bouncing around the table were impossible to keep up with. Even with Bryce, Mia, and Carter all within arm's length, I was feeling a bit overwhelmed. It was moments like these where I was startled by what my life had turned into.

"You okay over here?" I could feel Bryce's breath on my ear as he leaned in to make sure he could be heard over the crowd. The warmth of his breath made me want to squirm away. He nudged my knee with his under the table. "You're being quiet."

Not wanting to admit I was a little out of my element, I pushed my empty plate back. "Just trying to keep up with everything."

He glanced around the table, fondly taking in his friends, before he looked back at me. "There's a lot going on. Did you want to get out of here? Our hotels are close to each other. We can share a ride back."

Typically speaking, Mia and I preferred to stay within walking distance of the venue, but that wasn't always feasible. Which was part of the reason Mia had driven. Once we decided where we were going, we'd piled as many people as we could into her SUV and everyone else got a ride, knowing walking back was out of the question. Once we were at Bryce's hotel, though, I could walk the block or so back to mine.

"I shouldn't leave Mia," I argued. "It was my idea to come to dinner. She would have been perfectly happy hanging out in the room, just catching up."

Bryce glanced over my head toward her, where she was locked in what sounded like a heated debate about football. "She's having fun with Carter. She has her car; she can get back to the hotel on her own."

A loud laugh from somewhere down the table made me wince and wonder then when I'd started to get a headache. Bryce's arm wrapped around the back of my chair, thumb rubbing in comforting circles on my arm.

Relenting, and desperately wanting to get out of here, I turned to Mia and got her attention. "Bryce is heading back to his hotel. It's right by ours, so I'm going to catch a ride with him."

Both her gaze and Carter's flickered between Bryce and me, her lips turning down into a frown. "Sure, if that's what you want. Which hotel room will you be in when I get back?"

While the question was valid, it caught me off guard a bit; the way Bryce's arm tensed around me told me he'd heard it as well. When I looked at him over my shoulder, his jaw was set, but his focus was on his phone as he ordered us a car. I looked back to Mia. "I don't know."

Bryce didn't pull his gaze from the phone, but he did join the conversation. "If you want to come back with me for a bit, you can. Mia shouldn't feel like she needs to rush."

Mia's eyes narrowed at him. "Josie is also a grown woman. She can entertain herself in an empty hotel room for a couple hours if she wants."

He looked up from the phone. "Of course she can. Whatever she wants."

Both Mia and Carter stared at me, waiting for my reaction. My mind went back to the conversation we had as we left the airport. Going back to Bryce's room was the last thing I should do, but it didn't mean we'd end up sleeping together. I enjoyed spending time with him. Right now, all I cared about was getting away from the noisy restaurant before my headache got worse.

"I'll probably go back with him, watch TV, or something. Text me when you're on your way back to the hotel and I'll head over."

Mia rolled her eyes but said nothing else.

Carter let out a groan, earning his best friend's attention. "Someone let me know if I have to find another room to crash in."

"Fuck off." Though Bryce directed his statement at Carter, it was so low I doubt the other man heard it. Next thing I knew, Bryce was standing with the announcement our ride was here. He pulled out his wallet and handed cash to Carter. "This should cover both of us. We'll text you guys later. Let's go, Jos."

I quickly said goodbye to Carter and Mia, knowing full well they'd talk about us in our absence before following Bryce out of the restaurant. He was more anxious to get out of there than me. Neither one of us said anything until we were out in the humid Ohio night.

I also noticed there were no cars waiting at the curb for us.

Bryce let out a groan, pacing down the sidewalk a bit to avoid the view of the restaurant windows. With a grimace, I followed.

He wove his fingers through his hair before spinning to face me. He started a bit, blinking when he realized I'd followed him. "Sorry about that. I wanted to get away from them. I couldn't stand the way they were looking at us. Or me."

"How were they looking at you, exactly?"

"Like I was doing something wrong! Look, Josie, I would never force you to do anything you don't want to do, you know that, right?" I nodded, because of course I did. "So, if you want to hang out on your own, I will take you to your hotel. If you want to hang out with me, I will walk you back when you're ready. You call the shots. You always call the shots."

I reached out until I could tangle the fingers of my left hand with his right. He stared down at our joined hands before letting out a deep breath. He stepped toward me, closing the distance ever so slightly, relaxed by my reassurance.

Telling me I called the shots wasn't something he'd ever needed to tell me. I knew. In the way he hesitated, in the way he searched my eyes before he took a step closer, I knew. If I showed any signs of being uncomfortable, we stopped immediately. Despite the label of casual hookup, he was one of the few people I felt completely comfortable around. A fact he knew. Which could only mean he was seeing something in the way our friends looked at us.

Reaching up with my free hand, I cupped his cheek until he looked at me. "It doesn't matter what anyone thinks, or what we are. All that matters is the fact I know you and I trust you completely, Bryce."

He didn't look convinced, but he also didn't pull away. "I don't want people to think poorly of you because of me."

"I don't care what they think," I reiterated, stressing every word. "Mia said it herself. I'm an adult. I get to make decisions for myself. Let's go back to your room and hang out."

He relaxed even more, nodding as he pulled me closer with his free arm. I dropped my hand from his cheek and allowed him to pull me into a tight hug. No feeling compared to being wrapped in his arms, regardless of the voice in the back of my head reminding me it wasn't real. Not the way I wanted it.

As we pulled away, his lips brushed the top of my forehead, sending a sensation similar to an electric shock straight down my spine. Such a moment made whatever was between us harder. Moments when I get the smallest glimpse, the tiniest taste, of what it'd be like if he were mine.

About five minutes later, Bryce and I slid into the back seat of a midsize sedan, hands clasped together, and sitting far too close. In that moment, I knew he'd be texting Carter to find a different room to crash in. I knew I'd get an annoyed look from Mia when I made it back to ours. None of it mattered, though. The only thing that did was the person sitting beside me, and whatever piece of him he was willing to give me.

⁓ ele ⁓

The next morning, I attempted to hide my yawns behind a cup of coffee as we sat down on the uncomfortable concrete bleachers. It had been nearly two in the morning by the time I made it back to the hotel room I shared with Mia. Though I tried to sneak in without waking her, I knew she'd woken as soon as I stepped through the door. Mia was a light sleeper.

Neither one of us had done a lot of talking this morning.

"Isn't that your third cup of coffee this morning?" She didn't look up from the heat sheets in her hand. "You should have just brought the whole pot."

"Hotel coffee sucks," I said. "It's never strong enough, and it tastes like shit, but I still need it to get through the morning."

"You could have gotten a good night's sleep, then you wouldn't have to depend on your caffeine addiction to get you through the day."

I ignored the bite in her tone, taking another sip of the disgusting brown liquid as I scanned the deck for anyone we might know.

Apparently, Mia wasn't ready to be done talking, though.

"Please tell me he at least had the decency to walk you back. I swear I'll kill him if I find out he let you leave his hotel at two in the morning alone."

"Walked me to our door and everything." I hated the bite I could hear in my own tone, but I felt the need to defend Bryce. Especially after the conversation we had last night. "He's not an asshole, Mia."

"Never said he was. I don't trust him with you."

"And why is that, exactly? You were fine with him until last summer. What changed?"

"I was hoping he'd grow up and stop treating my best friend like a stop on his travel itinerary every meet we go to." When she finally looked at me, I could see the anger simmering. "Yet you're still hooking up and he's still refusing to admit he wants something more."

"Did you ever stop to think maybe I'm the one who wants to keep things like they are?"

"Oh, please," she replied.

I sighed. "Yeah, okay, it's not me. It sounded stupid even as I said it."

"That's my point, Josie. You get wrapped up in this same routine whenever you see him. I feel like I know the path this is leading you down, and I don't like it."

I wanted to agree with her. I wanted to call her out and tell her I'm not so naïve that I don't see how this is ending, but I didn't. I knew she was looking out for me, the way a best friend should, and I knew she worried I could see what was happening, but I couldn't bring myself to stop it. I couldn't walk away.

As fucked up as it was, having him now, knowing that heartbreak was coming, was still better than never having him at all.

"I love you for looking out for me, but I have to make my own decisions. I know what I'm doing, and I know what I'm chancing."

I've never had someone look at me with as much sympathy as Mia was right now. "Do you? If you know a choice is going to lead to a broken heart, why make it?"

"Because it's better than not knowing," I admitted, trying to keep my voice from cracking. "Even if I get hurt, at least I'll know. I'll know what it's like to have him, in whatever way I can."

Sighing, she slung her arm around my shoulders, pulling me closer. I leaned against her side, taking the comfort my best friend offered. I knew she understood where I was coming from, even if she didn't agree with how I was handling it. This was her way of saying she'd back off, trust me to make my own decisions, and be there for me through whatever the fallout ended up being. Which is all I ever needed.

"You make a fair point. I'll back off. Just make sure he knows I'll hurt him if he hurts you."

I grinned against her shoulder. "Oh, trust me, he knows."

Laughing, she gave my shoulder one more squeeze before releasing me. Our gazes drifted back to the deck, looking for anyone familiar. "I haven't seen Bryce yet. Did he say anything about scratching this morning? They're going to clear the pool in like twenty minutes."

Frowning, I surveyed the crowd for his familiar frame. "No, he told me he would see me this morning."

"Hopefully, he didn't sleep through his alarm. I already saw Carter, which tells me he wasn't in the room last night."

I scrambled for my phone from the bench beside me. I had a text from him asking how Mia was acting after last night. The text had come through about ten minutes ago, which meant he was at least awake.

"Oh, there he is," Mia commented as I typed out a reply. "Except he hasn't started warming up yet."

Feeling even more confused, I looked up and found where Mia was pointing. Standing on the deck—dressed and completely dry—was Bryce. He was talking to one of his coaches, looking at ease as he laughed at whatever was being said. I looked around again, trying to find his main coach, because I couldn't believe he'd be okay with Bryce not warming up.

Feeling a little sassy, I decided to send him a quick text.

Are you going to warm up or nah?

From my seat, I watched as he slid his phone from his pocket, glanced at it, and then looked directly at me with a sly grin. He said something to the coach before turning to walk the other way, typing away on his phone. Just as he disappeared from my sight, my phone buzzed in my hand.

Are you going to warm up or nah?

I'm going, I'm going. It's not my fault I had a bit of a late start today. Did you know you hog the covers?

Grinning to myself, I sent back a cheeky emoji before locking my phone and setting it back on the bench beside me. Mia was watching me. "What?"

She rolled her eyes. "For two people who aren't dating, you're disgustingly adorable."

I just grinned, not needing to say anything else.

Chapter 9

NOW

April 2023

Omaha, NE

"I always look for you, Josie."

I'm frozen in place, staring up at the building where Bryce had first spoken those words to me back in 2016. He'd just made his first Olympic team, our friendship was budding, and it was a few months after our very first kiss. Those words—and the moment we were surrounded in when he said them—were the first clue I had that this thing between was something more. The two of us could be something more.

I'd latched onto the words, ran with them, and gotten my heart broken. And now here we are, seven years later, and he's saying them to me again.

"I knew you were done," he says to fill the silence. "We had talked about how you were done. You'd posted goodbyes on all your social media, but I was still hoping. I kept hoping you'd decide to go to one last meet. I wanted to try to make things right."

I stare at Bryce, uncertain where this conversation is going. Uncertain whether I'm ready for where this conversation is going. I know I can't be the girl I was the first time he'd said those words, and I don't want to be the girl I was the last time we'd had a conversation in the confines of this place. But I also know I don't want to lose him.

"That's why I was so excited when I saw you at work," Bryce rambles. "I was thinking, maybe, I was finally getting the chance to fix what I'd fucked up."

The dangerous feeling of hope swoops through my chest, allowing my mind to wander to what might transpire if I give him another chance. Since walking back into my life, he's been nothing short of persistent, here at every turn, even when I want to avoid him. I've been worried about repeating the past, and he's standing here telling me all he's been trying to do is fix it.

He takes a tentative step closer while I'm still trying to wrap my mind around the conversation. "When we first saw one another two weeks ago, you told me you wanted nothing to do with me. You swore we'd never be able to have a civil conversation. Look at us now."

He makes making a solid point.

"I remember, but one or two civil conversations doesn't magically fix everything."

"No, it doesn't, but it does mean the possibility of us being able to get past this is there. And I'll take that."

My heart is pounding against my chest. "What are you getting at here, Bryce?"

To my surprise, he holds eye contact with me as he answers, "I told you I wanted to take this opportunity to make things right. I messed up, but I want to do this right, Josie. You and me. I want to do what I couldn't in the past. I guess . . . what I want to say is, will you go out with me? On a real date, with the potential for something more."

I blink, every inch of my body stiff like a deer in headlights. After years of thinking about this moment, I never imagined it'd happen like this. I never imagined it'd come when it was the last thing we should be doing. We aren't at a point where I'm ready to take the risk, plus I think the two of us need to get to know each other outside of the sport.

His smile falters a bit, which tells me he knows what I'm about to say.

"You're turning me down, aren't you?"

Biting my lip to keep from crying, I nod.

His smile crumbles further, and he ducks his head in a nod. He no longer wants to meet my gaze, not that I blame him. I know he's searching for an exit, but I don't want him to leave until I have the chance to explain.

"I'm sorry, Bryce." At the very least, my voice pulls his attention back to me. It's the truth. I am sorry I can't take the moment to see what we both can do with it, but now isn't the right time. "I just . . . It's not a good idea right now. You have to know that."

He opens his mouth like he was about to argue, but he relents instead. "Yeah, I do. I guess I was hoping we'd be able to move past what happened and find something new."

"I don't know if looking past it is the right answer, either."

"I know I was a dick back then, Josie. I'll be the first person to admit it, but we were also young. I didn't want the kind of relationship I want now. Back then, I was too young for that. I had just gotten out of a relationship when you and I started things up."

From the start of our situationship, Bryce hardly ever talked about his ex. The little I knew helped me understand how he went from serious commitment to not wanting to tie himself to one person. While I can't say I blame him for that, I'm the one who took the hit for the decision, and I'm not convinced I believe he's ready for something more now.

"I agree with you, Bryce. I understood then, and I understand now, but now it's my turn. I'm not ready to jump into something else with you right now."

"Why not? I want to do this right, Josie. I don't want to just hook up with you. We did it wrong the last time because we jumped into something physical and ignored the emotions we couldn't handle."

"*You* couldn't handle," I correct. "You were the one who couldn't handle the emotions."

His brow furrows. "What are you talking about, Josie?"

"I'm still not over what happened then. Whether you want to believe it or not, you broke my heart."

"Because I didn't want more?"

I consider lying. I consider brushing the question off, laughing about how I had a silly little crush on him, but I don't want to. "Yeah, but also because I did. I'm still learning how to be without you."

"But why do you have to be without me?" He holds his arms out like he's going to envelop me in a hug. I fight every instinct not to step into them. "I'm right here! And I'm not going anywhere."

"I can't take that chance again."

"But why?" He stresses the question, his tone voicing his desperation to understand.

"Because I was in love with you!"

He rears back slightly, a stunned look flashing across his features, eyes wide. I'd surprised him more than I'd surprised myself.

"And I was stupid enough to think you could eventually love me, too."

I watch a myriad of emotions pass over his features. I thought I'd feel more relieved after saying the words out loud, but the relief doesn't come. I feel as though I'd blindsided both of us, and he's grappling with the truth of them. They are out in the open now, and I can't take them back.

A couple of moments later, he lets out a shuddery breath, fingers combing through his hair. "I can't believe I just asked you out. I can't believe I didn't realize you felt that way." He groans, an earnest expression on his face. "God, Jos, I'm sorry."

The use of my nickname—the first time I'd heard it from him in years—had tears stinging the corners of my eyes once again. "Don't apologize, about anything. You didn't know."

"But I should have," he insists. I know he's going to beat himself up over this, but that's not what I want from him. It won't solve anything. "I get why you're saying no, Josie. I'd say it, too."

"I, uh, I need to go," he says suddenly with a glance at his watch. I wonder if he actually has somewhere to be, or if he's looking for an excuse to get away. "I'm happy I ran into you, though. I'll see you on Monday?"

I force a smile, despite internally freaking out about potentially having ruined everything. "Yeah, I'll see you on Monday. Enjoy the rest of your weekend."

My heart is still pounding as I watch Bryce give me a not-so-discreet once-over before he jogs the other way. He doesn't turn back, which is probably a good thing. If he did, I would have taken it all back and asked if we could try again.

I know I'm making the right decision, but I can't help feeling like my last chance is running away from me. The intense feeling of hope settles in the pit of my stomach, but I know better than to give in. I learned long ago: hope is a bitch.

Chapter 10

THEN

June 2017

Indianapolis, IN

"Did you see who's about to start signing autographs?" Mia didn't even glance up from her phone because she was answering her own question. "Obviously, it's Bryce."

"I noticed that." I kept my tone nonchalant as I checked the notifications on my own phone. We were in Indianapolis for National Championships, and I'd done a pretty good job of avoiding Bryce Clark so far. "We can go if you want. Have him sign some stuff for a giveaway. It's up to you, though."

"I thought you'd be jumping at the chance to see him." She nudged me with her shoulder, smirking. "What's going on, Josie? You've been weird since we got here."

"Nothing's going on," I lied.

"I think that's bullshit. Seriously, what happened?"

"Nothing." It wasn't technically a lie. Nothing had happened, and that was the problem. It'd been a year since Bryce and I last saw each other, and except for a few random interviews, we'd barely spoken.

She narrowed her eyes. "Does Bryce know you're here this week, Josie?"

"No," I admitted. As soon as her eyes widened in surprise, I started defending myself. "Look, we've hardly talked since last summer, and I'm trying to distance myself a bit. I don't think it's a good idea to make a big deal out of us being here, especially when he probably couldn't care less."

Mia rolled her eyes. "That's not true, and you can't hide from him. He's going to see you, or our posts, and he'll want to talk to you. You'll have to explain to him why you never told him we'd be here. I know he's asked what meet we were going to, and we've had this planned for months."

"I didn't tell him because we went too far last year, and I can't risk something like that happening again. He made it clear this thing between us won't ever amount to anything real."

"It's great you recognize that, but I'm not the one who needs to hear it. You need to talk to him, and you can't avoid it forever—you're both adults and you made the choice to sleep together."

"Yeah, well, I didn't sign up for this side of adulthood," I grumbled back.

"No one did, bud," she teased. "But that's life; you might as well get used to it. Plus, you've been spotted."

I stood straighter, turning to see Bryce heading right toward me, eyes narrowed into a glare focused on me. Hoping to ease some of the obvious tension, I gave him a smile, but he remained stoic. My smile was returned by his friend Ronan, though.

The closer he got, the darker his glare became. I didn't expect him to stop and talk to me out in the open, especially since the two Olympians had been spotted by people hanging around. Not five seconds later, he stopped in front of us, anger rolling off him in waves. His gray eyes reminded me of clouds rolling in over the river back home, bringing the threat of a nasty storm with them. His jaw was set tightly, no emotion evident in his features.

I'd never seen a look like this directed at me. He was pissed.

□And I could feel eyes on us. People were looking from Bryce Clark and Ronan O'Brien to us, wondering how we knew them. Ronan wasn't helping as he greeted Mia with a tight hug she seemed to melt into, which added another layer of confusion. Another layer I couldn't deal with right now.

□"We need to talk." Bryce's tone matched the look in his eye, sending a shiver racing up and down my spine. He nodded off to the side, indicating he didn't want to do this in front of the audience we had.

"He said something about needing to clarify something from the last interview you did," Ronan declared loudly.

I frowned, but Ronan raised a brow and cocked his head toward the girls behind him. They were listening, and he was creating a diversion.

He turned to face them. "Please tell me you follow Adair Swimming on social media and their website? If you want to keep up with the sport, they're the best blog."

In that moment, he was my favorite of Bryce's friends. He was the only one who'd been successful in putting the attention on himself. He also did it in a way that would give us more exposure in this community. Ronan O'Brien knew what he was doing.

"Can we get a picture with you?" one of the girls questioned, eyeing him as if she were mesmerized.

The look made me recall the first time I'd laid eyes on him. Ronan was one of the most beautiful human beings I'd ever seen. The problem was, he knew it.

He smirked at them. "Are you following Adair Swimming?"

With the group distracted, Bryce caught my gaze, and again motioned off to the side. I reluctantly followed him down the hall to a secluded area. When he decided we were far enough away, he turned to face me. He had a clear view of the group, who would eventually notice our absence and their curiosity would get the best of them.

"Were you planning on telling me you'd be here this week, or was it supposed to be a surprise? Because if it's that, you succeeded. I'm officially fucking surprised."

His tone held such a bite I felt the need to push back. "I didn't know you cared so much. I figured we'd just run into each other like we always do, and we'd go from there."

"Why did you decide to go with that plan instead of telling me you'd be here one of the dozens of times I asked? I know you and Mia; you've had this booked for months."

That sent a spark through me—although I couldn't pinpoint whether it was annoyance or warmth—because he did know me. At least a little. "I wasn't sure what our plan would be this week. I'm still not sure what it is."

Because we were working, too. We wanted to interview a couple of people, connect with others in the governing body of the sport, and seize opportunities to meet up-and-coming athletes. We worked our asses off at these meets, and he knew that.

While being a professional swimmer was literally Bryce's job, running a successful media outlet for the sport was something I was passionate about. We wanted to try and make this work, and we couldn't be successful if we didn't take the opportunities that were presented to us.

"But you knew you were coming," he challenged. "You didn't want me to know you'd be here, Josie, and I'm trying to figure out why."

"It's not like that, Bryce." Why did I keep lying to him? "It's not just about you."

"Then what is it like? Because it sounds like you're freaked out over what happened, despite the fact we talked about it, and are doing everything to avoid me."

"That's—"

"And instead of being an adult about it, you want to hide from me and not tell me when we're going to be in the same place. Real mature of you."

"Do you blame me?" I snapped back.

The question seemed to stop whatever part of his rant was coming next, as he frowned down at me, eyebrows furrowing. "What?"

"Do you blame me for not telling you or talking to you about this? I mean, honestly, Bryce, why would you expect me to?"

"Because we talked about this in the airport before I left Omaha! We talked about how we'd be mature about this."

"And then we didn't have a single serious conversation again. Last summer went a lot further than I expected it to. Things changed between us, and I tried to run from it back then, but you wouldn't let me. I thought, after our talk, things would be a little different. I didn't expect them to be more awkward than they were before."

He sighed, shifting the weight of his backpack. "You know I wasn't looking—"

"Oh, my God!" The way he glanced around to see if I'd caught anyone else's attention made me snap further. "That's not the point;

that was never the issue. Stop telling me where we stand like I'm some idiot who doesn't get it. I do, believe me."

"Then why are you mad at me?"

"Because I thought we could at least stay friends," I hissed, my cheeks flushing. "I thought you would stop treating me like a secretary you need to set an interview up with whenever we're in the same place and start treating me like a friend. I'm not an item for you to cross of your to-do list."

He stared at me, mouth opening, and closing in surprise. "I don't—"

"I know what you're doing, Bryce, I see it." I didn't want to hear whatever he was going to say. "You're using my position in the media to protect yourself. Keep me around without letting me in. So, you know what? Yeah, I'm here. I'll be here all week. If you have the chance to sit down for an interview, that'd be great. I'll send you a message and we'll set something up."

Just as I turned to head back, his hand closed around my wrist, keeping me in place. The firm, warm heat of his grasp was enough to stop me in my tracks. "And if I just want to hang out with you?"

I shake my head. "Sorry. I will be spending any free time I have hanging out with my friends."

"Josie," he muttered. "We're friends."

"No, I don't think we are." He dropped my hand as if I had burned him; it was a feeling I could relate to. "You should go. You have an autograph session to get to."

With nothing left to say, I made my way back to Mia and Ronan. Security had ushered the group of fans into the room where the signing would take place, so no one seemed to be paying them any mind right now. Just as I reached them, Bryce stormed past, heading straight into the autograph session. Ronan looked at me with wide eyes, his mouth gaping open. He looked impressed, but all I wanted to do was hide from the world.

"I don't know what happened back there," he began, choosing his words carefully, "but it looked badass."

I laughed, but there was no real humor in it. I glanced at Mia. "Can we get out of here?"

Without questioning anything, she grabbed her bag with a nod. "Ronan is going to sign some cards for us to give out."

I flashed him a grateful smile before walking out the door, knowing Mia would follow. I didn't look into the room where Bryce was doing his signing. I didn't pay attention to the few people who were giving me confused looks. I needed to get out of there. The atmosphere, the smell of chlorine, was suffocating me, which was a first.

~ele~

Later that evening, I was back in our seats, waiting for finals to begin. Mia had decided to take a walk around the venue, wanting to stretch her legs before she was stuck in the uncomfortable plastic seats for a couple of hours. I'd opted to stay back, watch our seats, and reply to some comments on our social media page.

Ronan had found me about five minutes after she left, checking in on me after earlier and to drop off the autograph cards he'd set aside for us. I was surprised to find a couple from Bryce as well. We chatted until he had to get back, and I was left alone again.

As Bryce went through his typical warm-up routine, he'd catch my gaze every now and then. Every time it happened, I'd promptly look away, focusing on my phone, or the heat sheets. Every time I looked away, it was a little harder than the time before.

About five minutes before the meet started, Mia reappeared at my side looking pissed off. I moved my bag off her seat as she approached. "How was your walk? Did you run into anyone?"

"No one," she replied, as she sat down. "I need to ask you something, though."

She'd never opened a conversation with me that way. We always said what was on our minds. "Sure, what's up?"

"How many people know about you and Bryce?"

My eyebrows rose. "I don't know, exactly. Carter and Ronan know for sure since they're his best friends. There might be a couple others, but I don't have a list or anything. Why? What happened?"

"No reason," she brushed me off. "I wanted to make sure he wasn't spreading crappy rumors about you and what's going on between you guys."

I knew he wasn't. Whatever happened between us didn't exactly paint him in the best picture, and he wouldn't run the risk of what would happen if it went public. He wouldn't risk his reputation, and I felt confident saying he wouldn't risk mine either. He wasn't that kind of person.

"I don't think he'd do that, but why do you think he would?"

"No reason."

"You know I'm not going to buy that." I searched her features, looking for any hint as to what she was saying. "What's going on? Did you hear something or run into someone on your walk?"

Her fake smile was unflappable. "Nothing like that. You know me, I worry about you. Especially after what happened this afternoon. I want to make sure you're good."

There was something she wasn't telling me. Someone she was trying to protect. I knew it wasn't Bryce, because she'd been looking for a reason to tell me to let him go. If he had said or done something, there would be no question whether she'd tell me. I didn't know who she was protecting, but it was clearly something she didn't feel was her business to get involved in. If I was okay, she would let whatever this was go and I wouldn't get any more information out of her.

Still, it probably wouldn't hurt to do some digging of my own, to find out who knows about what happened between us.

Chapter 11

NOW

April 2023
Omaha, NE

I spent the rest of the weekend reflecting on my conversation with Bryce in front of Riverview. The way it pulls in so many memories, the good and the bad, and how it is forcing me to realize I missed having him in my life. Even if I'm not ready to jump into anything romantic with him right now, but maybe we can at least try to be friends.

After all, he said he wanted the chance to do this right.

I want to talk to Mia about this, dissect every little thing that can go wrong, or right, if I were to pursue a friendship with him. Though I had a feeling she'd discourage me from the idea. If I decide to start something up with him again, I need to be the one to make the decision and see it through.

By Monday morning, I have made up my mind that Bryce and I can be friends. Starting there, we can work our way back to whatever is on the cusp of happening before it all goes to shit. It always seems like a great plan, but then Bryce seemed to do his best to avoid me.

I'm not used to being the one ignored and avoided in our relationship. Usually, the tables are turned. And I'm freaking out about it.

What if I've fucked up so badly that we can't move past it? I swore I'd never tell him how deep my feelings went back then, and then the words came tumbling out the very first chance they got. There's no going back from that. There's no way to make him see how uncertain I am about where we stand now, but I know he's hurt me more than anyone else has ever hurt me before.

Now he's doing what I've asked of him in the past—giving me space. And the space between us feels like an ocean. I want to be closer to him again; I want him back in my orbit.

By Wednesday morning, I've had enough of Bryce Clark going out of his way to give me space. He hasn't given me a chance to say hello, let alone tell him that I'd spoken too soon. So, on my way to work, I stop at my favorite café and get him his usual coffee—or what used to be his usual. Black with the smallest amount of sugar still seems gross.

He's the only person at the office when I arrive, hard at work already. With the mess all over his desk, it's clear he's been here a while, but his sleeves aren't pushed up his arms yet, which tells me he either has a meeting later or the stress hasn't gotten to him yet.

I clear my throat as I approach his desk, startling him. I watch him tear his gaze from the computer, eyebrows raising, gaze moving from me to the coffee in my hand. When his gaze meets mine again, I smile, and hold out the cup. He squints at it like caffeine is a foreign object. "What's this for?"

"A couple weeks ago, you told me you'd bring me coffee until I learned to like you again," I remind him. "Now it's my turn to bring you coffee until you learn to like me again."

His brows furrow, still staring at the cup. "I don't think there's ever been a single second where I didn't like you, Josie."

His words are like a shot to my heart, but I can't shake the unease his avoidance caused. "Okay, so you still like me, but you've been doing a damn good job avoiding me the last couple of days."

"I was trying to give you the space you asked for." His eyes don't waver from the coffee.

"I know, but asking for it was a mistake," I admit, hating how vulnerable I sound. Especially because we're at our place of work. My colleagues never see this side of me. I'm the employee who comes in, does her job, and goes home. "I don't want space, Bryce."

Lips pressed into a thin line, he stares back at me. "I have never gotten so many mixed signals from someone who doesn't want to date me."

I let out a groan, which also mixes with a little laugh. It's a weird sound, but it causes the corners of his lips to quirk up. "Ugh, I know! I'm sorry. I don't have a clue what I'm doing."

Bryce stands, leaving inches between us, before taking the coffee from me just to set it on his desk. My breath catches in my throat. It's been years since we've been this close to one another, but I'm taken aback to see he still has the same effect on me—goosebumps, heart thumping, and the thrill of knowing what it feels like to have his body pressing mine against the nearest flat, vertical surface.

And now is not the correct time to be thinking about anything along those lines.

"It's me, Jos," he murmurs, voice low. "Me and you. Just like it's always been. Tell me what you're thinking."

A week ago, I would have panicked at the realization of how he can still pull me out of whatever spiral I was heading down. Now, though, it's calming. It's a reassurance that, for the first time in years, I'm not alone. There's someone else by my side. And there was even a time in our lives when he understood me just as well as Mia. In some ways, even better.

I inhale a deep breath, looking up to meet his gray eyes, which are full of concern. "I want all of it back!" His frown deepens as the words stumble out of my mouth. "I miss being your friend, Bryce. I miss the two of us understanding one another the way others might not have. I shouldn't have asked for space because it's not what I want. I want you in my life."

His entire facial expression changes to the open, smiling man I know; it eases the tension from my shoulders. "Then we can do that; we can be friends. I want to be your friend, Josie."

I'm waiting for the other shoe to drop, waiting for him to say *but*, yet it never came. He's being sincere about wanting to be my friend despite my inability to give him what I now know he wants. It takes me back to every other big moment we've shared. I know now, as I did then, I'm the one calling the shots. Bryce will voice what he wants, but he will never pressure me into giving more than I'm ready to give.

I know him better than he wants to admit. He's a good guy—a good guy who could inflict a lot of pain on me. He's human and has the same complexities we all do.

"Good, that's what I want." I'm not certain if we can do this; if we can just be friends without getting tangled into everything else, but I want to try. "I'm sorry I can't give you what you want right now."

He's shaking his head before I can finish. "Don't apologize for that. Our roles were reversed for way too long. Now it's my turn to be patient and I'm happy to do it for you. For us."

For us. The words send another jolt of something I can never quite explain down my spine. He's being way more mature than I anticipated, and I'm beyond grateful for it. I hope he understands that by saying "not now," I wasn't saying "never." This is new territory for both of us.

"I'm not sure how we're going to pull this off," I say with a light laugh. "How are we supposed to be friends after everything that's happened between us?"

Amusement is evident in his eyes. "We were friends first, right? We'll do it the same way we did back then. We've always been just friends. Really, *really*, good friends."

"Bryce, no!" I huff, faking annoyance at his cheeky response. He chuckles as a million memories flash in my mind, proving just how good of friends we've been. "That's not what we want to accomplish right now."

Still grinning, he holds his hands up in mock surrender. "I'm kidding! Well, kind of, we were great at being friends before everything else. Let's go back to that—back to how things were before the meet in Mesa. How about we hang out this weekend? You can show me your favorite spots in Omaha."

Another memory shoots through me, and forms in my mind like it happened yesterday. Every detail slides into place, reminding me of the last time he'd said those exact words and how what followed was something I'll never forget. "Do you remember what happened the last time you asked me to show you around Omaha?"

To my surprise, and amusement, a faint blush coats his cheeks and he clears his throat. "I didn't mean it like that."

I can't pass up such a golden opportunity to tease him. "Oh, is it how you meant it that night? Did I miss the innuendo?"

His cheeks darken even further, jaw dropping open. "What? *No!*"

My resolve breaks, allowing a single giggle to escape. Once one sneaks out, and a look of confusion crosses his features, I lose it. I can't calm my laughter, even if I want to. Bryce pouts when he realizes I'm teasing him.

"I'm sorry," I say, giggling around the deep breaths I'm taking. "I couldn't help it. And the look on your face made it worth it."

He cracks a smile. "Is this the point we're at now? Can we laugh at the past?"

Though the question is asked innocently, it was enough to calm me down. Somehow, I manage to keep my knee-jerk reaction at bay. "At least some of it, yeah. The rest of it, maybe one day."

Now I'm the one saying a string of words that flashes memories through the both of us. A haunted look crosses over Bryce's features, letting me know his mind has taken him several states and years away.

"One day," he repeats, "but not yet."

Chewing at the corner of my lip, I shake my head. "No, not yet."

He nods once, but has a soft smile on his face. "I can work with one day."

The sound of approaching voices shatters what's left of our little bubble, catapulting us back to the reality of a life we never would have anticipated. A life I never thought I'd even tolerate, yet here I am, staring at the last person I would have ever expected to find here. What a surprise to our past selves we'd be.

"We'll make plans," I promise as the voices grow closer. "We'll give this whole being friends thing a fair shot, right?"

"Absolutely. In the meantime, we should probably do something we're paid to do."

I grin at the lame joke. "Have a good day, Bryce."

"Yeah, you too, Jos." He reaches for the coffee abandoned on his desk. "And thanks for the coffee."

He's started calling me by the familiar nickname again, and it feels good to be that person with him once more. I like Jos. She's fearless, brave, and someone I want to be. With him calling me Jos, I can almost believe I'm her again.

And the feeling of confidence, of being seen so perfectly by someone who matters to you, has me floating on a cloud the whole way back to my desk. Where my cloud is overshadowed by the presence of Sarah leaning against my desk.

"Hey." She looks up from her phone at my greeting, watching me approach with a frown. "What's up?"

She doesn't say anything, just watches me as I drop my bag in my chair and set about getting ready for my day. Being under her scrutinizing eye has me fidgeting with anything I can get my hands on, and I only let the silence last for a minute before I can't take it anymore.

I turn to her again, hands on my hips. "Okay, what's going on? I'm a little creeped out by the silent staring."

"I'm trying to figure out why it took you so long to get to your desk this morning."

I blink at her. "What?"

She shrugs, picking at a perfectly manicured nail. "Your car was already here when I got here, and I didn't see you in the cafeteria when I stopped for coffee. And I know you weren't utilizing the gym."

Self-consciousness causes my shoulder to bristle. "What the hell does that mean?"

"Please, you've never used our gym, Josie."

Yeah, because the people I work with are assholes. I have enough gym trauma on my own; I don't need to add to it. But I'll never tell her that, and the condescending tone she's using is sending me into the shy bubble I hate.

"I have a membership somewhere else, Sarah. Not that it's any of your business."

"So you've said," she replies coolly. "Where is it again?"

I glare at her. "It's a women's only gym out west. Now, what is it you need me for, Sarah? I have a lot of work to do this morning."

"I wanted to see how things were going with you and Bryce."

My back stiffens as I stand up straighter. "That really isn't any of your business, is it?"

"I'm looking out for you as a friend." She frowns sympathetically. "The day I tried to introduce you, it was quite clear to me he'd hurt you. I don't want to see history repeat itself."

Sarah is the last person I want watching out for me. We've been friends long enough for me to know to be cautious. She always has her best interests at heart. "That's considerate of you, but I don't think you need to worry. I'll be fine."

"I disagree. Josie, it's rather immature to get involved with someone who already has a history of hurting you."

I bristle at the use of my nickname. Clearly, she's taken it upon herself to start using my preferred name. "I know what I'm doing, Sarah. Thanks, though."

She doesn't look convinced, but her phone lights up in her hand, signaling an incoming call. She glances down at it before looking back at me. "If you insist. I need to get this."

"I'm fine. Thanks for stopping by."

"Just remember, history repeats itself."

She's already accepted her call and is walking away before I have the chance to say anything else. Once again, she got the last word in and felt proud of herself, despite how clueless she was.

Chapter 12

THEN

June 2017

Indianapolis, IN

The next morning, Mia and I got ready in silence. Both of us were lost in our own thoughts, though I wasn't as sure of where hers were wandering to; I was still dissecting everything that had happened the day before. As I dug through my suitcase, I kept glancing to where she was doing her makeup cross-legged on the bed—perfecting her black winged eyeliner in a way I never could. The triple moon tattoo I had inked into my ribs stood out against her pale wrist.

I'd always hated it when there was something between us I couldn't fix.

"If you keep looking at me, I'm going to mess up." She sighed as she lowered her arms. "What's up?"

I bit my lip, wondering if this was something I wanted to bring up to her. Maybe I was making something out of nothing. "I just . . . I want to make sure we're good."

She frowned at me. "Why wouldn't we be?"

I shrugged, refolding the top in my hands and setting it in my bag. "Things have seemed weird since yesterday, that's all."

"Which makes sense, because yesterday was weird," she said. "Josie, I have your back, you know that. You also know I'm always happy to ignore Bryce and drive him crazy, but next time give me a heads-up, okay?"

I nodded. "Yeah, I will. Although, I didn't even realize that was my plan until it was happening." She laughed, going back to her makeup. "And the other thing?"

Her smile faltered, but she covered it by focusing on what she was doing. "What other thing?"

"Whatever happened last night, with you. Are we good with that?"

"That had nothing to do with you, Josie. It had everything to do with the rumors I thought he was spreading about my best friend, that's all."

"And you're not going to tell me what made you worry about it in the first place?"

"There's nothing to tell," she insisted. "You should get changed if we want to get out of here on time."

A glance at the clock confirmed she was right. "You'd tell me if it was something you thought I needed to be aware of, though, right?"

"Absolutely. Now go get ready! But don't wear that shirt; wear the one with the open back and the cute jeans."

Laughing, I grabbed the outfit she mentioned and headed into the bathroom to finish getting ready. About fifteen minutes later, we were stepping off the elevator to grab breakfast before heading to the natatorium. As the lobby full of swimmers came into view, I cursed under my breath.

A bunch of them were Bryce's teammates, as indicated by the Georgia gear they were wearing. While Bryce had gone to school in Arizona, he'd moved to Georgia when his childhood coach was named head coach out there. It made logical sense. I always had a feeling he'd go back to him if given the chance, especially since it meant he and Carter would train together again.

"I'm guessing you didn't know they were staying here?" Mia questioned from my right.

"Nope," I replied, following her to the buffet layout. "We were too busy arguing to have a conversation, remember?"

"Well, I don't see him yet," she said, grabbing a plate as she glanced around the crowded room. "Maybe we'll get lucky. Maybe he's at the pool already."

"Don't get too hopeful."

I jumped at the voice suddenly behind me. With a beating heart, I turned to see Carter standing to my left, looking over the options like he didn't just scare the shit out of me. "What the hell, Carter?"

He grabbed a couple pieces of bacon, smiling apologetically. "I'm just telling you, he's about to come downstairs for breakfast."

Heart jumping into my throat, I turned to Mia with wide eyes. "We need to go!"

She shook her head, frowning. "Um, no. What we need to do is eat breakfast like the calm, rational adults we are. You aren't going to run away every time he comes around. If you don't want to talk to him, you don't have to."

Carter hummed in agreement. "But he's going to want to talk to you." Mia leaned past me to glare at Carter. "Hey, don't shoot the messenger, I'm just telling you the truth. As your friend, I'm giving you a heads-up. I'm still not entirely sure what even happened."

Mia almost looked gleeful to tell him. "My best friend told your best friend to get the fuck over himself." I groaned between them while she grinned proudly. "What? That's more or less what happened!"

Carter gave me an impressed look. "You did that?"

Meekly, I nodded. I didn't think it was that big of a deal or anything impressive, but Mia had a point. I'd told him what I thought he needed to hear. "Yeah, I guess so."

"Good," Carter replied. "He deserved it."

I'm not sure how he would know that, given the fact he wasn't around for what happened yesterday. Then again, Bryce was his best friend, and they were likely rooming together. Carter also knew things about him I didn't—things that would warrant a response like that. His response also made me think back to what Mia had said last night, asking me about what people knew about us. Now I was wondering if she had a point.

"I'm going to grab a table, Jos," Mia declared once her plate was full. "Before the rest of the swimmers come down and take over the lobby."

Nodding, I kept plating my breakfast. As soon as she left Carter and I to ourselves, I wanted to ask him about what he knew, and whether Bryce had been saying about us without my knowledge. The problem was, I didn't know how to do that. Sure, Carter and I had always gotten along well, but this was potentially interfering with a friendship that was twenty-three years old, and I didn't want to be that kind of person.

Still, I had to know. "Hey, Carter, can I ask you something? It's something I might not have any business asking you, so please tell me to go to hell if you want, but I need to know."

Carter looked a bit surprised. Which left me to figure out how to ask without outwardly accusing him of dragging my name through the mud.

"Um, does Bryce . . . Does Bryce make jokes about the two of us?"

His brows furrowed as he tried to work out what I was asking. I was trying to figure out another way to get my point across when his eyes widened in understanding. "No, Josie. Oh, God no."

I relaxed, the built up of tension dispelling. His reaction was enough proof he was being truthful and that he understood what I was asking. "Right, thanks. I didn't mean to accuse him or anything but—"

"Don't apologize," he cut me off, keeping his tone low despite no one else being near us. "*If* you were worried that was a possibility, I'm glad you asked. Look, I'll be honest with you. Bryce has given Ronan and me a very brief explanation of what's going on between you two. We know you've kissed, and we know you hooked up last summer. That's it."

The part Carter wasn't saying was the fact Bryce hadn't given them any details. He'd just stated a fact—we've slept together, which was a perfectly normal thing for two people in their twenties to do.

"Bryce is . . . Well, Bryce is Bryce, as I'm sure you know. He can be intense, and he can be a bit of an ass."

Carter was right. He wasn't telling me anything I didn't already know. Ever since last summer, when Bryce made his first Olympic team, there had been a new level of intensity in him. It was clear his focus was already on something that was still three years away. "Yeah, I've noticed that shift, too."

"I'm trying to get him to talk about it, but he's, you know." Carter explained what he meant with an eye roll. And, yeah, I did know. "That's not the point. Despite all that, he would never talk about you like that, Josie. I want you to know that. You're not a joke to him, even if he can't show it."

The last bit of tension left my shoulders. While I would give anything to hear those words from Bryce himself, hearing them from the person he was closest to was just as reassuring. "Thank you for telling me. Logically, I know it's true, but sometimes I get caught up in my own head. Especially around him, and especially after something like what happened yesterday."

"Bryce is my best friend, Josie, but I also consider you a friend. I won't take sides in something like this, so if something's bothering you again, talk to me. Okay?"

A wave of gratification washed over me as I smiled at him. "I will, thank you. That means a lot."

He chuckled, the sound coming out a little awkward. "Yeah, well, I know what he can be like. I just wanted to make sure you know it's not us and him against you."

"Well, that's good to know, but I wasn't too worried," I lied. "Besides, I have Mia on my side. She's my secret weapon."

I followed him over to the coffee station, desperately needing a cup myself. "You know, he actually is terrified of her."

He handed me the mug he filled up, and I took it with a quiet thank you as I reached for the creamer and sugar. "Good, that means my plan is working."

"Is your plan to scare him into shape or something?"

I shook my head as I fixed my cup of coffee. "An evil genius never reveals her plan, Carter. Thanks for the coffee and the chat."

"Anytime," he replied as he made his own cup. "I'll see you guys later."

When I turned to find Mia, I was taken aback to see Bryce standing off to the side. His jaw was set, eyes narrowed at Carter. The look on his face was one I'd seen once before, last summer in Omaha.

It had taken me a minute to realize what it was then, but now I recognized it as jealousy. He was jealous of Carter and me talking, of how we seemed to get along well. Which was ridiculous, because Carter had a boyfriend and I was not interested in Bryce's best friend that way.

Rolling my eyes, I went back to searching for Mia. There was no way I was dealing with this right now.

When I found Mia, she had already finished most of her breakfast. We discussed what Carter and I had talked about, and that Bryce seemed to be peeved when he saw us together. Just as I expected, Mia rolled her eyes, and made a comment about how his jealousy had gotten us into trouble before. Bryce didn't have the right to be jealous. I knew Bryce had to be behind us somewhere, because her gaze kept flicking over my shoulder as we talked. Stubbornly, I kept my head forward.

A minute later, she stood up. When I gave her a questioning look, she flashed me her phone and announced she needed to call her parents before we headed to the pool.

I glared at her back as she deposited her trash and moved across the lobby to step outside and make the call. How dare she leave me to the wolves? Figuratively speaking, obviously.

She wasn't even gone a full minute before Bryce was sliding into the seat across from me, a guilty look on his features.

"Nope," I said, shaking my head as I picked at my bacon. "Not in the mood to talk to you."

"That's fine. You don't have to talk. I'll talk and you can listen."

"And if I'm not in the mood to listen to whatever bullshit you have to say to me?" I glared at him, just wanting to finish my breakfast. "I don't have to listen to you, Bryce."

"Then I'll just sit here and talk. You can either listen or ignore me. It's your choice, but there are some things I'd like to say." My glare didn't move. "Please, feel free to finish your breakfast."

I pushed some potatoes around my plate. The only way to avoid him would be to gather all my stuff and move, which was the last thing I wanted to do. Plus, it would get the attention of everyone around us. I knew it wouldn't stop him. He'd just move with me and, when he realized I'd had enough, leave me alone until we could talk later. I was too annoyed to avoid the inevitable, so I might as well face it head-on.

"I want to apologize about yesterday, to start," he began. "I was out of line. You don't have to tell me what your plans are if you don't want to, we're not in a relationship. We don't need to keep tabs on each other. I also know that saying you should have told me you'd be here was hypocritical for that very reason. Why should I expect you to tell me what was happening when I've made it explicitly clear I wasn't looking for a relationship?"

"I'm glad you can acknowledge that, at least."

He frowned at my word choice, but continued, "I'm also apologizing for constantly pushing that fact. I don't think you're an idiot, Josie. I knew you get it, and there's no reason for me to keep bringing it up, but I just . . . I want to make sure that I'm not disappointing you."

I raised my gaze from my plate to stare back at him. The last thing he said was hanging between us for a few seconds as I tried to figure out what I wanted to say. There was a vulnerability in them that I rarely saw, and I wasn't sure how I wanted to respond to them. "You're not disappointing me, Bryce. Last summer took a turn I wasn't expecting, and that's fine. Whatever. What I didn't expect was to be treated like a business contact afterward. Especially when I thought we were friends."

He tensed. "I wasn't trying to—"

"If you regret that we fucked, just say it now, and we can both move on."

His jaw dropped open at the blatant way I put it. It was a defense mechanism for me, being vulgar, and crass in situations where I felt uncertain. The people closest to me were well-aware of this trait, but not Bryce.

As soon as he got over his initial shock, he was shaking his head. "I don't regret anything that's happened since I met you. Do you?"

No, I wanted to admit, *and I never will*. But was I ready to be that open and vulnerable with him yet?

His frown deepened, as though he could see the truth behind my silence. "If you regret this, then we part ways here, no questions asked. I never wanted to make you feel uncomfortable, Josie. I never want you to do something you don't want to do."

"I don't regret it," I admitted. I wasn't ready to let him off easily. "But it also doesn't matter what you were trying to do, Bryce. You still made me feel like someone that was quick and easy. I thought things had changed between us after last summer. You said things had changed. I wasn't looking for forever; I just thought we were friends."

"We were—we are." His eyes searched mine for doubt. "I was a jerk yesterday. I've been a jerk for the last year, and I want us to move past that. We can do that, right?"

I had two options. I could forgive him and see what would happen, knowing my heart would end up broken, or I could walk away and break my own heart. Like always, he was giving me a choice, and well, maybe there was a part of me that was a bit of a glutton for punishment because I wasn't ready to say goodbye to him just yet.

"We can move past it." I made the choice. Whether it was right or wrong, time would tell. I just knew I wanted him in my life as much as possible. For as long as I could have him. Still, I couldn't help but sneak in a slight warning. "You should be careful, though. Mia's pissed at you."

I held in the giggle as his eyes glanced toward the door she had just gone through. The look on his face was pure panic. "Oh, God."

"After everything that happened yesterday, she was telling me to avoid you. Then she started in on a rant about how I didn't know what you were telling people behind my back."

His panicked look worsened. "What are you talking about? I would never say anything bad about you behind your back."

"I didn't think you were, but I got confirmation this morning," I assured him. "Mia's protective. I don't know what made her so concerned randomly, and she wouldn't tell me, but she wanted to make sure I was okay."

"Do you think I should talk to her, try to set the record straight?"

I was shaking my head before he even finished the thought. "Absolutely not. Telling her there's nothing to worry about will just make her worry more, and she'll always worry about me the same way I worry about her. There's nothing you can do to calm her."

The only thing that would ever get Mia to back off would be for us to be in an actual relationship, but that wasn't something he was looking for right now, and I respected that. There was no stopping the feelings I had for him., but I wasn't going to force him into a relationship he didn't want to be in. At the end of the day, Mia's biggest fear wasn't even that he'd hurt me. Her biggest fear was that

I could hold on to an idea of what a future with him could look like but never get close to it.

And to be honest, that's what I was most afraid of, too.

Bryce didn't look convinced. Which made sense to me. He liked to be in control of what people thought of him; he liked to fix things when his reputation was targeted. Still, he trusted me enough to know I knew her better, and trying to prove himself to her would only make her distrust grow.

He relented as he relaxed into his seat. "Okay, whatever you think is best. All I care about is whether we're good."

"We're good," I promised with a nod. "But I don't think we should have a repeat of what happened last summer."

Without hesitation, he nodded, just like I knew he would. I was always in control of whatever happened between us—I knew it then and I knew it now. "Whatever you think is best."

"I appreciate that."

My resolve lasted all of ten hours. After finals that night, I found myself stumbling through the door of his hotel room, lips attached in a heated kiss as he pushed me against a wall, his tall frame encompassing me a second later. And I melted into him, exactly how I knew I would.

Chapter 13

THen

June 2017

Indianapolis, IN

The weird thing about swim meets was how quickly they went by. Blink, and one might feel like they missed the whole thing. Before we knew it, the team for World Championships had been named, and the meet was over, leaving us exhausted—both emotionally and physically.

This was the first meet we worked in an official media capacity, and I felt like we'd barely had any time to spend with friends.

"Josie Martin!"

I spun around at my name, just about running right into Mia, who appeared less than thrilled. I mumbled an apology before looking over her shoulder to see Bryce, Carter, and Ronan coming toward us.

Mia groaned. "Do we have to talk to them? I'm tired."

Ronan approached us with an easy, assertive grin that only men who knew they were handsome could pull off. "Where are you ladies off to?"

"I think we're going to grab some dinner, then head back to the hotel." Mia made a sound of confirmation. "What about you?"

"I think we're doing the same thing, right, guys?"

All the guys nodded in confirmation, and I wanted to suggest we all go together, but Mia had just told me how tired she was. I didn't want to be that friend, the one who forced her to do something social when her battery was drained. I'd be mad at anyone who did it to me. Although I could tell by the way Bryce was looking at me told me he was thinking the same thing. Forcing our friends to hang out because we wanted to wasn't fair.

Plus, there was nothing stopping us from hanging out alone.

"There's a chain restaurant a couple blocks from here," Mia declared, surprising us all. "Generic food that never fails and hardly any wait. I'll put our names in before we head out. Everyone in?"

Bryce looked surprised, but I shrugged. I was as unsure of what to make of this situation as he was. "Yeah." He cleared his throat. "Sounds great, Mia. Thanks."

Already typing away, she nodded. "A table for four?"

"Um, no, there are five of us," Ronan pointed out before anyone else had the chance to.

She glanced up, like she was surprised to find him there. "Right, I wasn't sure if you'd be joining us or if you'd have other plans." I knew my best friend well enough to know that she'd taken a hit at his tendency to hook up. From the frown on his face, Ronan knew it, too. "Okay, table for five."

Bryce and I frowned at each other, exchanging questioning looks to see if we were the only ones sensing this new tension. Ronan was frowning at Mia, while Carter was rapid-fire texting someone without paying us any attention.

"Okay, the table will be ready in twenty minutes," she declared, pocketing her phone. "Are we walking?"

"Yes," I decided for the group. "That gives me some time to grill Carter on who he's texting so furiously over there."

Everyone forgot about the awkward tension between Mia and Ronan as a bright, teasing grin bloomed on Bryce's features. "He's got a new someone. The jerk won't give me or Ronan any details, though. Please, grill away."

"Dude, seriously," Carter groaned, also shoving his phone in his pocket. "Can't you two drop it? I won't be on my phone tonight, I promise."

Mia linked her arm through his, pulling him closer. "No way in hell are we dropping this. Come on, dude, talk to us. You know, anything you say tonight is completely off the record."

I took his other side, which earned an eye roll from Carter. "So, naturally, you have to tell us everything."

Sighing, Carter shook his head while Mia and I began to lead him out of the natatorium, hoping Bryce and Ronan would take the hint and follow us.

"All right." He gave in. "His name is Ben, and he's British."

"Oh," I said, like this was the most important information he could give me. On his other side, Mia wrinkled her nose in distaste. "Don't look at her, Carter. People with accents have burned her too many times. She's jaded. Tell us more."

Laughing, he launched into the tale of how he and Ben had met one of the rare nights his friends had managed to drag him out. As we talked and headed toward the restaurant, the five of us broke into small clumps, Bryce and Ronan giving Carter the room to keep the conversation private if he wanted. When Carter didn't pull them in, Bryce hung back like the good best friend he was. Despite the way our heads were ducked together, voices low as we listened to the love story, I could hear pieces of Bryce's conversation with Ronan.

"Dude, Abrams is stealing your girl," Ronan joked, unaware of the spark he sent up my spine.

Your girl. Is that how his friends see me? As his girl? It's not something I'd ever heard Bryce say about me, and it certainly wasn't a title I'd use for myself. Maybe things were different now. We'd fought, we'd talked, and things seemed different. Maybe this was going to be it.

Bryce chuckled, the sound low, and deep, filling me with warmth. "That's okay. I'm happy they get along. Plus, he can steal her all night if it means he talks to someone about this Ben dude."

Eventually, Carter was ready for the focus to be off him. Still, he and Mia continued to talk, shifting the conversation to other topics while I drifted back to hover by Bryce and Ronan. As soon as I was at his side, Bryce's arm slid around my shoulders.

"Did my best friend tell you everything?"

I looked up at him when he pulled me in closer. Concern was evident on his face. "I did. He seems happy."

"Are you going to tell me any of the information he bestowed on you?"

My brow arched. "Bestowed? That's a big word for you, Clark." Ronan let out a loud, surprised laugh beside him while Bryce, who was used to my teasing, rolled his eyes. "And no, I'm not. The conversation was between me, Carter, and Mia. He'll tell you whatever he wants when he's ready."

Frowning, Bryce looked ahead to where Carter and Mia were still laughing. "We tell each other everything."□

There was always something unsettling about a friend keeping something from you, especially something big. It was a reaction, and a fear, most people acknowledged, and I wasn't surprised to see it written all over Bryce's face. Anyone who paid attention could tell their friendship ran deep.

"He's not keeping it from you, Bryce. He's not sure where things are going; it's early. He doesn't want to brag about someone he's not sure he can keep."

A different emotion flashed across his gray eyes, his protective streak also familiar to me. "But you promise me he's good? I worry, ya know? His last relationship was—"

"He's good," I assured him. "He's not going to keep it from you forever. Give him a chance to figure out what's actually happening."

"Can you three pick up the pace a bit?" Carter called from the entrance; he was leaning against the wall with his arms crossed over his chest. "I'm hungry."

"When are you not hungry, dude?" Bryce teased. "We're literally twenty steps behind you."

"I'm too hungry to deal with semantics, Clark," Mia warned from beside Carter. When she deemed us close enough, she pulled the door open. "You were slower than us, which is all that matters."

"Then let's go eat." Ronan reached for the door, taking it from her to hold it for all of us. Mia glared at him. "What?"

"I am more than capable of holding the door open for everyone, Ronan O'Brien."

Startled at her tone, and the obvious anger in her eyes, he dropped the door, thinking she still had it. Less than a second later, it shut against her shoulder and her glare darkened. "*Seriously*? I thought you had it!"

"Shit," he cursed, eyes wide, hands scrambling to grab it again. "I'm so sorry, Mia—"

Sighing, she wrenched the door from his grasp and moved aside to allow him to enter. "Just go inside."

Ronan glanced at us in helpless confusion before following Carter into the restaurant. Whatever was going on with the two of them clearly wasn't something he understood.

Mia caught my eye as soon as he passed and shook her head. "Josie, please don't."

The reality was I couldn't even if I wanted to because I had no idea what was going on. "All right, I won't. But we'll talk later."

It wasn't an option as I led Bryce past Mia and into the crowded restaurant. Whatever issue she had with Ronan was something I needed to know about; he was one of the last people in this sport we needed to isolate. People gravitated toward swimming because of athletes like Ronan, and that was the audience we wanted to target.

"Do you think she'll talk to you about it?" Bryce hissed the question in my ear as we stood at the hostess stand.

The girl finished gathering our menus and was motioning us to follow her when I glanced back at him. "Not a chance in hell, but I'll still try."

As though she knew we were talking about her, Mia shot another glare in our direction before following the rest of the group to the table. As soon as we were settled and various conversations started, any thought of the weird tension between Mia and Ronan was forgotten. Even between the two of them, the conversation seemed to flow more naturally.

Much later than any of us should have been out, we started making our way back to the hotel. Ahead of us, Mia and Carter were arguing about some statistic regarding the men's 1500 meter freestyle that I couldn't be bothered to listen to. Ronan was hovering nearby, listening but not contributing to the conversation.

I was still trying to piece together the weird tension between him and Mia when Bryce wrapped his arm around my shoulders. Warmth pooling in the pit of my stomach, I leaned against him as we walked.

He lowered his head until he could whisper in my ear, "Come back with me?"

Despite the voice screaming in my head that this was a bad idea, a shiver went down my spine at the low tone of his voice. His gaze was locked on me, waiting for my answer.

Once again, I was in a position where I knew I should say no, but everything in me wanted to say yes.

Saying yes wasn't necessarily a bad thing. People hook up all the time. Engaging in healthy, consensual sex wasn't something to be ashamed of, and I wasn't. What I was ashamed of was my inability to grasp the boundaries he was putting on the situation.

No matter how many times he told me otherwise, I would continue to want more.

I smiled softly. "Sure."

He tugged me closer, pressing a kiss to my thick waves as we continued to walk. □

When we got to the hotel lobby, Bryce pulled Carter and Ronan away from us, while I went over to talk to Mia. Carter was annoyed at having to vacate his room, but relaxed when Ronan offered him the spare bed in his.

As I pleaded my case, Mia narrowed her eyes, and crossed her arms in a weird mix of exasperation and disappointment. Eventually, she relented and sent me on my way with a reminder of what time we had to leave for the airport. Seconds later, Bryce was tugging me through the elevator doors. None of our friends followed.

Neither one of us said much of anything as we made our way back up to his room, but the butterflies seemed to be working overtime in my stomach. Stepping off the elevator, he took my hand, and led me down the hallway, not releasing it until we were through the door.

I stood inside the room as he locked the door behind him. When he turned back to face me, he looked as uncertain as I did.

"I hope you know I didn't invite you up here to—"

This time, I made the first move. In a couple of steps, I closed the distance between us, standing on my tiptoes to connect our lips. He froze for a second before kissing me back, his hand wrapping around the back of my neck, tilting my head to get a better angle as he deepened the kiss.

A startled gasp escaped me as the other hand moved to cup my ass, pulling me in closer. Melting against him, my own arms reached up to wrap around his neck.

"Bryce," I mumbled, breaths coming out in short huffs as he pulled away, lips trailing a path across my cheek toward my neck. "Bed."

The hand at the back of my neck swept down my back to join his other one at my hips. His lips returned to mine, his urgency obvious as he explored my mouth before our tongues intertwined. He slowly moved us backward until the back of my knees hit the bed.

His rough fingers skimmed beneath my shirt, dragging it up as they made a path up my ribs. Feeling rather impatient myself, I reached for the hem, parting from him long enough to pull it off. I bit my lip as his gray eyes scanned over the exposed skin. Then they drifted up to meet my own. In a flash of confidence I'd never experienced, I held his stare as I reached up to undo the front clasp of my bra, letting it fall down my shoulders. Bryce let out a quiet groan.

He leaned down, capturing my lips in a short, desperate kiss. Pulling away, he pushed at my hips until I sat down on the edge of the bed. "Lie down, Josie."

Helpless to do anything else, I followed his instructions, scooting back until I could rest against the pillows. I watched as he tugged his shirt over his head before turning away long enough to grab a condom from his bag. Then he was over me. Muscular arms caged me in on either side of my head, and I'd never felt so comfortable.

Resting his forehead against mine, his eyes watched me carefully. "You sure?"

My answer came by combing my fingers through his hair, pulling him down to me for another kiss. "Yes."

Chapter 14

THEN

June 2017

Indianapolis, IN

My eyes opened as I felt the bed shift beside me. The room was dark and still, indicating the sun had yet to rise. Just as I was about to drift back to sleep, my cell phone lit up the ceiling above me. I frowned, waiting for the light to go out. Although I didn't know what time it was, I knew it was far too late, or early, for Bryce to be awake right now.

The phone never turned off.

I startled him as I rolled over. "Time is it?" I mumbled, blinking up at Bryce. God, he's handsome. I rested my head against his arm, attempting to make my eyes focus on the screen. He didn't move it away from my gaze. "And what are you looking at?"

"It's almost four," he replied, scrolling through a document starting to look suspiciously like psych sheets.

"Are you looking at psych sheets right now?" I questioned. My eyes were able to focus enough to read the name he stopped on—Haurto Sasaki, his biggest competition. The Japanese swimmer was favored to win both of Bryce's signature events. Which also happened to be the only two events he'd be swimming at Worlds. "Bryce, why are you looking at this right now, babe?"

He stiffened at the endearment. "I couldn't sleep, so I decided to see what some of the top times are right now. You know how important it is to know what I'll be up against once I get to Hungary."

My frown deepened. He already knew what those times were, but that wasn't the point. He was panicking and I couldn't get a sense of why. "Yeah, that makes sense, but do you have to do it at four o'clock in the morning right after you finish the qualifying meet?"

He gave a casual shrug. "I have nothing better to do."

"You should be resting. It's been a long week; you don't need to be looking at that right now. You have plenty of time to prepare."

"You don't understand." He kept his gaze locked on the screen as he scrutinized splits.

Suddenly uncomfortable in the room, I sat up and swung my legs over the edge of the bed. With the sheet wrapped around my body, I grabbed my underwear, and his discarded shirt from the floor as I made my way to the bathroom. He didn't even glance up.

Knowing he wouldn't miss me, I took a few extra minutes to comb my tangled hair and wash the grime of last night's makeup off. When I left the bathroom several minutes later, I left the light on so the room would have at least a little light. I wasn't shocked to find him in the exact place I left him, eyes still glued to his phone.

I shifted my weight from one foot to the other. "I think I'm gonna go."

The murmured words seemed to break him from whatever daze he was in. Bryce looked up at me, surprise swirling in his gray eyes. It was a look I'd seen before, no matter how hard he tried to hide it; it told me he didn't want to be left alone.

"What? Why?"

Now it was my turn to shrug. "You seem distracted and like you want to be left alone."

He blinked at me. "It's four o'clock in the morning, Josie. You can't leave."

"I'm staying in this hotel, Bryce," I replied, exasperated. I guess it was nice to know at least a part of him cared about me. "I'm not leaving the hotel; I'm taking the elevator down a floor."

Before I knew it, he was out of bed, phone forgotten on the nightstand, as he crossed the distance between us. My breath caught in my throat as he approached me.

He must have pulled his underwear back on when he grabbed his phone, as the black boxer briefs were low on his hips, showing off the defined muscles he worked hard for. I kept my gaze from drifting any lower. I already knew I'd give in to whatever he said next.

When he reached out to me, I had no other choice but to take a step closer.

"Don't leave," he murmured, voice deep as he gripped my hip to pull me against his chest. I wrapped my arms around his neck as his lips brushed my forehead, then my cheeks, and, finally, my lips. "I don't know when we'll see each other again."

I wanted to point out we could change that. We could make more of an effort to see one another outside of a meet, but I knew doing so would be counterproductive to getting him to open up about whatever was going on inside that head of his. That part of him that always seemed impossible to reach.

"Do you want to talk about it?"

His eyes fluttered closed when my nails brushed against the skin. "You can talk to me. Tell me what's got you freaked out tonight."

Eyes opening, he looked down at me, reaching up to push the bangs from my eyes. "I need this to go perfectly. Not like last summer."

My brows furrowed as I tried to figure out the hidden meaning behind his words. I knew he wasn't happy with the results of last summer, but I didn't think he'd see it as something to be ashamed of. "You won a silver medal at the Olympics. Why are you acting like it was some huge disappointment?"

"Because it should have been gold."

I almost made a joke about how cocky he was being, but I knew this wasn't him being overly confident in his abilities. In fact, it was quite the opposite. He was angry with himself for not winning. "That's not how it works, babe. You can't manifest a gold medal into existence."

"I know, but I trained like hell to be on that team, and I ended up being a failure."

"Whoa, what? Who says you're a failure?" The word hung in the air between us. "No one thinks you're a failure because you got second. You should have heard me screaming at my TV. I cried."

He stepped away from me. I wanted to reach out, pull him back in, and let him feel my arms around him. But I knew better than that. It was clear he wanted some space.

He sank down on the edge of the bed, shoving his fingers through his hair. "You know the history the US has in that event. I fucked it all up."

I stepped forward tentatively. "You did not. Bryce, you swam a hell of a race. Your training did exactly what it was supposed to do. You got on the podium."

"You don't understand."

The words hit me like a slap in the face. It was the first time someone had said them out loud to me. No matter how many times I said it to myself, hearing them would always be different.

I kneeled in front of him, my hands resting on his knees. He dug the palms of his hands against his eyes. "You're right," I said, keeping my tone low and soft. "I don't understand, but that doesn't mean I don't want to help. So, help me understand."

When he looked at me, his eyes were a little bloodshot. "I've dedicated my whole life to this sport. I worked hard to get here, against all the odds. Against so many people who told me it'd never happen. I proved them all wrong; I made the team. And then I fell short."

I was struggling to wrap my mind around what was being said. While the idea of post-Olympic depression was being discussed more openly, it was the first time I was having a conversation about it with someone I knew. Someone I cared about. The first time it'd made its way into the sport's media, I'd read everything I could on the subject. I was curious about it. What did someone do when they got that dream? What did an Olympian do when it turned out to be everything they wanted it to be? What about when it fell short?

Now Bryce was opening up to me about those questions, looking for guidance, and I didn't know how to help him.

"No one wants to go to the Olympics and barely miss out on a gold medal," he continued. "Maybe that's the problem, knowing I was that close to making it happen and I couldn't."

He was right. This was something I didn't understand; it was something I could never understand. It pained me to know he was feeling this way, because where I saw something to be celebrated, he saw failure. I didn't know how to help him cope with that, or if I could even help at all. Would he let me if I could?

"Have you talked to anyone about this? I think you should find someone who can help you with this. You don't need to deal with it all on your own."

"I've talked to some of my friends and my coach a bit," he admitted. "They know I'm putting extra pressure on myself. They're aware of it."

While that wasn't what I had been leaning toward, knowing he was at least talking to someone eased my worry. Even if he wasn't being completely honest, I trusted his coaches to keep an eye on him. They would know if something more needed to be done.

Still, I knew the world of professional sports could be unforgiving for athletes and wanted to stress to him how okay it was to ask for help.

"Maybe you need to talk to a professional. That's more along the lines of what I was thinking."

"I don't need a therapist," he groaned. "I'll be fine. Seriously. I just need this to go well."

"And then you'll be fine." I watched as he relaxed ever so slightly. "Until the next one, right?"

He opened his mouth to argue, but closed it just as quickly when he couldn't find the words. While I wasn't aiming to hurt him, or even call him out on his bluff, I knew he saw what I saw. The words hit the very spot he was trying to ignore. He could push me away all he wanted, but in the end, nothing would get better if he didn't deal with this.

He knew that, but I wasn't sure he'd do anything about it.

"That's not how you want to live your life," I whispered. I tried to get him to look at me, but he wasn't budging. "You know it'll catch up with you in the end."

"I'm fine, Josie," he said, and I wanted to scream at him. He was the furthest thing from fine. "Or . . . I'll be fine."

I couldn't make him listen. I couldn't make him open up. Getting mad at him would only result in him further pushing me away. So, I yielded, and decided to let it go. "Okay, if it doesn't get better, please talk to someone. Promise me?"

He stared at me with an intensity I had never seen before. "I promise."

Before I could question anything else, he was leaning down to kiss me. His warm, soft lips moved against mine in the all-consuming way I'd never encountered with anyone else. It was the kind of kiss that could pull me from reality—make me feel like I was floating. The kind of kiss that should be the result of more than a hookup. This was the kind of kiss people wrote novels about, and it was always like this with us.

As it got deeper, I melted into the kiss a little more. His tongue traced my bottom lip, coaxing my mouth to open. As soon as his tongue tangled with my own, he reached out for my hand and pulled me up until I was straddling his lap. His firm body pressed against mine as he gripped my hips.

Combing my fingers through his hair, I shifted closer until I felt every inch of his solid body against me. He was the first person I'd ever felt this confident with—assertive enough to take control and to ask for the things I wanted. As a woman with curves, I never would have guessed an Olympic athlete would be the first person to make me feel beautiful, but here we were.

I gasped as his hands gripped me tighter, grinding his hips against mine. As soon as I pulled away from the kiss, his lips moved to my neck. I released a small whimper, head tilting back.

Fleetingly, I wondered how we always ended up here.

He kissed his way up to my ear, teeth grazing the skin as he went. "Do you want me to walk you down to your room?" He leaned back to look up at me. "Or do you want to stay?"

I pressed a kiss to his cheek as I stood back up. "I'll stay, but we need to sleep. It's been a long week for both of us."

Nodding, he stood and pressed a lingering kiss to my forehead before stepping past me to go to the bathroom. I crawled back into bed and pulled the covers over me. While I waited, I took a minute to look at my phone and read through some notifications. When I heard the bathroom door open, I put the phone down and sank down onto my pillow.

I watched as Bryce made his way back over to his side of the bed. He stopped at the nightstand long enough to plug his phone in, then slid in beside me. Warmth spread through me as he pulled the covers over himself, cocooning us both in.

"Goodnight, Bryce," I whispered, closing my eyes.

He wrapped an arm around me, pulling me against his side while his fingers rubbed over my bare arm. Trying not to grin too much, I laid my head against his chest. Cuddling was something new for the two of us, and I knew it couldn't mean anything, but I was going to bask in it for as long as I could.

Saying goodbye until who knew when was the day I dreaded the most during these trips. Not only did I have to say goodbye to Bryce, but I also had to say goodbye to Mia, too.

I stayed with Bryce for as long as I could, basking in the early morning. When Carter showed up an hour before they needed to leave for the airport, I decided it was time to hangout with Mia while I could. Bryce walked me back to our room, pulling me in for a quick kiss and a hug before we parted.

As Mia and I packed, she avoided the topic of Bryce. No tension or weirdness existed between us, but it was clear she wasn't in the mood to talk about any swimmers. Our flights weren't until later in the afternoon, so we stopped for lunch and to shop before heading to the airport.

The airport was busy, but I managed to get my bag checked quickly and found a bench to wait for Mia. I'd agreed to walk her to her gate, giving us as much time together as possible.

I was scrolling through my photos, deleting those that were blurry, when someone called my name. Glancing up, I spotted Ronan coming toward me, dressed in black shorts and a gray T-shirt, and a baseball cap to cover up his messy hair. I was willing to bet no one in that airport knew who he was, but everyone seemed to be paying attention.

"Hey," I said as he shrugged off his backpack and plopped onto the bench beside me, long legs stretched out in front of him. "What are you still doing here? I thought the Florida guys left last night."

"I had some brand stuff I needed to do and an interview," he told me. "What time are you out of here?"

"Not for another three hours, but Mia rented the car, and she leaves in an hour."

He nodded, adjusting the brim of his cap. "You and Bryce get everything talked out? You seemed fine at dinner."

"Yup," I assured him. "We talked it all out. We're good."

"You know he's always excited to see you, right? Whatever meet you're coming to is his favorite one of the year."

Something in the pit of my stomach fluttered, unable to ignore the hope that shot through me at those words. Still, I had to remind myself they weren't coming from the person who mattered. "People keep saying that to me, but he never does."

Lips pressed in a tight line, Ronan shook his head. "He can be a bit of an idiot. He's got this idea of how he's supposed to act and what he's supposed to do and be. I don't understand why a relationship doesn't work into whatever plan he has, but he's not budging."

"You all have insane pressure on you," I defended, "and since I'll never understand it, I have to trust he's making the right decision."

"Yeah, but you're his . . ."

I raised an eyebrow. "I'm his what?"

He smirked at me. "I don't know. I was kind of hoping you could fill in that blank. Any time we ask him, he says you're his Josie. I don't think he even knows what that means."

I knew I sure as hell didn't.

"I don't have the correct term to fill in that blank. We're friends, but sometimes we're more? I don't know how he wants it explained."

He shifted, facing me. "Carter and I know the basics, nothing more than what you just said to me. Most of us know you're friends, obviously, but I don't think they know there's more."

The last ball of nerves that had been nestled in my stomach since the beginning of the week eased. "Thanks, Ronan. I needed to hear that."

"Don't mention it." He glanced down at his phone to check the time. "I need to head out, but can I say one more thing that you might need to hear?"

"Yeah, sure," I replied, fighting back the urge to laugh. What could Ronan O'Brien possibly have to say to me? "What's up?"

"Do me a favor and don't forget you have just as much say in what happens between the two of you as he does. Don't let him be the only one running the show here."

I gaped at him. Despite being one of the older swimmers on the team, he wasn't known for being deep or mature. He was happy to live a pro-athlete lifestyle. He liked to party, knew he was hot, and he had no problem never being seen with the same woman more than twice.

He stood, grabbing his backpack as he looked at me. "Take it from someone who's been him. He's going to hurt you. And that's not fair to you."

"If you know it'll hurt, why do you do it?"

He shrugged, like nothing could touch him. God, swimmers, and their confidence. "Haven't you heard? I'm the team asshole! Bryce just thinks he is."

I could see the cockiness I always attributed with him waver. "Ronan—"

He shook his head. "I gotta go, Josie. It was good seeing you, though."

"Yeah, you, too."

I watched as he turned to walk toward security. He had only taken a couple of steps when my stare caught Mia stepping away from the desk to head toward me. Ronan's steps faltered as he spotted her, too. Then he turned back to me.

"One last question," he said, close enough to talk at a normal volume. "Why does Mia suddenly hate my guts?"

With that one simple question, realization crashed into me. Mia's concern about what Bryce was telling people hadn't come from him. It had nothing to do with anything she'd overheard him say. Maybe it had nothing to do with him at all. It still had something to do with Ronan, though. The way Mia acted whenever Ronan was near was different from anything I'd seen before. She'd even tensed up when he was brought up in conversation. It was never about Bryce; it was about Ronan. He was the one she was mad at. I just had no idea why.

Which was why I didn't have an answer for him.

"Maybe she heard you were the team asshole?" I offered, trying to tease, but also trying to convey the truth—I don't know.

His smile faltered slightly, but he quickly replaced it with an amused grin. "Damn, scared another one away, and I didn't even do anything this time. Have a good flight, Josie."

He turned and walked right past Mia as he made for security. Though the two of them had known one another for years, no one would ever have guessed it, as they avoided each other like strangers. She was rolling her eyes as she neared me, but Ronan looked back at her with an expression that almost looked hurt.

As soon as he realized I was watching, he looked away.

"What did he want?" she questioned, looking down at her phone.

"Just wanted to make sure Bryce and I had a chance to clear the air."

"Well, you were in his room having sex all night and morning," she commented. I rolled my eyes. "So, you obviously made up."

"And I know you're not mad at Bryce, you're mad at Ronan." Like I'd expected, she tensed up at his name. "What did he do?"

She glanced behind her, where we could barely see him as he started to disappear in the crowd. "He existed. Trust me, that's enough."

Whatever happened, it had been bad. It took her another moment to even look at me. "Well, I don't think we're getting rid of him. We'll probably see him next meet."

She shrugged. "And I'll deal with it then. Right now, I'm happy to hate his guts."

Except we didn't see him at the next meet.

In a shocking twist of events, Ronan O'Brien announced his retirement a few months after Worlds as allegations of doping started to creep into social media, which was made worse by his silence. The quieter an athlete was, the more people wondered what was going on.

When a story broke that he'd refused to take a drug test, people assumed it meant he was doping. Mia and I attempted to jump to his defense, but it was hard when we didn't have any answers, either. He wasn't responding to messages. He announced his retirement, explaining he had been on medication he knew would be flagged on the test, and had declined to take it.

What was more confusing than anything was the fact he retired because of it. We knew there had to be more to the story, but it was one of those things we would never quite get answers to. When I approached Bryce, he'd replied it was Ronan's decision and, as far as he was aware, there was no intentional doping involved.

Although Mia swore it never bothered her, we never saw him again and never got real answers to what happened. And something about his absence bothered her. She had questions she'd never get answers to. If anyone understood what that felt like, it was me.

Chapter 15

NOW

April 2023
Omaha, NE

"Do you remember the first time we met?"

I instantly grin, the memory flashing through my mind as if it were yesterday. We had both been so young, both of us awkward, both of us full of big dreams and no idea what the road ahead had in store for us. Now, we're both adults with careers, trying to move on from the past and make a friendship work during a happy hour on a Tuesday evening.

"Oh, absolutely," I confirm, unable to tamper my grin. "Do you?"

Laughing, he nods. "I'd just broken up with my ex who I swore I was going to marry."

"I believe the exact words you used were 'I was just naïve enough to think I'd found the one at eighteen.'" I make the same exaggerated grossed out face he'd made all those years ago. He laughs harder. "I never met her, but I'd heard stories about her. Everyone seemed convinced you'd end up married, but weren't shocked when it ended."

"She wasn't as bad as she sounded," he argues. "Yeah, Carter hated her, but she had good moments, too."

I pick at the appetizer between us. "Everyone does, but I knew she was the reason you were so hesitant to start anything real between us."

He takes a pull from his beer to think over my statement. "I was a kid blinded by a love that came way too young to understand it. At least, it was love on my end. I was scared it'd happen again. So I decided it could wait. Which, after everything we've talked about, makes me feel like a bigger dick than I already do."

"Well, you know what they say about hindsight."

"Yeah, I do. Now we'll never know what could have happened if I hadn't been the idiot incapable of letting people in."

Sipping my margarita, I shake my head. "You can't think like that. No one gets a redo, and you'll never have answers to those questions, so don't bother thinking about them. Things happened, we made our choices, and now we have to live with the consequences."

My words come from experience, even if he doesn't know it. I've played the what-if game more than enough times to know it never yields new answers, or provides a new perspective—it will drive someone crazy. It's a path that's never worth going down because no one can go back. Moving forward is the only way, hopefully in a way that allows more chances.

He watches me carefully, with a contemplative look in his eye. I shift in my seat. "Do you regret it?"

A sob almost breaks through before I have the chance to stop it. Regret will never be an emotion I feel when it comes to him. "No. I probably should, though. I was naïve back then."

He nods, maybe in agreement, or maybe he's thinking over my answer. I give him a couple of seconds, waiting to see if he will continue the conversation he'd started. It's one we need to have. When he still doesn't say anything, I ask, "Why? Do you?"

Our gazes lock again, but his face remains blank. "I have a lot of regrets about that time in my life. Things I wish I'd done differently."

The response feels like a punch to the gut. It's a literal reminder not to ask a question if I'm not prepared to hear the answer. While I'd always known Bryce meant more to me than I did to him, it's disheartening to hear it echo in his words. Hearing him say it out loud is a reminder he had been prepared to walk out of my life at any given moment. "Oh, I see."

"All of those regrets have to do with swimming, and the person the sport made me. None of them have anything to do with you or us."

I stare blankly at him. "Oh, I see."

The grin that overtakes his features causes the corners of his eyes to crinkle, causing my stomach to do the annoying flip-flop thing it always does whenever he smiles at me like that, open and genuine. "Did I render you speechless?"

I laugh. "Honestly? I'm not sure yet. I'm still trying to process your answer."

And as I do, he decides to hit me with another nugget of truth designed to rock my world. "The only regret I have when it comes to you is that I couldn't give you more."

I can tell I'm going to need a therapy session just to process everything he's said to me in the last three minutes. At the very least, a long conversation with my best friend and a large glass of wine.

"I didn't know how to own up to what I was feeling," he admits. "I didn't know how to own up to the fact I was lost. I was so lost."

From here, it's like I can physically feel the conversation shifting around us. We are entering into a topic we've tiptoed around the entire time we've known one another—the mental health aspect of his entire career, the injury, and the retirement. He's ready to acknowledge this dark cloud that hangs over us.

I'm not going to let him shut down the conversation this time, especially since he's the one bringing it up. "I understand, Bryce, really. I guess what I don't understand is why it took you years to push me away. Why wasn't it over before it even started?"

He tears the edge of his napkin. "I don't know. I always felt this pull to you, and the deeper into it we got, the more I became afraid of being alone."

"Being alone? Bryce, people constantly surrounded you. I could never get you alone." The excuse is hollow to my own ears. Being alone while surrounded by people is something I know intimately, and it sucks. "That wasn't the right response. I'm sorry. Let me try again . . . I get what you're saying, but there were so many people in your life who would have been happy to be there for you."

He shakes his head. "Not the way you were."

"You never let me in."

His gaze remains serious and unwavering. "I had just started seeing a therapist the last time we met. Hell, I still am. I was at the point where I knew it was going to get worse before it got better. I pushed you away because I refused to take you down with me."

Bryce is practically known for being terrified of his feelings. He doesn't want people to know when he's suffering; he doesn't want them to see him in pain. When I think about him like that, I reflect on the night in Indianapolis when he'd shut me out. To the point I was ready to walk away. The panic in his eyes at the thought of me leaving has stayed with me. Along with the feeling I should have pushed harder, done more to get him to open up to me.

It took me months, and several therapy sessions of my own, to come to the realization that I can't force people to open up. They have their own choices to make, and I was never the one he wanted to lean on in those moments. I had to respect that.

"I knew I had to end things," he continues, watching me carefully. "I hadn't talked to my therapist about you yet, but I knew I needed to let you go. I had to do it in a way where you would walk away without looking back. You wouldn't have given up on me unless I hurt you. It makes no sense now; it's one of my biggest regrets, but it's what I thought I needed to get better back then."

"You're right about me not giving up on people." Even now, I can't shake the memory of that day. "I never gave up on you, even when you pushed me away. I tried so hard—for years—to get you to talk to me. I saw the pressure you put on yourself, but you refused to acknowledge it."

"It scared the shit out of me, Josie. I never wanted to be found by someone as much as I wanted to be found by you."

"Bryce—"

"I took advantage of the fact I knew you'd always be there, hoping I'd eventually be ready to let you in, but I couldn't get there, and I'm sorry for that."

"You don't have to apologize."

"No, I do," he insists. "Because I was scared, and I hurt you."

"Scared of what exactly?" He's being so open with me, so honest about the feelings he had for me back then, and I want to get as much information as I can. I want to understand.

"The very last thing I wanted was to take you down with me."

I hold his gaze, hoping he can see the truth in my eyes. "You should have given me a chance. I'm a good swimmer."

He smiles with the shake of his head. "I don't doubt that. You were this ray of sunshine, and I knew I would snuff that out. How selfish would that have been of me?"

The full extent of what he's saying hits me, hard. I already know how he'd struggled with post-Olympic depression, but he's sharing just how much it affected his life. How he couldn't get away from it, how it consumed him. Even then, I'd known how guilty he felt about his mental health state, which is one reason this hasn't been discussed until more recently. Most athletes fall into the same thought process as the general public. They have everything, they're Olympians—what can they possibly be sad about?

But what does one do when the biggest, most implausible dream comes true? Where do they go from there?

"And you said that you were getting help with this?"

"I have a therapist who does virtual visits," he explains. "It took a while; I was too stubborn to admit I needed the help."

"I distinctly remember you telling me you didn't need a therapist." My mind drifts back to that dark room in Indianapolis. "I tried to get you to understand back then."

"I wasn't ready to listen to anyone then. I fell into that trap where I had nothing to be upset about, that everything was in my head, and I needed to learn how to deal with it. Finally, one day, I was with some of the guys, and they were talking about how they'd gotten help after Rio . . . It just kind of clicked. I wasn't the only one going through it, so I had nothing to be ashamed of."

"You needed to hear it from someone who was going through it. You're right, though, there's nothing to be ashamed of. You can be the biggest advocate for mental health, but it's still hard to admit you need help."

"When I first started, I kind of figured it'd be something that magically went away after a couple of sessions." He frowns. "Now, four years later, I'm still working on it. Something new always seems to come up."

"That's life," I reply. "People have such a stigma about mental health and who it should affect. I've never understood it. Everyone can, and will, struggle with it at some point. This idea that certain people should be better than that or immune to it is bullshit."

He gives me an amused look. "I never realized how passionate you are about this. I knew Mia and you were supporters of more awareness, but it's nice to see you so fired up about it."

"I am! I wish you would have given me the chance to say it to you all those years ago. It's a cliché, but it's true—it's okay not to be okay."

"I wish I would have been in a good enough place to hear you say it," he says. "To be honest, I wouldn't have believed it back then."

His ability to acknowledge that makes me realize just how much shit he'd gone through. Had I been paying so little attention as to let this go unnoticed—

"I know that look on your face, Josie," he cuts in. "Stop blaming yourself. I made sure to keep you at arm's-length because I knew you would see right through my façade."

I swallow, looking at him like I expect him to vanish at any minute. This is the conversation I've wanted to have with him for so many years, but was never given the chance. "I'm going to say something that the Bryce I knew wouldn't like."

He raises an eyebrow, looking intrigued. "Well, there's a very long list of things it could be, so let's have it."

"I saw you, Bryce," I say. "No matter what you think, I saw you. I just couldn't reach you, not the way I wanted."

His eyes widen before he breaks eye contact. He swallows to clear his throat. "Uh, Jos—"

"I saw you then," I continue, wanting him to hear me. "And I see you now. I've always been on Team Bryce, and I always will be."

When his gaze meets mine again, there are tears swimming in his gray eyes. "Like I said, you were the only one I ever wanted to be found by. You still are."

There is a fleeting moment where I find myself wondering why I'm not dating this man, but I know this is where we need to be right now. We need to learn how to be friends again before we can be more. Plus, I'm still not sure if I'm ready to jump into anything more with him.

"I'm right here," I promise.

"That almost sounds like you're agreeing to be friends."

"I'm at happy hour with you, aren't I?"

He laughs, relaxing. "Do you think that we could ever be more?"

I know we can be. That has never been the problem. The problem was always whether we should be. That is still the big question mark. If I am the one asking, I will want an honest answer, so that's what I decide to give him. "I don't know, maybe."

While I know he doesn't like the answer, he doesn't challenge it. Which tells me he knows I'm being truthful with him. Neither one of us knows where the future is heading. Our focus should be on the here and now. And right now, I want him back as my friend.

"I'm good as friends for now." He grins. "I'll take that maybe and make it my mission to make it a yes."

I ignore the flutter in the pit of my stomach. "I don't know if I'll be ready for more anytime soon."

"I'm patient. Should we get another drink?"

"You are the furthest thing from patient Bryce Clark." I laugh while he grins back at me before finishing his drink. "But, yes, we should."

✦✦✦

Later that night, I find myself lounging on my couch with my phone held up above my face. Mia is staring back at me, a purple face mask smeared across her face. I'm too tired to even walk into my bathroom to find a mask, let alone practice self-care. After the evening I spent with Bryce, I need someone to rant to.

"I'm terrified this is getting too real." I frown. "I feel like I'm on a slippery slope and there's no way to prevent myself from falling."

"So then, maybe you should let yourself fall."

I stare at the phone in silence for a few seconds, waiting to see if she heard what she'd just said. "Who are you and what have you done with my best friend?"

Mia laughs. "I know, I know. I can't believe I said it either, but it's true."

No matter how hard I try, I can't wrap my mind around the fact she's telling me to go for the very man she'd spent years telling me to run away from.

☐"I don't know what's happening here, Mia. I feel like I'm in the twilight zone or something. You were always the one who told me to run for the hills when it came to Bryce."

"No, I never said that." She waved me off. "I told you to be careful around him because I saw the hold he had on you. I didn't want my best friend to get lost because she was too caught up in a guy. I wanted you to be careful."

"But I still got my heart broken."

"And you fixed it, Josie." I'm still trying to wrap my head around what she's saying. "You proved to yourself you could live without him, and I'm so proud of you for doing that, but this is also a second chance. Those don't come around too often. The question you have to answer right now is whether you want to continue to live without him."

A rush shoots through me. It's a feeling I can't quite put my finger on. Mia might have a point. When I last saw him, I'd been convinced everything was over between us forever, and we would never see one another again. At the time, that's what I needed to be true. Having it be true allowed me to move on and get to where I am now.

Now everything is different and not having him in my life might not be the best option anymore. But I'm still hesitant on whether I should risk it.

"What if he breaks my heart again?"

She sighs, almost like she knew the question would arise. "It's a risk you'll always be taking with dating. At least with him, you already know you can heal from it."

"I'm not sure I can. What if I can't survive him again?"

"You and I both know you can. The thing I'm not sure you could live with is yourself, if you let this chance pass you by."

It's so easy to recognize with Bryce here right now, and to pretend he isn't going anywhere. I'm doing to him what he had done to me, taking his position in my life for granted. There's nothing keeping him here if something else came up. Nothing except me.

"The Bryce Clark you just told me about is not the same person we knew," Mia continues. "This version is giving you a chance to know what it'd be like to have him the way you always wanted. I think you owe it to yourself to get some answers."

When I'd called her, I expected this conversation to go very differently. I'd expected her to assure me I'd made the right decision, that Bryce is the last person I need to get mixed up with. Instead, she's doing the exact opposite, and it's causing a tightness in my chest.

I'm terrified to put my heart back on the line for him again.

But she has a point—if I want answers, this is my chance to get them. And it might be my last chance. And I've been telling myself I need to take more chances. "If he breaks my heart again, please remind me of this conversation. Remind me I'm saying yes, because I deserve to know what it could be like."

"Even if that happens, I don't think you'll regret this."

"Well, let's hope I don't have to find out. I can't believe I'm going to agree to this—to go out with him."

"If you ask me, it's about time the two of you attempt to do this right."

After years of doing everything backward, skirting around putting any sort of solid label on things, I'm left unsure what taking it seriously will even look like for us.

"You should text him," Mia replies as brightly as she can with the mask on. The purple of the mask seems to put a spotlight on the mischievous glint in her eye. "Right now."

"Mia," I groan, feeling my cheeks heat up.

"You told me you exchanged numbers, so don't even think about lying. Plus, I know you. If you don't do this now, you're going to talk yourself out of it."

"Fine," I grumble, sitting up a little straighter and pulling my phone closer. I'm sure I look spectacular all up in her face, but she's my best friend. I don't care, and she has a point. "I'll text him."

She's quiet as I type out a quick message:

> Hey, I've been thinking about what we talked about tonight . . . Still up for that date?

"There, it sent." As soon as I hit send, my phone buzzes in my hand. One message follows another. "That was fast."

"I'm not at all surprised," she teases.

Ignoring her for a moment, I focus on the messages.

> Hey, I've been thinking about what we talked about tonight . . . Still up for that date?

> Damn, that didn't take long. I told you I was patient.

> In all seriousness, absolutely. Prepare for me to woo the shit out of you.

"Ugh," Mia groans in disgust. "I was hoping you'd stop making that face when he said something to make you swoon."

Looking back at the screen where her face matches her tone, I stick my tongue out. "Bryce Clark has never made me swoon."

Mia rolls her eyes. "Who do you think you're trying to fool here?"

"All right, fine, he has." I point a finger at her. "I want you to remember you were the one who talked me into this."

Another text came through.

> I'll bring you coffee tomorrow morning. Goodnight, Josie.

At my bright, cheesy smile, Mia let out a loud sigh. "What have I done? I'm going to regret this forever!"

Maybe she will, but I can only hope I won't.

Chapter 16

THEN

August 2016
Omaha, NE
Rio de Janeiro, Brazil

From where it sat on my bed, my phone lit up with a picture of Mia and me from last month. Barely taking my eyes off the TV, I accepted the call, and put it on speaker. "I'm losing my shit, dude."

Her laugh echoed through my room. "Yeah, I knew you'd feel that way. Hence, the phone call. No one should have to sit through their boyfriend's first Olympic race alone in their bedroom."

"He's not my boyfriend, Mia." I groaned. "But I am happy you called; I don't want to do this alone."

"He's your something, though. Why aren't you watching this with your parents? Isn't your mom a huge Bryce Clark fan?"

I relaxed as the TV cut to a quick update on what was happening in the other sports. Sports I couldn't care less about. "She is, but they have company over tonight. It's my dad's boss. They want to talk about the future of the company or something. So, I'm stuck on my own."

"Is your dad's boss aware of the fact you might lose your mind? I mean, I stood next to you when he made the team, and you were screaming your heart out."

"Shut up." The camera panned back over the pool, a couple minutes away from the start of the 400 individual medley. My heart was practically in my throat. "I'm probably going to cry."

"Probably? I'm absolutely going to cry."

Well, at least we're doing this, like everything else, together.

The camera showed the athletes waiting to be introduced, getting in the zone for their race. The commentators were discussing the history the United States had with the 400 IM. All of it was stuff Bryce had heard countless times, but I was grateful he couldn't hear it right now. The last thing he, or Carter, needed would be to hear the worry they were expressing we'd fail to medal in our signature event. They had more than enough pressure on themselves.

"Jeez, they're being harsh." Mia's voice startled me. I'd almost forgotten we were on the phone from being so focused on how Bryce was staring straight ahead. "It's ridiculous."

I said nothing as the view on the screen once again switched to the still pool.

"One of them is going to be on the podium," Mia continued. "I have no doubt in my mind. I'm just not sure if it's going to be Bryce or Carter."

I wish I could be that confident in what was going to happen, but this field was stacked.

As the athletes were introduced, the commentators announced every single split Bryce would need to take gold. With each one listed, my heart beat wildly against my chest. I tried to tune them out to focus on the athletes they were introducing. Bryce had the second time coming from prelims, so he was the second to last to enter, Carter being introduced before him.

The crowd went wild for both Carter and Bryce, the camera briefly showing their families before focusing on the top qualifier being introduced. Haruto Sasaki from Japan was Bryce's biggest threat and had been for years. As he entered the arena, the crowd was thunderous, even over the TV. The camera showed Sasaki, and I watched his shoulders tense ever so slightly before he took a deep breath and continued to strip off his warm-up gear.

"Your boy needs to get out of his head," Mia warned, and I couldn't agree more. I wasn't even willing to argue with her about the title she gave him. Not now. "The race he should be worried about is his own."

"He's been under a lot of pressure with trying to beat Sasaki tonight." I didn't know why I felt the need to remind her of something she's known for over a year. Something we'd heard commentary on countless times. "But you're right. He doesn't need to be focusing on what's happening in the lane beside him."

The whistle blew, signaling the arena to quiet down as the swimmers stepped up on the blocks. I watched Bryce shake his arms out, proving just how tense he was, before he relaxed slightly. My breath was caught in my throat, eyes trained on the screen as I waited for the race to start.

"Take your mark."

Mia sucked in a sharp breath, neither one of us breathing or making an audible sound as we waited for the buzzer. A second later, they were off.

"That was a shit start, Carter," Mia muttered.

I agreed but couldn't find it in myself to say anything, as I was too focused on lane five. Just as I expected, he was overtaken during the butterfly leg and was fifth going into the backstroke, which was where he'd make his move.

"The way he swims this race stresses me the hell out," Mia grumbled. "He has such a strong backstroke. I'm still shocked he didn't make the team in the 200 back."

"Me too." I couldn't offer much of an opinion. And the only interruption I offered between mumbled out variations of "come on, Bryce" and "let's go."

As they turned to the breaststroke leg, he'd moved from fifth to third, with Carter trailing behind him. This was Sasaki's weakest leg, so while it wasn't Bryce's strongest, it was a chance to close the gap before they went into the freestyle. Bryce started creeping up on Sasaki, Carter creeping up on Bryce.

In the background, the commentators were talking about what to expect in the last 150 meters, but I wasn't listening to a single word they said. The race was close, Sasaki staying slightly ahead of a breakout French swimmer, while Bryce was a couple solid strokes from taking over second, and had half a body length on Carter.

"That's it, Bryce!" I cheered at the TV, Mia's voice echoing mine, as Bryce moves into second place about twenty-five meters out from the wall.

A few seconds later, Carter took over third after some impressive underwaters heading into the freestyle. "Yes, Carter!"

By the last fifty meters, I was kneeling on my bed to get closer to the TV, to be more involved in the moment that was happening a world away. Mia and I were screaming together to urge them to go.

And then it was over.

Sasaki hit the wall first, the arena erupting in screams and cheers. Bryce hit the wall second, only a couple hundredths of a second behind him. Lastly, Carter had taken over the French swimmer to finish in third place with a couple tenths of a second separating him and his best friend.

Bryce and Carter were Olympic medalists.

Mia and I were both screaming, crying, and cheering. I watched as Sasaki celebrated his win before the camera flashed to a happy-looking Bryce congratulating the Japanese swimmer. Pulling each other into a quick hug, they grinned brightly at each other, but as they separated, something in Bryce shifted—there was disappointment mingled in his excitement. Leaning against the lane line, he pulled his goggles off, heaving to catch his breath. With each deep breath he took, his smile dimmed a little more, taking mine with it.

It brightened back up when Carter turned to congratulate him. They hug before shifting their gazes back to the screen, breaking down their final time and splits. I watched as Bryce's smile started dimming again.

My heart ached for him.

"Good lord, Bryce, stop making that face," Mia whined, and my gut twisted at her words. "I can't handle the face. I wonder what's going through his mind."

I didn't have to wonder, though. Somehow, I knew. I knew how disappointed in himself he was. Yes, he was an Olympic medalist, but he hadn't accomplished the goal he'd set. For the first time since 1992, the gold medal in the men's 400 IM was not going home with the US, and he'd missed it by hundredths of a second.

"Please don't ask them stupid questions."

Shaking my head, I forced myself out of my head and focused back on the TV, only to realize I'd missed them getting out of the pool and making their way over to the media lineup. I didn't get the chance to respond to Mia before the interview started, and they were promptly asked a stupid question.

"So, no gold for the US in the men's 400 IM," the woman interviewer said, grimacing slightly. I watched both Bryce and Carter's eyebrows shoot up in surprise, but they quickly recovered before she turned to face them. "To have lost such a legacy on your watch, it must be a hard pill to swallow."

Both Mia and let out loud, annoyed groans. At this point, we shouldn't be surprised by the post-race interviews—by how unnecessarily targeted the questions could be.

Although the comment was directed at Bryce, Carter was the one who answered. "The reality of this sport is you never know what's going to happen. No matter how hard you train and plan, you have no idea what the other athletes have in store. We showed up, we swam hard, and got on the medal podium. I won't speak for Bryce, but I'm happy with it."

The reporter took the bait, holding the microphone out to Bryce, who finally cracked a timid smile. "I agree with everything Carter said. Yeah, we both had different goals coming into the race, but they didn't pan out that way. I'll learn from this race, like I do with every other race. Right now, I'm ready to celebrate our first Olympic medals."

Carter laughed as Bryce clapped him on the shoulder, both flashing real smiles.

"So, you think there's room for improvement?" The question wiped the smiles right off.

"There's always room for improvement," was Bryce's well-practiced, diplomatic response.

Carter jumped in before Bryce had a chance to continue. "As he just said, there's always room for improvement and that's something we'll be discussing with our coaches as we focus on the future."

She hovered her mic by Bryce, who remained silent until she brought it back to herself. "Thanks for talking with me, guys, and congratulations!"

With polite nods, they both mumbled out their thanks before heading off deck. The camera followed them, showing them talking, and laughing as they disappeared from the public eye.

"How are we feeling about what we just witnessed?"

Leaning back, I considered Mia's question for a second as I muted the TV. I wasn't sure if I wanted to answer her for myself or if I wanted to consider the way I knew he was reacting. "I'm so proud of him. Carter, too, obviously. They both swam great races."

"I agree, a silver, and bronze at the Olympics is nothing to be ashamed of. Now, how do you think Bryce feels about it? Honestly."

I picked at the corner of my blanket. "He's disappointed in himself, I think. He wanted gold; he knew America wanted him to take the gold, but that's not what happened. My guess is he's already planning on cracking down to prepare for 2020."

"I was worried that's what you were going to say," Mia admitted.

"Yeah." I frowned at my blanket. "I think it's safe to say whatever might have happened last month is back on pause."

"Jos, you don't know yet." She was being supportive. I knew him, and I knew I had no hope of breaking into his world right now. "You need to talk to him about it."

"I have, and he told me his focus was getting a gold medal at the Olympics. He's not there yet," I argued. "He might one day. So, I'd rather be what he needs me to be, a friend or whatever, and figure out everything else later."

She groaned. "I swear to God, the two of you will spend forever dancing around each other."

"Maybe we will, but that's for us to decide. I want to make sure he stays in my life, however it's meant to happen."

Bryce Clark could be in my life however he wanted to be; I wasn't about to be picky. The only thing that mattered was he was there—at least I'd get to have him in some way.

I knew she didn't agree, though. She worried I was setting myself up to get hurt, and I probably was, but that was my choice to make. I was choosing to keep him in my life, no matter what the cost to myself was.

I was sure I could survive a broken heart. I was less sure I could survive losing him.

"Are you going to text him?"

I hesitated. "Do you think I should?"

I'd always been so careful to never come across as too much. As too clingy. If we talked outside of a meet, Bryce was usually the one who initiated contact, unless I knew of a specific reason we would need to talk. Even then, it was always in relation to the blog and was kept professional. I followed his lead.

"Yeah, Jos, I think you should," she replied. "He just won an Olympic medal, and he's probably disappointed. I think he needs a friend right now. Stop overthinking this."

"Overthinking things is my specialty." I laughed.

"Not when you're with him; it's not," she countered. "He'll want to hear from you."

I picked up my phone, found our text thread, and started typing.

Congratulations! I was watching and cheering the whole time. I know it's not what you wanted, but it's something to be proud of. And I am so proud of you!

I hit send, but never received a message back.

The next time I heard from Bryce was nearly a month later, when things had finally settled down and he was back home. This time, he was reaching out about a post-Olympics interview we'd discussed ages ago.

Once his smiling face appeared on my computer screen, things snapped back to normal.

Except we didn't talk about the Olympics, not really. And neither one of us brought up what happened in Omaha again. And I had to find a way to be okay with it.

Chapter 17

THEN

June 2016

Omaha, NE

"How are you feeling over there, bestie?"

I laughed dryly—the answer was obviously not good. The Riverview Convention Center was packed with people, music pumping through the speakers, as the pool a few rows before us cleared in preparation of naming people to the 2016 Olympic team. Bryce's best shot at making the team was minutes away, and I could not sit still to save my life.

Between the quick, fleeting hug after prelims, and the dozen or so messages we'd exchanged since, I knew Bryce was on edge. He was staring down his dream, ready to reach out, and grab it. Meanwhile, I was in the stands worrying about all the ways this could go and how to handle whatever happened.

"I need you to breathe, Jos," Mia muttered in my ear. "I can't have you passing out on me on top of everything else going on right now."

I let out a shuddery breath, then another, and another, until I was breathing at a more normal pace. "What if he makes the team tonight?"

I knew the question had caught her off guard. She had probably expected me to ask about what I'd do if he *didn't* make the team, which was a real possibility, but I didn't want to focus on the negative right now. Either way, everything about our relationship with him—both professional and personal—would change regardless of the outcome of tonight, or even this week, was. And I needed to be prepared.

"Then you scream and cheer for him until you lose your voice. You be part of the moment, Josie, as much as you can be and then you go from there."

The answer calmed my racing heart ever so slightly. "And if he doesn't make the team tonight?"

"Then he tries again later in the week," she reminded me. "And you be there for him as much as he'll let you, and as much as you want to."

Her advice made sense, but this was so different from anything we'd ever experienced. Four years ago, I sat in these seats watching this meet and my love for swimming was ignited in a way I never expected. Now it's what we do, and it's the first time we're experiencing a meet this monumental while it involved people we care about. They were chasing everything they've given their blood, sweat, and tears for.

We weren't just another face in the crowd. We were—in some small way—part of their story. Part of the history being made.

"It's weird, though, right?" I said. "I mean, we're part of this for so many people, but we're also not part of it at all."

Mia frowned, sensing the spiral I was on. "I think it's a hazard of the job. Though it's unofficial, we're still covering the meet and writing about these people, and their accomplishments. It's hard to figure out where we fit in to the grand scheme of things."

I'm sure she was hoping to calm me down, keep me from worrying to the point where I wanted to hide away from everyone we cared about, but it brought me back to a fleeting thought I'd had in Mesa a couple months prior: How much do we matter to them? Did they view us as friends in the way we did with them? Or were we another way for them to get their names floating around social media as they tried to make the most of their career within the sport? After all, isn't that what we're out here trying to do, in our own ways? Chase an impossible dream when all the odds were stacked against us.

And then there was Bryce. The very man I knew was off limits, despite how everything had changed between us the last time we saw each other. He was the person I couldn't let my mind wander to for very long. I knew what he wanted in his life, and I knew I couldn't provide it for him, but I also wasn't ready to let him go.

There was nothing more terrible than staring at a man I could see forever with, when I was just someone passing by to him.

"Do you worry we might be getting too involved sometimes?"

"Oh, girl, I think that already happened to you," Mia teased, but I could sense a bit of fear in her words. She was worrying about the very thing I was. I was getting too involved, too quickly. "But maybe that's not such a bad thing."

"Whatever happened between Bryce and me back in Mesa can't go any further. You and I both know that."

She didn't look convinced. "The two of you kissed in Mesa, Josie."

"And he immediately made it clear that he wants to focus on making the team and isn't looking for anything serious."

"That might be what he said in Mesa, but it might not be what he'll say in Omaha." She winked. "If he makes the team, he won't be able to use that as an excuse anymore. Yeah, he has to get through the games, and that's what his focus should be on, but he can also look to what comes next, to what he wants going forward. Which could be you."

The problem with leaving things the way we did after Mesa was that I didn't have answers, despite having so many questions. I didn't know what I meant to him. I didn't know what he thought of me. My insecurities had plenty of room to come out and play. In the span of an hour, I could convince myself that I was a beautiful person who he would be lucky to have, only to crash at the thought of someone like him never actually caring about a woman with curves like mine. Or that I was too much for someone like him. And that was a dangerous game to play—one I was never plagued by when I was with him, but those moments did exist when I was on my own.

When deep in insecurities, one's memories could take on a fuzzy edge. start looking for moments that supported the narrative my subconscious told me, and it was hard to get them back into focus. Sometimes, impossible.

Before I could reply to Mia, the lights went down, and a different song started pumping through the arena as the introduction video began on the jumbotron. My nerves spiked back up and didn't calm until Mia reached for my hand, squeezing it tightly.

Here we go, I thought to myself. *This is it.*

In a flurry of screams, cheers, and tears, Bryce had made the team. He was the first person to be named in the 2016 Olympic Team, and I was still having trouble wrapping my head around it. As he'd glided to the wall, I had stared at the pool with my mouth gaping open. His victorious yell somehow echoed over every other person cheering around me.

He did it. Bryce Clark was an Olympian.

After the medal ceremony, which had brought another wave of tears for both Mia and me, I kept checking my phone like the hopeless person I was. There was a small part of me that thought he'd text me. Maybe he'd want to see me, want me to celebrate with him. Be part of his moment. Which was ridiculous because I had no idea when he'd be released from his press obligations, or when his coaches, and other officials would be done with him so he could see his family. And, most of all, this was a moment that should be shared with them; not some girl he barely knew, but kissed one time in Arizona.

I was reminded of a rather intrusive thought that had snuck in as I watched him launch himself at Carter, who'd come in second. It kept beating against my subconscious as he graciously accepted the medal. *There's no place for you in this moment.*

If I knew that, why was I torturing myself by checking my phone?

In between races, I took a moment to scan the crowd. As I took it all in, I felt the prickling sensation of being watched from behind me. When I turned my gaze over my left shoulder and looked up, my eyes landed on Bryce. He was standing in an aisle a section over, ensuring he wasn't blocking the view of anyone else as he talked with his family. Except, he wasn't all that engaged with them, distracted despite his mother speaking to him. Because he was looking directly at me.

I felt my cheeks flush as we made eye contact. When Bryce realized he'd gotten my attention, he tilted his head toward the nearest exit, indicating I should meet him in the concourse. After I nodded, he turned back to his family with a blinding grin. He focused on them long enough to say goodbye before he headed into the hallway.

"Go say hi to your boy and bring me back a drink." Though Mia didn't even pull her gaze from her phone, she somehow knew what was going on. "Something with caffeine, please."

I scowled at my best friend. "I wish you'd stop reading my mind, Mia. It's kind of creepy."

"Then stop being so easy to read and say whatever's on your mind," she teased back. "You always make the same face when you're not sure how to tell me whatever it is you want to say, and I'm too impatient to wait for you to figure it out. Now, seriously, go. You don't know how soon he has to be back."

Before the next race started, I stood and exited the row. As I climbed the steps to head toward the concourse, I felt butterflies erupt in the pit of my stomach at the idea of getting to be part of this with him. As soon as I entered the bustling hallway, I found Bryce off to my right, leaning against a wall. Apparently, I wasn't the only one who'd noticed him, though.

A small gaggle of age group swimmers, probably pre-teens, sur-rounded him. I held back for a while, smiling as I watched him with the kids. He chatted as he signed a cap before glancing up at me. A few seconds after he turned his attention back to the kids, they were thanking him, and dispersing so he could walk over to me.

The closer Bryce got, the more his smile grew. I could feel myself doing the same until it hurt. Eventually, his arms wound around me in a tight hug. I laughed as he picked me up to swing me around. It took everything in me to keep my tears at bay. I was so damn proud of him.

He held me for a moment longer, both of us ignoring the curious stares from those who passed.

"I was going to give you my medal, but Mom took it," he admitted once we had separated.

I ignored the way my heart skipped a beat at the comment. It wasn't unusual for swimmers to give away their medals, but they usually gave them to someone important to them or to a fan. I never would have expected to be given his medal, but I was swooning over the mere idea that I'd even been considered.

"She said something about not trusting me with it." He rolled his eyes, but the tiniest grin spread across his features. "She forgets I'm technically an adult."

"Or she's worried you'd give it away," I replied. "If you had it, I wouldn't have gotten it, anyway. You would have given it to one of those kids before I even entered the hallway."

A faint blush coated his cheeks before he ducked his chin, confirming I was right.

An awkward silence settled between us. It was the exact silence I'd anticipated after wondering how I was supposed to act around him now. I couldn't help but worry that both nothing and everything had change. How was I supposed to tell him how proud I was without it being too much? How do I convey my emotions without coming across as clingy?

Was this the moment when he'd tell me it's been great, but this mounting friendship was over now that he'd achieved his dream? Because I'd do it. I'd step back as he continued this journey to bigger and better things.

"Did I see you crying when I got out of the pool?"

My jaw dropped as I looked up at him. How could he possibly know that? Sure, Mia and I were close enough that he could see us from the deck, but only if he looked for me. With everything else going on around him, why would he do something like that?

Bryce laughed triumphantly at my reaction. "I knew it!"

"But how?" I questioned him, wanting to put him on the spot as well. "There's no way you could know that with everything going on!"

His triumphant look dropped. He shrugged, suddenly avoiding eye contact. "Because I looked for you."

"Oh," I breathed out. "I hadn't expected you to say that."

Blush returned to his cheeks, and he shrugged, full boyish charm on display. "I always look for you, Josie."

Now I was blushing. In the last year since we'd met, I'd noticed how his gaze seemed to find me, no matter where we were. It was evident in the day-to-day happenings of a busy meet, and it was evident in the photographic evidence we had collected. I'd never let myself think about it too much, despite how much Mia teased me. I knew if I let my mind wander, I'd end up falling for him in a dangerous way. I knew how shitty unrequited love could be, and I could already feel it creeping into my life. I didn't want to add more fuel to an ever-growing flame.

"I could tell you and Mia were both crying, maybe more than my mom." He was grinning down at me, full of mirth.

"This is a huge deal, Bryce! We've watched you work so hard for it, and we're both so damn proud of you. That's why we were crying, and I'm sure we'll be crying again."

"Which means I'm nothing special," he teased. "Just another guy who made the Olympic team."

"Exactly," I teased back. "I mean, look around. Did you do something that remarkable?"

Laughing, he pulled me in for another hug. "I need to head back, but I wanted to see you."

There was another thing I couldn't let myself think too hard on. "I'm glad we got to see one another. Can I talk you into taking a picture?"

After Mesa, I realized we didn't take a lot of pictures together. In the four meets I'd been to since we first met, he had been at three, yet I only had one picture of us. From the first time we met. I didn't know if it was something we avoided, knowing people might question how relaxed we were with one another. Or if we were too wrapped up in the moment to document them.

But this one needed to be documented. I wanted to remember this forever.

"Are we needing a professional one or one where we're just us?" The fact that he knew the difference told me I was on to something with my speculation.

"How about both?"

Nodding, he moved inside my side as I got the camera pulled up on my phone. Without any kind of communication, we started with the one I'd later post on social media. His arm draped around my shoulder, a casual smile in place. I had the chance to take two crappy pictures before he took my phone to use his height to get a better angle. Once he took a couple shots, we both looked through them before deeming them acceptable.

"Now that we've done the ones where we pretend not to like each other, come here."

I moved into Bryce as he tugged me to his side, holding the camera above us. It took every ounce of my willpower not to melt against him, to take what he wanted to give me in this moment without needing more.

Although we posed for a couple pictures, I didn't get the chance to look at them until we parted ways and I'd returned to my seat. Scrolling through them, I couldn't stop my smile. We looked good together, and we posed together in a natural way. None of the photos looked forced—the pose was comfortable, our expressions genuine and bright. My favorite, though, had to be where he pulled me in close until I was beaming at the camera, and he was staring down at me with a soft smile.

It almost looked real.

I wanted to make it my lock screen or wallpaper, but I knew I couldn't. That wasn't something friends did, not when they looked like that in a photograph. As much as I could kid myself, it wasn't real, and nothing was going to change that. Especially not a picture.

"You forgot my drink, didn't you?"

Groaning, I looked over at Mia with an apologetic look. I knew I had forgotten something. "I'm sorry, we got talking, and it slipped my mind."

"It's fine." She glanced at the picture on my phone before meeting my eyes. While the photo made her smile, I could see the worry hidden beneath it. "Do we have a problem here?"

Sighing, I looked back at the photo and nodded. "Yeah, we have a problem."

I was falling for him. Fast and hard, there was no stopping it now.

Chapter 18

NOW

April 2023
Omaha, NE

I stand a little straighter as I spot Bryce approaching me from across the street. He looks handsome in his pale blue button-up shirt, but that's because he's come from work. His sleeves are rolled up, revealing the dark ink of a forest designed in a band around his forearm. I find myself drawn to it the moment I see it, wondering what else he has inked since we last saw one another.

"I can't believe you wouldn't let me pick you up," he grumbles, strong arms pulling me into a hug as soon as he reaches me. "We're finally doing this right, but I still don't get to do it right."

I laugh against his shoulder before we separate. When I squint up at him against the evening sun, my stomach swooping at how happy he appears. His dark blond hair is a little messy, probably from running his fingers through it all day, but his eyes are bright, and he seems relaxed. "You had a late meeting and I live in Central Omaha. You're ten minutes late as it is. It'd have been impractical for you to pass the restaurant just so you could make a chivalrous point."

The mischievous glint in his eye is how I remember it from the first time I met him. It's a reminder we are still just Josie and Bryce.

"You're right. Besides, when have we ever done anything practical?" He pulls the door to the restaurant open, stepping into the crowded brewery after me. We take our spot in the short line to the host stand. "I'm glad you suggested this place. I've always wanted to try it. I haven't had the chance since I moved, and every other time I was preoccupied."

"Do you expect me to believe you were too busy becoming an Olympian to try a restaurant?" I tease, earning a grin in return. "The food is great; the atmosphere is better."

He says nothing else, but his hand brushes against mine. A second later, he's tangling our fingers together. Glancing down, I stare at our joined hands, suddenly a bit emotional as I recall the last time we did this. Out of everything I missed, I never thought this would be the thing I craved—the steady pressure of his hand in mine. Now that I have it back, I don't want to let it go.

When we step up to the host stand, I don't miss the way the woman's gaze locks on Bryce. She even stands up straighter. As he requests a table for two, her smile widens as she instructs us to follow her. She never once acknowledges my presence. She makes small talk with him in an attempt to flirt. Meanwhile, Bryce gives polite replies, barely engaging with her.

When we reach the booth, she sets his menu down and attempts to flirt again, but he brushes it off by sliding into his seat, eyes scanning the menu. She hands me my menu with a huff before stomping away. I resist rolling my eyes while he frowns at her retreating back, as though trying to make sense of the situation. This wasn't the first time someone ignored me while I stood beside an attractive man.

Hell, it wasn't the first time it had happened with Bryce.

"That was a little rude, right?" Bryce questions. "Please tell me I'm not imagining it."

"It was nothing." I brush the comment off because the last thing I want to do is bring up body insecurity on a first date. It isn't a side of me Bryce knew.

It took me a long time to get here, but I love my body. I know I'm beautiful, desirable, and I feel confident in my skin. But, like everyone else, there are moments when society's fucked up beauty standards creep in and make me insecure about my stomach, hips, and thighs. I am never that person with him, though. Mainly because he never makes me feel that way. It's almost like he has a sixth sense for when my thoughts are straying to not-so-healthy places, because he's never failed to pull me closer and do or say something to make it go away. I never once doubted his attraction to me.

He's the first, and admittedly only, man I've never had insecurities around. I've been searching for the same comforting acceptance for years and have yet to find it. There always seemed to be snide comments about what I ate, or if we should go out to dinner when we could take a walk instead, and even comments about how they'd never have to worry about me stealing their clothes. With every man since Bryce, my confidence hasn't been celebrated; I missed the way he enhanced it.

"It's not nothing," he argues. "We're clearly together, and she flirted with me the whole time, ignoring you completely. I don't understand why people think acting that way is okay."

I glance up from my menu to find Bryce grimacing. I don't want to pull him into the self-conscious side of my life, but it isn't something he's going to let go. "You're an attractive man, Bryce. People are always going to flirt with you, especially if they think you can do better than the person you're with."

Anger flashes in his eyes as he scoffs. "And who would be better? Her? *Please.*"

I shrug. "I'm sure she thinks so. Women like me don't get guys like you."

He balks at that, like he can't believe what he's hearing. "Women like you?"

"You know, fat, curvy, thick, whatever you want to say. Regardless of what you call me, bigger girls don't date professional athletes."

"Says who? Please tell you me you don't believe that bullshit, Josie."

Outside of the sport, Bryce has never cared what the world thought of him. Yes, as an athlete, he has an immense need to prove his worth, but who he's dating, or what he does in his free time has never been up for discussion. Nor has he ever felt the need to feel the need to comment on the lives of the people he cares about. I've seen it with both Carter and me.

With any other guy, calling myself fat, curvy, or thick would result in them telling me I shouldn't be hard on myself. Or, worse, it would be followed up with "You're not fat, you're beautiful," like fat can't also be beautiful. Instead, Bryce looks at me like I matter to him, like he didn't give a shit what anyone has to say. He looks at me like I'm one of the most important people in his life, no matter what else we're surrounded by.

And he's looking at me the same way now.

"No, but sometimes it's hard to ignore." The way he regards me makes me want to be open, honest, and vulnerable. "It's not the case when I'm with you. It never has been that way with you."

He reaches across the table, taking my hand in his. I fight back the weird feeling creeping up inside me and the flutter in the pit of my stomach. The feeling is a reminder that we can't pick up where we left off; this can't be like last time. If we're serious about making this work—about seeing where we could go—we have to work at it. That meant talking about real things in ways we never had before. Like body image issues.

It's not something I ever let myself think about when with him, and I'm not sure how I can open up to him now. Back when we were getting to know each other, I kind of fell into a manic pixie girl role with him—this bubbly, quirky girl that doesn't let anything touch her. Was I ready for him to truly see me as I am?

"So, what's good here?"

His question startles me out of my thoughts. When I look at him, he's already staring at me. No matter what else has happened, what is going through my head, the foundation is still the same. I need to calm down.

Taking a deep breath, I calm myself before pointing out various favorites on the menu. This is a first date; we don't have to get into the hard-hitting stuff yet. For now, we can just talk and enjoy each other's company, which is something we've never had an issue with. It's the part that should be easy. Everything else can wait. We don't need to bring up the past. We need to get to know one another here and now.

After ordering, I lean back in against the booth and take a moment to ground myself in the moment. If twenty-one-year Josie knew this night was coming, she'd be freaking out; twenty-nine-year-old Josie needed to calm the fuck down.

"When Sarah tried to introduce us, it was the biggest shock I've had while working at Hunt & Sloan. You were the last person I would have ever expected to be working across the building from me. I never thought corporate Bryce would be a thing."

He pauses as he raises his pint glass. "You knew I studied business and swimming couldn't last forever. What did you think I'd end up doing?"

I scrutinize him for a second while he takes a pull of his beer. "Not corporate sales. Honestly, I'm not sure what I expected, but I was also surprised to see how soon you jumped into a career after retiring. I figured you'd travel or something."

"I thought about it, but I was sick of never being home. Then this opportunity came up, and I'd heard wonderful things about the company, so I applied. I needed a fresh start. I didn't expect to end up in Omaha, though. That was definitely a surprise."

I can't help but laugh. "Didn't you know where you were applying? Usually, the posting tells you if you have to relocate somewhere."

His grin causes a glint in his eyes. "Don't be a smartass, Josie."

"Oh, pot meet kettle." I laugh, motioning between us. "Did you forget who you were talking to for a second?"

His own laugh sets off a swarm of butterflies in the pit of my stomach. "Fair. For your information, I didn't apply for the Omaha office; I applied to be in Baltimore."

The reality of what could have been crashes into me. He was supposed to be somewhere else. Would we have ever found one another again if he hadn't come back to Omaha? Were we even supposed to find each other again? Or was our last meeting supposed to be the way things ended between us? Recognizing I'm spiraling into a mess of what-ifs I don't need to get caught up in, I focus on him to block those thoughts. "How did you end up in Omaha, then?"

"They filled the position in Baltimore with someone local," he explains. "They told me they had a position opening in Omaha and asked if I'd be interested. I took it because Omaha has always been good to me. It seemed like the best place to go to for a fresh start."

I want to ask if he ever thought about me during the decision-making. Did he ever wonder what would happen if we ran into one another? Did he look me up on social media prior to coming out here? Despite thinking them, I'm not about to ask those questions. I don't want to make him think I've spent the last two years pining over what never was.

"But I was shocked to see you at work, too," he comments, pulling me from my thoughts. "I didn't think you'd stay in Omaha. Let alone wind up in a corporate position here."

I've been more vocal about my plans than he has. It's no secret I want to move somewhere new and exciting; I want to write and create my own life. After growing up in Omaha and venturing less than three hours away for college, I want to see the world. Yet, at twenty-eight, I'm still here, working a job I barely tolerate, and nothing has been published under my name since I stopped writing articles for Adair Swim Blog.

And no one is more disappointed in me than myself.

"Things kept coming up," I say, knowing it's an excuse. "My family needed me here, and I needed a stable income. I just haven't ventured out yet."

The look in his eye tells me he wants to say more—probably point out I've basically given up on my dream, but I know he won't. It also isn't true. I still hold those ambitions. They are just on pause, and I allow myself to inch closer to them whenever I can.

"Life happens, and your priorities shift. I'm happy to know you haven't given up on writing. I always thought you were talented. Not that I have the experience to back up my claim."

"To be fair, you've also only read my professional writing," I point out. "Writing fiction is completely different."

"I always preferred your articles over anyone else's. Mia's too. You both had a way of writing where it was obvious you saw the person first and their accomplishments second."

"And maybe that's why Adair Swimming never took off the way we wanted," I joke in a kind of self-deprecating way. "We always thought people put too much emphasis on medals and never enough on the people who make the sport what it is."

"I learned the hard way what happens when you focus too much on medal count. You always saw me, Josie, which was both the only thing I ever wanted and the thing that scared me the most. Trust me, what you have to say matters. It always has."

I lean back, stunned. He said the very words every writer wants to hear. It's the confirmation from someone who knows me but doesn't owe me the pleasantries of reassuring my dream—that their craft is good. There's a difference between friends and family supporting me and someone who believes in what I'm doing. Despite everything we've gone through, and everything we're heading toward, Bryce doesn't owe me compliments or blind support. For him to say something like, I know he means it.

Flushing, I fiddle with the edge of the napkin sitting on the table beside me. In this moment, it is the most important thing in the room because I've never been able to take a compliment. "Thank you for that."

He looks a little surprised to hear me thank him, but he doesn't know the gravity of those words. "Of course. I'm still hoping I'll get to read your book someday."

Bryce reading a book I've written is another thing I've never considered. Writers are known to pull inspiration from the people, places, and events they've experienced, whether, or not they want to admit. Though I try not to, I always find little pieces of him in the heroes I write. While they might not be noticeable to everyone, I'm sure they'd be obvious to him. I'm not sure there will ever be a time when I'm ready for him to see that.

Besides, wouldn't it be another way of handing him my heart, hoping he won't break it again?

"Yeah, maybe one day," I finally agree.

We slip into another awkward silence, both of us opting to glance around the crowded restaurant instead of at each other. I can't help but worry this is how it'll be between us forever. Will we always be torn between moving forward and reflecting on the past? Old habits are hard to kill, and I'm not sure how to keep us from slipping back into them, even though I know it's the very last thing we should do.

Thankfully, any awkwardness is cut short by the server bringing our food. Just like old times, the distraction serves the purpose of getting us out of our heads so we could turn our focus back to one another. At least for now.

Chapter 19

THEN

June 2016

Omaha, NE

Mia and I pushed through the doors of the Riverview Convention Center and stepped into the sticky Omaha night with a sigh. We'd just finished the last session of the 2016 Olympic Trials and had hung around the venue to secure a couple quick interviews with newly named members of the team, as well as some up-and-comers who had made a splash on the scene during the past week. The meet was over, our work was done, and now we could relax.

"Here's the plan." She turned to face me. "We go out, have a few drinks, leave at a respectable hour. Then, once we're back at the hotel, we crash, and I'll sleep so hard because it's been a week and I'm so done."

Honestly, it sounded like heaven. I'd be perfectly okay heading straight back to the hotel, but we were too young not to celebrate the end of such a huge event.

"What time do we have to be at your parents' for Fourth of July tomorrow?"

"Not until the afternoon; we get to sleep in."

"Thank God," she groaned with a wistful look. "I'm so excited to sleep."

I laughed, the crosswalk light changing as we approached it. We crossed the street with the few people still lingering around Riverview. "Me too. I feel like we haven't slept for a month. I'm actually a little surprised we're going out."

"We're in our twenties, Josie. We need to socialize!" I almost pointed out our age difference to mess with her—she was nearing twenty-five and I'd barely had a chance to be twenty-two. "We've had a long week, but we need to go out. We never know who we'll run into, and we should celebrate something like this. With that being said, I have no intention of staying out all night."

I wanted to be out. I wanted to experience what it was like to celebrate a meet like this, but I was also more exhausted than I remember ever being. Knowing Mia, we'd be back in the hotel and in bed before midnight, which helped my mindset. Neither one of us were party people, but we knew when it was important to be part of the moment, which was why we were heading to the Old Town Brewery, the designated hangout for athletes and fans. It wasn't the first time we'd been here, as they'd hosted a couple of events throughout the meet.

As much as I wanted to hang out with Mia, my mind kept drifting back to Bryce. How was he celebrating his first time making the Olympic team? For all I knew, he could be back at the hotel sleeping or even preparing to head out of Omaha. We'd had few interactions throughout the week, and I didn't want to text him in case he had other things going on.

I refused to be the needy girl he wanted to avoid.

"Hey!" Mia called, pulling me from my thoughts. When I glanced over at her, her gaze was trained on someone behind her, someone we'd passed. "Wasn't that Will Jacobson?"

"Where?"

We both stepped to the side, Mia pointing me in the right direction.

Sure enough, Will was a couple of paces behind us, waiting for someone else to catch up with him. I nodded in confirmation. "Yeah, that's him."

"We should go say hi!"

Which was the absolute last thing I wanted to do. Especially on a street corner at almost eleven o'clock at night. "What? Aren't you the one with the rule about not ambushing people on the street?"

She shrugged. "I'm tired. My manners don't exist right now. Besides, I want to know if what you and Bryce say about him is true."

Before I had the chance to respond, she was walking back to where he stood, and I had no other choice but to follow her.

Will Jacobson was a lesser-known swimmer who was the same age as Bryce and me, having just graduated college, and he was known as a piece of work.

While most athletes we knew were determined to stay in the sport for however long it took to achieve their goal, Will couldn't wait to get out of it. He claimed he loved the sport, but he had other goals and aspirations he wanted to achieve. And he constantly bragged about them.

This was the only chance he gave himself to make the Olympic team, and if he didn't make it, he was hanging up his goggles and heading to med school.

It was no secret that Bryce hated Will for a reason I could never pinpoint, except for being a pompous ass. When I'd met him in Mesa and set up an interview a couple months back, Bryce had warned me I was about to encounter a jerk and he hadn't been wrong. It was honestly the worst interview I'd ever conducted, and writing the article had been torturous. Now, this would probably be the last time I'd ever see Will Jacobson.

As we approached, Mia pushed me in front of her. "You talk to him first. He knows you."

"Seriously?" I grumbled under my breath, glaring at her over my shoulder. The last thing I wanted to do was talk to him, and now she was making it seem like it was all my idea. "You owe me."

"Yeah, yeah." She waved me off. "I'll buy you a drink."

We were already too close to abandon the plan; he was staring right at me as he pocketed his phone. I plastered on the fakest smile I could muster. "Will, hey!"

"Josie!" He pulled me in for an awkward hug, and I wanted to squirm away from him. Something about him didn't sit right with me, which was true long before Bryce told me of his distrust. "I knew you guys were here, but I wasn't sure we'd get a chance to talk."

"It's been a bit busy, hasn't it?" I asked, stepping back to motion to Mia. "I'm glad we saw you, though. I wanted to introduce you to Mia."

"Ah, the other half of the dynamic duo," he replied with a toothy grin. "It's nice to meet you."

I stood back as the two of them shook hands and made obligatory small talk, the thing I dreaded about this job.

They pulled me into the conversation when they started talking about the article I wrote about Will. It'd been getting a lot of traction this week, despite him not making the team, and was even quoted by another major media outlet within the sport. Our article had even been linked. As Mia tried to talk about the week, Will changed the conversation to the topic of his future plans.

He'd barely missed making the team, coming in third to Ronan O'Brien's second place in the 400-meter freestyle. I knew it was making people question his decision to retire. He'd been close, and he was only twenty-two. Why give up now?

"Honestly, I didn't expect O'Brien to go that hard," Will commented, making Mia shift from foot to foot. Ronan was our friend, and one of Bryce and Carter's best friends. "This is what? His third time? He should have retired a long time ago."

Ronan had made his first team at eighteen, straight out of high school, and he was nowhere near needing to retire. He'd made the team in three events, two of which he placed first for.

I could tell Mia wanted out of this conversation, especially because he was insulting someone we knew. "I mean, he's only twenty-six. I don't think he has to hang up the goggles just yet. It was a damn close race, though."

Someone called my name before he could reply. Looking past Will, I spotted Bryce walking toward us from the hotel across the street.

Will glanced over his shoulder before turning back to us with a frown. "You know Bryce Clark? I didn't realize."

That was a load of bullshit. Bryce was one of our most often interviewed athletes and we also posted pictures with him when we went to meets. "Yeah, he's a friend of ours."

Bryce's towering form stepped between us, pulling me into a hug. He whispered a quick greeting against the top of my head before placing a kiss on the same spot. His actions made me freeze, but when he stepped back, Will was fuming beside us while Mia watched.

"Hey, Mia," Bryce greeted before giving her a side hug.

"Oh, you both know Clark," Will said under his breath as Bryce stood with an arm slung over my shoulder.

"Obviously," Bryce scoffed, looking at Will. "How are you doing, Jacobson?"

Will straightened up, but he was still a couple of inches shorter than Bryce. "I'm doing fine. How's Abrams?"

Mia and I exchanged a look at the mention of Carter. The two of them had trained under the same coach in Georgia.

"He made the team, didn't he?" Bryce shot back. "So, you're friends with Josie and Mia?"

Bryce knew we weren't friends with him, and he was trying to push Will's buttons, but I didn't know why.

"It's kind of hard not to know them, right?" Will asked, his gaze lingering on Bryce's arm around my shoulder. He didn't pull me any closer to him, but it was obvious whatever friendship Will claimed to have with me was nothing in comparison. "I've been following their blog practically from the beginning. I'm assuming you read the articles she posts?"

Bryce nodded. "Now that you mention it, I remember the one she wrote about you." He glanced at me. "It was all about how he was going to be done swimming if he didn't make the team—something about medical school?"

"There are more important things than swimming, Clark," Will hissed.

He barely looked at Will, waiting for me to confirm he was remembering the correct article. Once I did, he turned back to Will. "She did a great job of making you sound like less of a pompous dick than you are. Be sure to thank her for it."

Having never heard Bryce talk to anyone like that before, my eyes widened. It was obvious they didn't get along, but he'd always kept it professional when he should. Yet here he is, calling him out for what he was.

Will was seething. "You got a problem with me or something, Clark?"

"You know I do," Bryce shot back. "What I don't get is your need to insert yourself into everyone else's business, while also making yours everyone else's. We get it, you're going to med school. Stop shoving it in people's faces like you've got it all figured out and no one else does."

"I call out the truth. I expose facts."

I had a feeling there were two conversations happening here—one was related to the current situation and one about whatever it was that pissed Bryce off in the first place.

"Swimming won't last forever, man," Will warned. "Don't be the guy who doesn't know when to walk away."

Bryce snorted out a laugh. "Says the guy who didn't make the team."

"Says the guy who knows what he's doing with his life," Will corrected, fists clenching at his sides. "The one who won't peak before thirty. Good job with that business degree, man. Your future looks promising."

I stared between them, wondering if Mia and I should step in, but it was like watching a train wreck. I couldn't turn away even if I wanted to.

"Thanks, dude," Bryce replied. "I'm sure it'll look even better with a couple of Olympic medals next to it."

For a split second, I thought Will was going to lunge at Bryce. Apparently, I wasn't the only one, as Bryce pushed me behind him.

"Okay, that's enough!" Mia declared, stepping between Bryce and Will to prevent them from pummeling one another. Bryce took a deep breath beside me. "I think we should all go our own ways; this conversation is going nowhere."

I nodded, giving Will a polite smile. Bryce pulled me a bit closer to his side. "I agree with Mia. It was good to see you, though, Will."

His anger grew at the way I dismissed him as he scowled at Bryce. Eventually, he glanced back at me to say, "Yeah, you too."

Mia clapped her hands together once to ensure she had everyone's attention. "Seriously, Will, good luck with everything!"

He barely gave her a nod before turning to walk away without another word. I hadn't realized how tense Bryce had gotten until he slumped beside me, arm slackening against my shoulders instead of resting there. I was pulled into his side, his face buried in my hair.

Mia waited until Will was out of earshot before she turned back to us. "So, you were right, he's an ass, and Bryce doesn't just dislike him, he hates him."

"That was a lot," I agreed, nudging Bryce until he lifted his head to look down at me. He did so with a tired groan. "What was up with bringing Carter into it?"

"They've never gotten along," Bryce said.

Mia's eyes narrowed into a glare. "Is he homophobic? Does he have a problem with him being bi?"

Bryce hesitated for a split second. "It's a problem with Carter in general. There was a huge thing freshmen year, and it's only gotten worse. He doesn't like talking about it."

That was all he needed to say for us to know it was dropped. Neither one of us would push him, or Carter, to talk to about something they didn't want to discuss.

"It wouldn't have gotten that bad if Bryce hadn't stormed over here and add to what was already an uncomfortable conversation," Mia said.

"I did not storm over," Bryce whined. "My coming over here had nothing to do with you guys talking to him. I wanted to see you."

A slow smirk that could rival Bryce's was creeping up the corners of Mia's mouth. "No one said anything about it having to do with Josie. Although now that you bring it up, I'm wondering if it did. Did you come over here just because Josie was talking to him, Clark?"

"W-wha—*No!*" Bryce stuttered out, shifting beside me. "No way! Why would I do that? I am not jealous!"

I tried to fight back a grin; Mia was enjoying this too much. "I never said you were jealous, but you just did."

"Well, uh . . . I didn't—" he stumbled over his words before frowning at me. "She's trying to trick me."

"She's not. She's just asking you questions." I grinned back at him. "You're the one getting all jumbled up."

He rolled his eyes. "It's not my fault the guy sucks!"

"You should get a gold medal for deflecting attention," Mia replied, exasperated. "No wonder the people who interview you never feel like they get answers to their questions."

He flashed his signature fake, media-pleasing grin as he shrugged. "What can I say? I learned from the best on how to avoid unwanted attention."

My gaze drifted up to him. "Is that what we are? Unwanted attention."

"Absolutely not. I came over here to find out what you were up to tonight."

Mia playfully rolled her eyes. "I think our plan was to get some drinks, then head back to the hotel to go to bed."

"Sounds like a great plan." He nodded, stuffing his hands in the pockets of his jeans. "It's been a long week, right? We're all tired."

"Oh, for the love of God," Mia grumbled out, startling us both. She looked at me, her eyes glimmering with amusement and annoyance. "It's obvious he came over here to ask you to hang out tonight. I don't know why you're both being awkward about this. You kissed in Mesa."

Bryce's eyes widened. "You told her?"

"She tells me everything, Clark," she reminded him, while my cheeks warmed. "Don't ever forget it. Now, why don't the two of you decide what you want to do tonight so we can go from there?"

"I don't want to impose." Bryce frowned.

"We are literally doing nothing." Mia sighed. "I guess I'll do this for you—Jos, Bryce wants to hang out with you tonight. So, go. Do whatever you want to do, and I'll be fine."

I opened my mouth to argue. Seeing Mia was just as rare for me as seeing him was; I wasn't quite ready to give up time with her in favor of spending time with a guy. Plus, I didn't love the idea of leaving her on her own.

"Whatever you're thinking, stop," Mia cut into my thoughts. "I'm not hanging out with you two. I can't handle the two of you pretending you aren't into each other. I'm not being a third wheel tonight." Bryce and I frowned at each other. "I'm walking away from you. Bryce, please make sure she gets back to the hotel safely. Please don't do anything stupid. I'll see you when I see you."

She was already turning away from us, heading toward Old Town Brewery, as Bryce and I stood there for a second, stunned.

"Should we follow her?" Bryce asked.

From the start of our friendship, I've admired Mia's strong capability to take care of herself. The bar was less than a block away from our hotel and she would be surrounded by people we knew and trusted. She had no problem handling her own safety. Besides, we were the kind of friends who needed quiet time, even when we hadn't seen each other in months. Our social batteries drained quickly doing this, so we spent most evenings sitting in our hotel in compatible silence. Mia knowing we both needed a night out on our own, doing what we wanted, wasn't surprising.

"Honestly, I think she'd kill us if we did." I grinned at Bryce. "I'm sure she'll find some friends, have a drink or two, and then head back to the hotel to crash."

A grin finally broke across his features. "If you're sure, let's go ditch my friends, then."

He reached for my hand as he led us back to the hotel. Now that he knew we had the night to ourselves, he seemed eager to get away from everyone else and focus on me—on us. His handsome face, the feel of his hand in mine, took me back to the two of us hanging out in Mesa a couple of months ago. It was only the two of us then, and that was when I realized my feelings were more than a crush.

Back then, he'd assured me that someday it could happen. It—us and our relationship—could be real.

Chapter 20

June 2016

Omaha, NE

"Bryce, wait!" I laughed as I struggled to keep up. He led me down the sidewalk, weaving us between groups of people. I was aware of certain people eyeing us as we passed, along with people who had no idea an Olympian had walked by them. The toe of my sandal caught on a crack in the sidewalk. "Seriously, Bryce, I'm going to trip."

At my warning, he came to an abrupt halt and caught me when I stumbled against him. "Sorry." He wrapped an arm around me. "I guess I'll walk like a normal person."

Grinning, I pushed my auburn bangs from my eyes. "That's all I ask."

The way he was grinning told me he was still riding high on the adrenaline from this week. Perhaps it should have been a reason for me to be a bit concerned, but instead, it was something I wanted to revel in. I'd never seen him this relaxed, this happy.

His other arm wrapped around me, pulling me against him. He leaned down, capturing my lips in a brief kiss. It was over almost as soon as it started, and it took everything for me not to chase his lips. Electricity coursed down my spine at the briefest of touches.

"Come on," he murmured. "Let's go find my friends and tell them I'm celebrating with the person I want to be with tonight."

How could a girl say no? Everything around us melted away. As far as I was concerned, we were the only two people on the street, maybe in this city. In the wake of his biggest dream coming true, Bryce was choosing to celebrate with me. He wanted me to be part of this.

"If you're sure," I breathed out.

"I am," he promised, taking my hand again. "Come on, let's go tell the guys."

This time, he led me to the sidewalk at a normal pace. I could see Ronan, Carter, and a couple of other guys sitting around a table at the hotel's outdoor patio.

"Hey, Josie!" Carter greeted, standing to meet us. "I was hoping I'd get to see you again before I left tomorrow."

"Hi!" I broke free from Bryce long enough to hug his best friend. "Congratulations on making the team! I'm so excited for you."

"Thank you." He chuckled as he pulled away. "I wasn't sure it'd happen this time around."

"Bullshit," Bryce declared over my shoulder. Ronan had come over to join us and we exchanged a quick hug as well. "We both knew it'd happen this way."

Although Carter laughed, the relief was evident on their faces. I'd been in the sport long enough to know that any of them could plan all they wanted, but the meet might not go according to plan. Know what an opponent had in store was impossible. This week had given us some surprising wins and heartbreaking losses. Every single person that had stepped up to those blocks had a plan, and it either worked, or it didn't. We were lucky everyone we cared about had done what they'd come here to do.

"Yeah, well, we're lucky it worked out the way it did," Carter commented.

"This conversation is getting way too deep for me," Ronan groaned. This was the third time he'd made the team, and he seemed more interested in getting drunk than reflecting on what almost didn't happen. "Why don't we have drinks in our hands yet?"

Carter rolled his eyes. "Because you're literally on a sidewalk, man. Are you coming out with us, Josie?"

"About that," Bryce said before I had the chance to speak. "I'm ditching you guys to spend some time with Jos. Alone."

Ronan groaned again. "You can't be serious right now. We're getting drunk. We deserve to get drunk. She deserves to get drunk."

"Shut up, man," Bryce said, tightening his grip on my hand. Though we've never talked about it, I knew the dynamic he had with Ronan. Ronan was like the older brother Bryce never had; he looked up to him but sometimes his teasing got under his skin. "I'll be with you for over a month. I just want to hang out with her."

I wish I could have prevented the little flutter my heart did at his words. Deep down, I knew there was nothing serious about them. No matter what he said, we were just two people who were barely friends and hung out when we could. Even though there was something more between us, we weren't acting on it. In fact, Bryce seemed determined to ignore it.

Carter's features mirrored the same worry I could never quite keep at bay as he glanced from our joined hands to me, then to Bryce, who was jokingly arguing with Ronan. The next time his gaze met mine, I gave Carter a reassuring smile. Somehow, it made him frown even more. Apparently, I wasn't fooling anyone here.

And his worry made sense. Carter was Bryce's best friend; he knew what his outlook on relationships was like right now. He was also a good guy—the type of guy who didn't want anyone to get hurt.

"So, where's Mia tonight?" Carter asked, both of us ignoring the two idiots still arguing in hushed tones beside us. "Did she head back to the hotel?"

"No, she headed down to Old Town," I replied, motioning to the brewery down the street behind me. "I don't know how late she's planning to stay out, but there are a couple of people she'll want to see who are supposed to be there."

The mention of my best friend snapped Ronan's attention back to us. He squinted down the street. "Mia's there?"

Nodding, I tried to swallow the guilt about leaving my best friend.

"Should we try to meet up with her?" Carter asked, turning to Ronan, who nodded.

The last unease I had about the situation evaporated. There was almost no one I trusted more than Ronan and Carter, and at least she wouldn't be alone.

"You ready?" Bryce's voice was right by my ear. With a slight jump, I squirmed away at the feeling of his breath ghosting over my ear. He chuckled deeply, which sent a jolt of something through me. "We'll talk to you guys later."

Bryce was tugging me away from the group before anyone could say anything else. This time, though, I followed, and kept up with his pace. "Where are we headed?"

"Show me your favorite place in downtown Omaha," he told me. "I haven't had the chance to do much exploring."

As soon as we had left his friends, a bright grin was back on his face. I found myself wanting to do everything I could to keep that look in his eyes. Nothing could touch us. And I wanted to keep it that way for as long as possible.

"Well, in that case, follow me." I tugged him across the street to head up to the Old Market.

The voice in the back of my mind urged me to remember every single second of tonight because it was going to be the kind of night Taylor Swift would want to write a whole album about. It'd be magic. If this was all I'd ever get, I was going to make the most of it.

*

Bryce and I spent the evening wandering the streets of downtown Omaha. We'd stopped at a bar in the heart of the Old Market, but then, after a drink, decided the loud atmosphere wasn't what we were looking for. We talked about any and everything that came to mind. Occasionally he'd we'd steal small kisses, but nothing ever escalated.

He opened up about how he was worried about the games next month, stating he'd hoped to make the team in multiple events. I assured him I'd be watching the whole race to cheer him on, which seemed to help him relax as the rest of the night unfurled.

We talked about our dreams, our goals, our families, and I did everything I could to prove that Omaha wasn't as boring as media made it out to be. It wasn't easy, given it was past midnight and most of the city was closed. Still, he listened as I told him stories about my favorite places, why they mattered to me and how, even though it was home, I longed to get away. He told me about how he missed his family but missed being close to Carter more. He'd never been without his best friend, and the decision to go to separate colleges had been hard.

It was the exact kind of night I never thought I'd share with Bryce; the kind that leaped off the page of romance novels. One I'd be pulling inspiration from for a long time.

I never wanted it to end.

"We should head back," he said as I tried to fight off a yawn. "You told me you were tired. I don't want to keep you out forever."

His right hand was on the small of my back as we looked over the edge of a railing and into the Missouri River. His left arm rested on the railing, his watch illuminating the time. It was almost two in the morning. I couldn't remember the last time I'd stayed out this late, but I wasn't ready to call it done yet.

I turned to him, ready to tell him just that, but the exhaustion was written all over his face, making the decision for me. "Let's head back."

I'd always found it strange how the moments we wanted to last forever go by the quickest. Within ten minutes, Bryce and I were walking through the eerily still lobby of the hotel. Before I even knew it was happening, we were in the elevator and his hand was hovering over the buttons as the doors slid closed.

I leaned against the opposite wall for a couple seconds, as I waited to see what he'd do. "Mia and I are on the third floor."

"Right." He still didn't push a button.

For the first time since I've known him, I couldn't pinpoint what was running through his mind. It was becoming increasingly obvious he wasn't ready for the night to end, but this was Bryce. This was the man who, just a couple months ago, told me he was too focused on getting an Olympic medal to have anything serious with anyone. Prolonging the night would cross all the lines he didn't want to cross.

"Are we just going to stand in an unmoving elevator?" I tried to make sure my tone was teasing without showing the uncertainty I was feeling. My stomach felt like it was on the floor at my feet and my chest was wide open for him to take my heart. "What if someone else gets on with us? Will you let them hit a button?"

He laughed, low and deep in a way that sent a shiver up my spine. His eyes landed on me, and the smile on his face melted away as an intensity I've never seen came over him. His expression was similar to the way he looked in the lead up to a big race, but something about it was just slightly different. Slightly darker. Heat pooled in the pit of my stomach.

No one had ever looked at me like that. Like they wanted to lay me out and take me apart piece by excruciating piece. I didn't know I wanted someone to look at me that way until I was under his gaze.

"Bryce?" His name came out as a whisper, almost breathless. I had no idea who I had become in his presence; this woman was a stranger to me, but I had a feeling I liked her. She was confident, beautiful, and felt wanted.

The way his gaze darkened, his hand balling into a fist as he fought the urge to touch me, told me he liked her, too.

"Come back to my room?"

I knew what he was asking. I also knew that no matter what my answer wound up being, he would respect it. If I said no, he'd hit the button for the third floor, and walk me back to my room with no hard feelings.

But if I said yes—everything would change.

No, my answer should be no. I should reach past him, hit the button for my floor, and call it a night. But here in the elevator, it was the last thing either of us wanted.

"Yeah." The single word answer surprised us both.

His eyebrows raised. "Yes?"

Not pulling my gaze from him, I sucked in a deep breath as the butterflies erupted in my stomach. "Yes."

In the blink of an eye, he had hit the button for his floor and was crowding me as it began to make its ascent. Although he had me bracketed against the wall with his arms on either side of my head, he wasn't touching me. I knew he was giving me one last chance to change my mind, to duck out from under his defined arms and put space back between us.

But I couldn't.

Regardless of what this would mean in the long run, I wanted him. And I wasn't ashamed of it.

Reaching up, I placed my hand against his cheek and stood on my toes, closing the last bit of height difference until I could place a kiss to his lips. Though it was chaste, it seemed to snap the last bit of his resolve.

One hand shot down to grip my hip as he pressed against me, deepening the kiss with his other hand moving to the back of my neck, angling my head the way he wanted as the wall supported me.

He surrounded me in a way I'd only ever dreamed of, and I still wanted more.

A gasp escaped me as his tongue flicked against my lips, seeking entrance. As entered my mouth, I arched against him, nails scraping against his scalp. The resulting groan he let out rumbled through my body, sending a shot of heat barreling through me. Wanting him to groan again, I repeated the motion, pushing my chest against his a little harder, nails scraping a little rougher.

He pulled away long enough to utter a whispered "fuck" against my lips before he was claiming them again. His grip on my hip tightened, pulling me impossibly closer, his hips swiveling down in a grind against me. I could feel wetness pooling between my legs and had to pull away to breathe. His lips moved to my neck instead.

"Bryce." His name came out in a surprising whimper. A second later, I knew what his insufferable smirk felt like against my skin, but it was gone almost as soon as I felt it. I gripped his hair tighter, trying to pull myself closer. He nipped and sucked at the soft skin on my neck. My head rolled back, giving him more access.

Then the elevator door was sliding open, and he was stepping away from me. A shiver went up my spine at the loss of his body heat. Both of us were panting. He was taking me in with stormy, half-lidded eyes as he took my hand and backed out of the elevator, pulling me with him. He pulled me in for the briefest of kisses before pulling me down the hall.

It was the kind of kiss that made me believe I could have him.

As we walked down the hall hand in hand, I tried to calm my heart. Then he was pulling out a room key when I was hit with a realization—athletes room together during meets. I didn't know who his roommate was, but I knew for damn sure I wasn't in the mood to have an audience.

"Bryce, wait." I grasped his arm as he pushed open the door. The room was dark inside except for the warm glow of a lamp.

Startled, he turned to me. "What? What's wrong? Did you change—"

"No, but what about your roommate?"

His brows furrowed before he realized what I was saying. "My roommate is Ronan and there's no way in hell he's coming back to this room tonight. I think he booked his own somewhere, you know, in preparation."

In preparation for his own night, not the night I was about to have with Bryce.

"Are you sure you're okay?"

I tensed, wondering if I had ruined the mood. But his gaze was all earnest and caring. I'd give anything to keep his attention on me like this, but right now, my mind was preoccupied. I wanted him. I wanted to see the fire return to his eyes. So, rather than answering, I cupped his cheek again as I pulled him down for another kiss.

Almost instantly, he deepened it, and pulled me further into the room. With the door closed behind us, he moved his hands down my back and over my ass, then he was lifting me up. Startled, I broke the kiss to let out a gasp, legs wing around his waist as I grasped at his shoulders. Before I could say anything, he pressed me against the wall, lips moving below my ear, sucking softly.

His hips grinding against my aligned core, I moaned his name. Fuck, I never wanted this to end.

"I've wanted to do this since we met," he breathed against my skin. "Fuck, Josie."

My mind was reeling as I tried to focus on the feeling of being in his arms. There was a part of me, the insecure part, which thought he shouldn't be holding a fat girl against a wall when he was about to go to the Olympics. But I couldn't bring myself to push him away because God, I wanted it.

He wanted to ravish me—he wanted to do everything women like me were led to believe we'd never get. Not only did Bryce want me, but he was also an Olympic athlete. He was the man I'd been told I could never have. Fuck society for making me believe I deserved less simply because I weighed more.

One of his hands drifted under my shirt, his rough fingers ghosting over my ribs in a way that pulled me from my thoughts. Now wasn't the time to think about the insecurity society and media had gifted me with. Right now, all I needed to think about was the feeling of his hands on me, drifting where I wanted him, and figure out why we're both still wearing clothes.

"You're perfect." He ducked further to place kisses along my collarbone.

With a blissful sigh, I leaned back against the wall. The thoughts I could never quite silence reminded me I wasn't perfect, but I also never would pretend to be. Bryce wasn't perfect. But right now, we were both perfect. This moment was perfect to each other, and that fact would probably keep me going for years to come.

Moving my hands back to his hair, I tugged his head back to reconnect our lips. As his tongue swiped across my lower lip, I dropped my legs from his waist. He groaned against my mouth, but got my point when I started tugging at his shirt. We parted long enough for him to pull it over his head, revealing all the muscles I'd seen countless times but never got to touch.

He let out a different groan when my nails scraped down his abs, feeling the ridge of each one as I went. His pupils were blown so wide it was hard to distinguish any color in them. Holding eye contact and feeling bold, I did something I never expected of myself. I pulled my dress over my head, letting it fall to the floor beside me. While my bra and underwear weren't anything sexy, because I'd never anticipated the night to take such a turn, he didn't seem to care.

He stepped forward until I was surrounded by him, groaning as he ground against me again. It had never been like this before, and I wanted more of him.

"Bryce," I gasped, dragging my nails against his back. "Bed, please."

Nodding, Bryce pulled away long enough to grab my hand. He never broke eye contact as he pulled me toward the bed. The moment we reached the bed, Bryce reached behind me in search of the clasp of my bra. Seconds later, it was sliding down my arms. His lips landed on my cheek. His hands went up to my breasts, cupping them as he started kissing a path to where he wanted them most. Where I wanted them most.

It took him a second before his lips were closing around my breast. I couldn't help but whimper when he sucked. My trembling hands reached for the button of his jeans. As soon as I popped it open, he stopped everything to stare down at me.

We were both gasping for breath, but I knew what he was doing. Biting my lip, I nodded once.

Smirking, he eased me onto the bed before turning to a bag sitting on the floor behind him. As he dug through it, I moved further up the bed until I was against the pillows. My gaze never left his bare back, content to watch the well-defined muscles move beneath his smooth skin.

When he turned back to me, he had a condom, and a small bottle of lube. He tossed both on the bed by my side for easier access later. A second later, he'd finished what I'd started, kicking his jeans to the side before crawling up the bed between my legs, all hard muscle with small tattoos and extreme hotness.

"Bryce," I breathed as his fingers slid up my thighs.

"Look at you," he murmured, body covering mine until I could feel every inch of him. "You're beautiful."

My arms wrapped around his shoulders, nails scraping against the muscle I'd been admiring. His lips found mine again, licking into my mouth. One hand gripped my hip, pulling me as close to him as possible. His hard length pressed against where I needed it the most.

My head dropped back to the pillow, mouth dropping open as his lips returned to my neck. His hand moved down until he could cup it against me. I arched up against his touch, needing to feel some kind of pressure. "Bryce," I moaned as his finger circled my clit. "*Please.*"

"I got you, baby," he whispered against, pushing a finger inside. I let out a deep moan while his other hand reached for the discarded condom.

As another finger slid in beside the first, I arched off the bed, pressing against his firm chest. Tilting my head, I silently pleaded for a kiss. A plea I wasn't sure he'd answer. But his lips captured mine before his fingers worked to stretch me open, and all I could do was melt.

Arms around his neck, pulling him closer, I gave myself over completely to this moment and to the man above me, never wanting to let go.

Chapter 21

NOW

April 2023
Omaha, NE

The night draws to a close, and I'm left even more unsure of where Bryce and I stand than before. All night I alternate between feeling comfortable around him to cowering in on myself like he's a total stranger.

It doesn't take me long to realize I'm not the only one doing it.

Neither one of us is solely to blame for the awkwardness. We both contributed to it in equal measures, but knowing it's getting to him is surprising. The man who has always been the epitome of cool, easy confidence is unsure of himself? If it's true, what hope do I have?

"I'm glad we did this." We are walking back to my car, a gesture he'd insisted on despite it being in the opposite direction. "I had a nice time."

"Me too." It seems like the automatic reply, the one to ease the blow of the inevitable "but" I know is coming.

I'm glad we did this, but I don't think we should do it again.

I'm glad we did this, but I get why we never did it back then.

I'm glad we did this, but . . .

Yet, it never comes. There's no declaration of regret, even as we keep walking through the Old Market with our arms linked. To anyone passing by, we appear to be a normal couple enjoying a cool spring evening. No one knows the history we share; they don't know I can't ignore the weird tension between us. No one knows we are trying to navigate a new landscape.

It's a reminder we can be and do anything we want here, away from the past. We are miles away from any place with memories that haunt us and the people we were back then. This might be our chance to move forward. Why can't we get out of our own way?

When we finally reach my Jeep, he faces me, and my arm slips out of his grasp to fall to my side. His tense smile does nothing to calm the anxious beating of my heart. "I'm sorry I got weird a couple of times tonight."

I guffaw. "We both did, and I'm sorry, too."

He bites the corner of his lip. "Do you think we can get past it? The weirdness?"

God, I hope so. How cruel does the universe have to be to give me everything I've ever wanted, only to snatch it right back from my grasp?

"I think so," I admit. "It'll take work, but I have faith in us."

"I keep thinking about all the times you asked me for this, and I couldn't give it to you." The frustration he feels reveals itself with a grimace, reinforced when he pushes his fingers through his hair, disheveling it. I want to comb it back in place. "I'm going to fuck this up."

Sympathy twists my heart. "You're not even giving yourself a chance, Bryce. Yes, we have history to sort through, and it'll be hard not to fall into old habits, but I think we can do it. I wouldn't be here if I didn't think we could do it. *We* want the same things this time around. We just have to work to get there. Together."

He watches me closely, considering my words. "And that's what you want? For us to make this work?"

I blink at him. "It's all I've ever wanted for longer than I care to admit. I'm not asking for perfection, Bryce. I want you to be honest with me. About where we've been, where we are at now, and where we're going. I can't question where I stand in your life ever again. If that's going to happen, we should say goodbye now."

He takes a small, tentative step toward me, reaching out to curl a hand around my hip. "It won't happen again. And, in the spirit of being honest, you should know I've missed kissing you. I wanted to kiss you the first day in the office."

Every single one of my nerve endings are on edge. "I probably would have slapped you if you tried."

His eyes brighten, causing the butterflies in my stomach to twirl. "And now?"

"Since we're being honest," I coyly reply, "I'm a little angry you haven't kissed me yet."

Like a scene in a movie, the world around us fades as he becomes the only thing I can focus on. His gaze momentarily drops to my lips before gray eyes are meeting mine once more. I'm itching to feel his lips against mine again, to melt against his strong, firm frame in a way I've longed to for the past two years. Now that it's within my grasp, my patience is waning. Each breath I inhale seems to take an eternity.

After what is probably only a couple of seconds, I can't take it anymore and close the distance between us. Everything that happens after is complete and utter instinct. My arms wind around his neck, his left hand cupping my cheek, while his right hand pulls me closer.

When his lips finally brush against mine, tentative at first, before becoming more demanding. His touch feels like coming home.

As a writer, I know that's about as cliché as it can get, but there's a reason clichés stick—nine out of ten times, they're true.

As much as I want it to last longer, go deeper, now isn't the time. Anything more than this simple, chaste kiss beside my car will feel like we are going backward. I know if one of us suggests we continue this somewhere else, the answer will be yes. That won't be a mistake, necessarily, but I'm mature enough to understand it isn't the best decision we can make right now.

Bryce must feel the same way, as he pulls away a second later. He inhales a deep breath before pressing one more kiss to my lips before resting his forehead against mine, thumb tracing along my cheek. Gray-blue eyes open to meet mine, both of us smiling like idiots. "I missed this."

"Me too." I kiss his cheek just as he's about to straighten to his full height. "I honestly didn't think I'd ever get to do it again."

"Well, we did, and we'll do it again. At least I hope I haven't scared you away from a second date."

I shake my head. "Not at all. I was hoping you'd ask."

"Good," he breathes, pushing a loose curl away from my face. "In the spirit of being honest . . . I'm not sure when we'll make it happen. The rest of the week is going to be hell for me."

"Me too," I agreed, grimacing at the massive to-do list I know I have tomorrow. "We'll figure something out. I have faith in us."

He glances down at his watch. "Did you want to call it a night or hang out a bit longer?"

"How about we get some ice cream?" I offer, knowing it's one of his favorite treats. "The Scoop is still open, and it's still as amazing as it was back in 2016."

"You had me at ice cream." He smirks, reaching for my hand to interlace our fingers. "Just remember, I don't share."

I laugh as he leads me toward the heart of the Old Market, where the ice cream shop is. The awkward tension dominating our night has vanished as we fall into talking about work, life, and even little memories from the past.

Once we have our ice cream, we slide into one of the slightly sticky, uncomfortable wooden booths in the little ice cream parlor. As I get about a third of the way through my favorite dark chocolate ice cream, Bryce glances at it from across the booth and asks how it is. Grinning, I take another bite, and happily sigh. For most of my life, I've been convinced there's no problem this ice cream can't solve.

"That good, huh?" Bryce teases with raised eyebrows. Before I can even blink, he reaches his spoon over to steal some. I gasp at him, but he shoves the bite in his mouth. "Wow, okay, it's actually good."

"You can't just steal people's ice cream, Bryce Clark!"

Instead of apologizing, he holds out his mint chip. I dig into his ice cream. Apparently, we are going to have that kind of relationship. Weirdly, I'm okay with it.

Chapter 22

June 2016
Omaha, NE

I awoke to sunlight streaking through blinds that were never quite closed, making me groan and roll away from the offensive light, only to be stopped by a strong, solid arm around my waist. I froze as memories of last night came rushing back to me, the reality of what had happened hitting me full force. I'm not in my room, I'm not alone in bed, and we're both naked beneath these sheets.

I took a few deep breaths, trying to calm down and figure out what my next move was going to be. This wasn't some drunken hookup, after all. We had made the choice, a couple of times, and we did so sober. What we failed to think about last night was the consequences of those actions and what they would mean moving forward.

Bryce didn't want this. I'd wanted this since the moment I first laid eyes on him. Now we were fucked.

He wasn't my first, but he was only my second, and I knew enough to discern I wasn't a hookup person. I couldn't pretend this never happened, not the way I knew he'd want to. But what was I supposed to do? How could I deal with this and keep him in my life the way he wanted to be in it? How could I sleep with an Olympic team member from a professional standpoint?

Shit, shit, shit.

Beside me, Bryce released a light snore. If things were different, I'd snuggle up against him and drift back to sleep, reminding myself to tease him about the snoring when we awoke next. As it was, right now, I needed him to stay asleep until I figured out what I was going to do.

The arm he'd draped around my waist tightened, bracing me against his bare chest and—*Oh.*

I needed to get the hell away from him before I did something stupid. Every inch of him rubbed the curves of my body, and I wanted to melt against it. I wanted to turn in his arms, kiss my way down his chest until I could wrap my mouth around—

No, I scolded myself. *That would be a very bad idea.*

"Josie?" Of course, his sleep-heavy, barely awake voice had to be deep, grave, and hot. Pairing that voice with how he nuzzled his face into my wavy hair was torture. "You good?"

No, I wanted to scream at him. *I'm the furthest fucking thing from good! How am I supposed to deal with this now?* "I'm fine. I just need to use the restroom."

I needed to get out of here. Or at least as far away from him to get my shit together.

Reluctantly, he released me from his grip by rolling onto his back. I lay frozen for a couple of seconds, wondering if I wanted to do this. What if I got up and everything changed while I was in there? What if he made the choice for me, and he wanted me to go?

It didn't matter. I needed to do this. I needed to wrap my head around everything, and I couldn't do it with his arms wrapped around me. Besides, I knew what was going to happen next—he was going to want to pretend it was nothing.

I had to get away from him.

When I turned to him, his head against the pillow as much as it could be at an angle, one eye barely cracked open to look at me. "Hurry back."

Nodding, I pressed a lingering kiss to his cheek before sitting up and grabbing his discarded shirt from the floor. I pulled it on. It wasn't baggy, but it wasn't too tight. It'd do for now. Bryce's breath evened out as I tiptoed to the bathroom, picking up my own clothes as I went.

I shut the door behind me, wincing as I turned on the harsh lights, and quickly took care of business before stepping in front of the mirror, letting out a small gasp at the reflection staring back at me. I looked well and truly fucked. My auburn curls were a mess, the light makeup I'd worn out was smudged and a series of bruises littered my neck and collarbone.

I hadn't realized how sensitive of an area that was for me until Bryce had and proceeded to make use of it.

As I washed my hands, I kept glancing at my reflection, not able to tear my eyes away as I thought through my options. If I went back out there, I could find Bryce ready to part ways. If I went back out there and he was asleep, I could crawl back into bed and pretend everything was fine. I could ignore the fact that, eventually, we would have to talk about this.

Or I could leave and avoid the inevitable conversation until Mia and I decided to go to another meet. I'd never run out on someone before. It wasn't my style, but I knew where this conversation would go, and I wasn't ready for it. If I left, I'd have months to prepare. If something had changed, he hadn't told me. Which meant he either still didn't want a relationship, or he didn't want one with me.

I took one last look in the mirror before I reached for my clothes to change. Once I was dressed, I exited the bathroom to find Bryce sprawled out across the bed, fast asleep. He was lying on his stomach, bare back exposed to me, and had his face buried in the pillow I had abandoned moments ago. Fighting the urge to crawl back into bed, I found my bag on the dresser, checked to make sure my phone was in there. The hardest thing I'd ever done was turn and walk out.

~ele~

Two days later and barely awake, I was walking through the airport parking lot with Mia so I could say goodbye to her. The sun was peeking through the clouds, and the exhaustion from the meet and the mental gymnastics I'd done since hooking up with Bryce had me dragging. Something Mia seemed worried about, but also hadn't pressed.

Despite bragging about sleeping in, Mia had been awake when I stumbled into our hotel room just after six-thirty. She didn't ask questions or say a single word when she took me in, just opened her arms to hug me as I cried from the emotional whirlwind. We promptly did not talk about it.

"Have you heard from him?"

Until now, apparently.

Stifling a yawn, I shrugged. "He's texted and sent a couple DMs."

Her eyebrow arched. "And you haven't answered any of them?"

"Nope." I didn't regret sleeping with him, but I knew better, and it shouldn't have happened. "We both want different things; it was a mistake. And I think we both need some space."

"But it did happen." We crossed the street, heading toward the entrance of the airport, Mia's bag rolling obnoxiously against the pavement behind us. "Nothing is going to be solved by ignoring him. I'm not saying you should get back in bed with him—please don't—but I think you should talk to him. The two of you could still be friends."

"Can we, though? We crossed a lot of lines the other night and I'm not sure how we move past that."

"Because you want more, right?" Mia knew better than anyone. She knew the answer to her question long before I was ready to admit to myself. Now she wanted to hear me say it. "I get it, Jos. I know what it's like to want someone you can't have, even to cross lines like that."

"What? Who—"

"It happened a while ago, not important." She waved me off. "We're talking about you right now, and I don't want to see you set yourself up to be hurt, but I think it'll bother you more to pretend this never happened. You know you're going to see him again, so just handle it."

The doors to the airport slid open as we approached, her words settling between us. A part of me wished I could be that brave, wished I could pick up the phone and tell him what happened didn't matter, or even that it did, but confrontation, and I had never been friends.

"I know you're right," I admitted, stepping off to the side to finish the conversation in the quiet airport. "I can't do it right now."

"Why?"

A groan escaped before I could stop it. "Because, Mia, he's about to go to the Olympics! He doesn't need the girl he hooked up with in Omaha breathing down his neck about their future. Especially because he's made it painfully clear that there is no future."

"Okay, fine." She raised her hands in mock surrender. "You don't have to call him. But what if you had the chance to talk to him in person before the games? Would you do it?"

I rolled my eyes. "Yeah, sure, totally. If he was still around and wanted to talk, I'd talk to him."

"Then let's talk."

"Holy shit," I cursed, practically jumping out of my skin as I turned to face Bryce. "What the fuck, dude?"

An amused smirk pulled across his lips. "Did I startle you? I didn't mean to."

"I think I'm going to go check my bag," Mia declared, looking between us. "Give you two a chance to talk."

I turned to glare at her, but Mia was already walking toward the check in area, leaving me alone with the last person I wanted to be alone with. Facing him, I took in his attire—black sweats, a Team USA hoodie, and a baseball cap. There were slight bags under his eyes and a wariness to his body that suggested he'd be content to collapse into a bed. When he saw me staring, his smirk dropped into a soft smile.

"So, I'm assuming you went back to your room the other night?" He didn't sound mad, but there was an accusatory snark to the question. Under the annoyance, though, there was obvious concern. "At least we were staying in the same place."

"I got back okay. I should have told you I was safe; I didn't want to intrude any longer."

He stuffed his hands into his pockets, eyes narrowing in confusion. "And how would you be intruding?"

I didn't have an answer, so I just kind of shrugged and did my very best to not look at him. "I didn't want things to get awkward."

He laughed, light, and easy. My heart sank

a bit. "And you thought it'd be less awkward for me to wake up to an empty bed? With no idea of where you went or when you even left?"

It was subtle, but his façade cracked with those words. He wasn't reacting the way he wanted to; he was pissed at me. His tone said it all. He probably had a right to be.

"I don't know, maybe? I panicked, Bryce. It happens to the best of us."

"Of course it does, but I'm trying to figure out why you panicked. Did something happen? Did I do something to fuck it up? I didn't mean to push you into some—"

"You did nothing wrong, Bryce. Everything that happened was something I wanted."

"Then tell me what's going on, Josie. Why did you leave?"

I closed my eyes, counting to five as I tried to gather the courage to be honest with him. I hated being vulnerable. I didn't want to give him or any guy ammunition to use against me. When I opened my eyes, he was staring down at me. "I didn't panic, necessarily. I got scared."

"Okay," he breathed a sigh. "We can work with that. Why were you scared?"

"You told me months ago you weren't looking for anything serious, and then you reminded me several times throughout the week. Then we slept together." I wrung my hands together. "Maybe it's not a big deal for you, but it is for me, and I can't just move past it."

"What are you talking about? It's a big deal for me, Josie," he argued. "You have to remember I dated my ex for years. I'm only twenty-two now and people thought we were going to get married. Sleeping around isn't something I do."

"But you're okay doing it with me. You told me you didn't want a relationship, but then you sleep with me. What am I supposed to think?"

"It's not you." He frowned. I swore if he followed it up with "it's me," I would kill him. I didn't even care that we were in an airport. "I don't want to hook up with random people. I made it pretty clear I want you, but I also cannot get involved in a relationship right now. Especially long distance."

"I know," I assured him, "and I respect that, but I don't sleep with people who I don't mean anything—"

"You *do* mean something to me, Josie." He ran a hand through his hair. "You mean more than I ever intended you to. I can't be what you want me to be right now. I would never ask you to do something you aren't comfortable with, but can't we go back to what we planned in Mesa? Stay friends and figure everything else out later? I don't want to lose you."

We'd be doing everything on his timeline, the very thing Mia was worried about, but I didn't want to lose him either. I didn't want to know what losing someone like him was like.

"I'm not saying we pretend it didn't happen, either," he continued. "We just . . . We move on. We see what the future holds for us. And go from there."

I couldn't understand why we kept having this conversation in airports, but maybe it meant there would be a day we didn't have to.

"Okay," I agreed, a little reluctantly. "We'll stay friends and maybe one day, this will go where we want it to."

"Yeah, maybe one day." He stuck his hand to me. "In the meantime, are we friends?"

Rolling my eyes, but unable to hide my smile, I shook his hand. It was different this time, because now I knew what his hands felt like when they were all over me. I'd never forget it. "Friends."

He looked down at our joined hands before dropping the handshake, returning it to his pocket. "I should get going. We board in thirty minutes."

That was more than enough time to get through security and to your gate here, but I didn't tell him that. Mia stood off to the side, checking her phone. She was leaving about the same time. I was saying goodbye to both of them. "I should head up with Mia, so I can say goodbye."

Bryce slung an arm around my shoulder as we walked toward Mia. "I'll head upstairs with you guys."

I shouldn't lean against him, but I felt comfortable snuggled against his side. Almost like I belonged there.

Silence settled around us as the three of us made our way toward the escalator. The adrenaline from the last week had long since disappeared and we were all feeling the exhaustion. Bryce more than any of us. We had spent the last four years hyping ourselves up for this meet. Now we were all a little unsure of where we went from here. Sure, the Olympics were next, but what happened when we were on the other side of those, too? No one knew what the next several months would bring. We had hopes and ideas, but that didn't mean they were guaranteed. Even though Bryce and I were parting on good terms, I had a million questions running through my mind. Questions I didn't dare ask or voice put to the universe.

When reached the top of the escalator, Mia and Bryce were each required to go a separate direction, and I was torn. The decision was made for me when he removed his arm from my shoulder to envelop Mia in a tight hug. They murmured to one another before he was back in front of me, large hands cupping my cheeks. I was trying not to cry.

"I'll see you soon, okay?" The question was whispered, and all I could do was nod. I expected him to kiss my lips, but he didn't. Warm lips pressed against the top of my head before he pulled me into a hug.

"Kick ass in Rio, okay?"

After a nod, he pulled away from me to head toward his terminal. I watched him walk away for a minute. He never once turned back. It wasn't until he was nearly at security I realized that he never said goodbye. He just assured me he'd see me later.

Wordlessly, I followed Mia to her terminal. It wasn't until we had said our tearful goodbyes that I thought back to her goodbye with Bryce. "What did you and Bryce say to one another?"

"Nothing much," she admitted. "I wished him good luck, promised we'd be cheering, and I told him not to break your heart. He told me he wouldn't."

Even then, standing in the airport, I knew the promise was out of his control. It was out of my control—no one knew what the future held. And it was pointless for two people to pretend they were incapable of hurting one another.

"Think he's going to win a medal?"

"He's going to try like hell," Mia confirmed. "And if he does, he'll be just as insufferable as he was before. I don't know what you see in him, but the heart wants what it wants, I guess."

Laughing, I pulled her into another hug. "I'll miss you, best friend."

"We'll be on the phone with one another in less than five hours," she teased, hugging me. "But I'll miss you, too."

I stood there longer than I did with Bryce, waiting until she was through security before I headed back to my car. Stepping into the humid air, I choked back a sob as the reality that it was over crashed around me. Everyone had gone back home. Everyone I cared about was on their way back to their real lives or the Olympics, and I was still here. I wondered if it was always going to be like this. If they would move on and I'd stay still.

I didn't want that for myself. I just hadn't quite figured out how to have anything different.

Chapter 23

NOW

May 2023

Omaha, NE

One thing I hadn't anticipated after reconnecting with Bryce was the way my inspiration would come back. Out of nowhere, I constantly feel the need to write and, even more surprising, new ideas are coming to me in waves. After we stopped talking, my writing didn't suffer. The desire to write is coming back. It's stopped feeling like a chore, and I'm remembering why I love it.

When I sit down to write on Thursday evening, after a rather long and taxing week, my phone rings. I almost ignore it, but Bryce's name flashing on the screen catches my attention.

We haven't had a chance to catch up much since our date, both of our schedules packed full of work commitments. Things are finally calming down for me and I'm hoping, since he's calling, he's out of the thick of it as well.

Accepting the call, I lean back in my comfy desk chair. "Hello?"

"Hey, Jos," he greets warmly, the old nickname rolling off his tongue. I can't remember the last time he called me that. "Is this a bad time?"

I shake my head even though he can't see me. "Not a bad time. I was going to get some writing in, but you're not interrupting anything." I glanced at the clock; it's almost eight. "What's up? Please tell me you're not still at work."

"I just left," he admits, and a second later I can hear his turn signal. "I can literally still see the parking lot in my rearview mirror."

And he'll be seeing it straight on in less than twelve hours. This is the beginning of something I've both seen a hundred times and experienced in the short year and a half I've been with the company.

"You're overworking yourself, Bryce. You'll end up with burnout. Haven't you ever heard of work-life balance? Because you need to find it."

"That's the bad thing about being a professional athlete for as long as I was; it's not a skill you learn," he says with a chuckle. I remember how he'd text me throughout the day, starting before the sun came up, and continued through multiple practices and other commitments within the day. "But I am trying, which is why I'm calling you. I wanted to discuss the second date we talked about a lifetime ago."

I find myself smiling like an idiot. "And by a lifetime, you mean Monday?"

"Obviously," he replies with a hint of amusement in his voice. "Look, I know last time it got awkward, and you might be a little wary about jumping back into it, but you were the one who said we needed to work at it, so let's work at it."

"What did you have in mind?"

"Don't hate me, but I took the liberty of taking a look at your work calendar," he begins. I'm sure he thinks peeking at my calendar is an invasion of privacy, but there's a reason I keep it public. I work with so many different departments, it's easier to let them look at my calendar and decide the best time for a meeting than try to schedule it myself. "I saw we're both going to be off at our normal time tomorrow."

As much as I want to see Bryce, I almost let out a groan at the mention of tomorrow. As he knows, I had a long week and was looking forward to a Friday night in. It's too early into whatever we are to tell him I'd prefer to spend the night in with comfy clothes, a movie, and takeout. We aren't even thirty yet, so it's a little pathetic to say I need a night like that to recharge my battery.

I say nothing and opt to see what he has in mind before I decide anything.

"I don't know about you, but I don't feel like going out."

I relax instantly, remembering he prefers nights in sweats as much as me. "I want to see you."

"Not going out sounds perfect." Cuddling on the couch with a movie? Sign me up. "Tell me more about these plans of yours."

He chuckles at the excitement I'm sure he can hear in my voice. "How about you come over, I make us dinner, and we hang out? We can watch a movie or something—I want a chill night."

"You cook?" I'm not able to hide my shock. Despite his athlete days being behind him, I still picture him as the kind of guy who lives off decent takeout options.

He laughs again, this time more openly. "Yeah, I'm decent at it, so I won't kill you or anything. I had to learn. I couldn't eat trash forever and although I trained on campus, they stopped letting me into the dining hall after I graduated. So, what do you say?"

It all sounds perfect, and I'm itching to see this domestic side of Bryce and his hidden skills I never fathomed. I want to be selfish, though. I have purposely planned my week around not leaving my apartment on Friday, and I'm not fully ready to give it up. I will if he isn't cool with it, but I still have to try.

"It sounds amazing, but I do have one small request."

"Name it."

"Can we do it at my place? I don't have to be in the office tomorrow and was planning on not leaving at all. If you'd rather do it at yours, I'm game. I just wanted to ask."

"We can do it another night, Josie," he offers, his tone gentle. "If you don't—"

"It's not that. You're not ruining my plans; you're actually making them better. We both had a shitty week, and I want to spend time with you. I just thought we could do it at my place. You're cooking, I want to host."

He hesitates for a moment. "All right, yeah, let's do it at your place. I'll bring everything I need grocery-wise. I'm assuming you have everything I'll need to cook?"

"I mean, my kitchen is equipped with everything a normal twenty-eight-year-old woman would need," I tease. "If you're planning to go all Gordon Ramsey on me, I suggest you bring anything normal people wouldn't have."

"I'm definitely not that good. I'll stop by my house after work to get everything and change. I should be over around six?"

"Sounds like a plan," I confirm. It will give me time to make sure the apartment is ready after my workday. "I'll text you my address as soon as we hang up."

"Great, you also get to pick the movie," he decides. "I'll see you tomorrow, Josie."

"Have a goodnight," I reply, still grinning like an idiot as I listen to him bid me a goodnight as well, voice soft, and warm, before I end the call.

———ee———

The next day, my phone rings as soon as five o'clock hits and I press send on my final email.

"No way you're done already," I accuse as soon as I accept the call.

Bryce's deep laugh fills my ears. "No way you're still working." Shutting my laptop, I sigh at his teasing. "I'm heading to the elevator now. Come on, Josie, we had a plan."

"I know, I know. I had one last email to send before I closed my laptop, but I'm done now."

"Good." I can hear the chime of the elevator from somewhere near him. "We might have a small problem with our plan, though."

"What's going on?"

"Remember how I told you I'd get everything we needed last night?" I mumble out an agreement. I have a feeling I know where this is going. "Well, that didn't happen. Instead, I picked up dinner, and thought I'd swing by my place to eat and change before heading toward the store."

"And you fell asleep on your couch, didn't you?" I laugh as I shut my laptop. "Are you thinking you'll be over closer to six?"

"Yeah, it'll probably be right around there. Or, and feel free to say no, but I thought I could swing by and pick you up? I know you said you didn't want to leave, but—"

"Yeah, absolutely, let's do that," I reply before I could stop myself. "I actually need to grab a few things, so it works out."

"Great, I'll be there in about twenty-five minutes with traffic."

"Sounds good. Text me when you get here."

Once we hang up, I take a couple of minutes to tidy up my workspace since it's the first thing anyone sees when they enter my apartment. I had tidied up the rest of the apartment last night, but I do another quick lap to make sure everything looks good. Once I'm done, I change out of the baggy pajamas I've worn all day to replace it with a simple pair of leggings and a matched cropped T-shirt. He said we are going for comfy and casual, so I'm leaning into it.

The last step is a glance in the mirror to make sure my curls aren't a total mess or look dead inside. I'm not wearing any makeup, and I don't plan to. Just as I shut off the bathroom light, Bryce texts me to let me know he's here.

I try not to race downstairs to meet him.

As soon as I slide into the passenger seat, Bryce leans over, and kisses me. Grinning as we part, I sit back in my seat and pull on the belt. As he drives out of the parking lot, I glance over at him and realize he either brought clothes with him to work or he stopped at his apartment on his way here. He's dressed in gray sweats and a black sweatshirt, with a backward baseball cap on his head.

I grin at how much he looks like the boy I first fell for.

"Where's the closest grocery store?"

Snapping back to reality, I direct him to the closest one. During the drive, we mostly listen to music and talk about our day. Before long, we are walking into the store, Bryce momentarily leaving to get a cart.

I don't know what Bryce needs for dinner, so I allow him to lead us through the store, chatting as we go. I hate grocery shopping with a passion, but it isn't so bad with him. By the time we have everything we need, the store is a little more crowded, and a line has formed at checkout. As we wait for our turn, we debate over what movie to watch.

"Excuse me," a small voice says from my left. I turn to see a young boy no more than nine, staring up at Bryce with wide, amazed eyes. Bryce looks a little surprised to see the attention directed at him. "Are you Bryce Clark?"

Gray eyes flick over to me before settling on the boy again. I wonder how often this happens to him. "Uh, yeah, I am."

The kid breaks out into a toothy grin. "Awesome! Can I get a picture with you?"

▢Bryce shifts his weight from foot to foot, but he nods. The kid waves someone over and I look up to see a woman who must be his mom approach with a phone ready. People are watching in confusion as Bryce squats so he can be more level with the kid.

As soon as the pictures are taken, the kid starts telling Bryce about his recent swim meet. Knowing this can take a moment, and Bryce won't interrupt the kid no matter how badly he wants to, I move us out of line.

"It was nice of him to agree to this," the mother says, flicking through the pictures. "He's basically Noah's idol."

"He loves interacting with fans." Or he used to, but the tension in his shoulders makes me doubt it's still true. "He doesn't mind."

He looks desperate for an escape.

The mom focuses on snapping pictures as she lets Noah talk his ear off for another few minutes. Eventually, she reminds him we probably have other things to do, so the boy thanks Bryce for the advice and his time before following his mother across the store.

As soon as they are far enough away, the tension leaves Bryce as he reaches for the cart and maneuvers us back into line. He doesn't say a word.

"I didn't think that would still happen." Outside of a swim meet, Bryce hardly ever had someone approach him, even at the height of his career. This is the last place I would have expected it to happen. "Is it a regular thing?"

He leans against the cart, shaking his head. "No. Definitely not here."

That's the end of the subject.

He drives back to my place in silence, minus the music he plays. As our joined hands rest on my thigh, I keep thinking back to the last time I saw Bryce like this, the way he spoke to me and the way his words aimed to hurt me.

Every time I look over at him, he's this person I don't want to remember, and I hate it. He doesn't fully relax until we are back in my apartment, already starting on dinner. I try to relax with him, but I'm too caught up in the past.

Watching him interact with Noah brings back memories of the way Bryce had once interacted with the group of boys seconds after breaking my heart. He'd known what he'd done, but he was nothing but nice with them, and I had to see that. I could see through it then, I could see through it now. Will I ever be able to get it out of my head?

"How about you tell me why you've been walking on eggshells since we got back?"

He's setting up everything he needed to cook dinner, while I'm perched at my island trying to get out of my head and figure out what he's making.

I force myself to relax, but he notices. "Yeah, exactly like that."

I try to brush off his concern. "I don't know what you're talking about, I'm fine."

Leaning against the counter in front of me, he frowns. "No, you're not. You've been off since that kid approached me. If we're going to make this work, we both have to talk about what's bugging us, right?"

He's right, obviously, but I don't know how to tell him about the thoughts running through my head. How am I supposed to stand here and tell him I can't shake what happened between us? That every time I tried, something pulls me back to those days, to the way he treated me like I meant nothing? And how do I make him understand I'm still trying to figure out how best to work through it?

"I know," I reply when he starts chopping some green peppers. "And we've done a good job of talking about the past, but it's mostly been from your perspective. I don't know, maybe it's harder for me to be open about my side than I expected it to be."

His brows furrow. "What does that mean? You don't want to talk through stuff with me? Because it kind of seems like it, which won't end well for us."

I sigh. "I don't know what you expect from me here. The last time I tried to have a serious conversation with you, you said I wasn't worth your time anymore. You humiliated me; it doesn't make me eager to try again."

As soon as the words leave my mouth, I know I've opened a door I won't be able to easily close. I know we need to have this conversation. I've been thinking about it since I saw him in the office the first time, but I don't want it to happen now, when we were on the verge of an argument.

Besides, a part of me always hoped he'd be the one to bring it up, seeing as he caused the pain. I know how it made him feel, but we've done very little talking about how I feel. Will he eventually want to know?

"I thought we talked about this, Josie." He sets down the knife to focus on me, but his tone sounds tired. "We cleared the air, that's why we're here. We're moving on."

But we haven't talked. He talked, and I listened. I let him tell his side of the story, the reason he had said the things he did, and the way he had managed to deal with the consequences. Not once have we ever talked about the impact that one moment had on me, though. Now it's the very thing standing between us and, as much as I want him here with me, I'm not sure how to move past it.

Can I move past the very real possibility he might leave me again?

"I'm not sure I can." The words crash down around us. Bryce stands straighter but says nothing. Meanwhile, words tumble out of my mouth. "And we didn't talk about it, not really. You talked about it. You talked about the way you felt, the way you regret what happened, and how sorry you are. But we never talked about the way all of it affected me."

Fear flashes in his eyes. He will never admit it, but I see it. Now I know why we haven't talked about my side of things. Because it meant he would have to confront the pain he caused me. Which I know was something he isn't sure he can do. Despite the harshness of his words, I know hurting me is the last thing he wants to do.

But that didn't mean it didn't happen. He needs to stop running from the consequences.

"Do you have any idea how much you humiliated me?" I go on. "How each word felt like a knife in my chest?"

He swallows thickly, looking anywhere but at me. His comfort level didn't matter anymore, though. This conversation is necessary.

"I knew it was coming," I admit, watching as his gaze snap back to me. "I knew whatever we'd been doing was over, but I wasn't prepared for how much it would hurt."

"Do you think I didn't know what kind of impact I would have on you? That it didn't kill me to know the pain I caused you?"

"Of course not, because I know you." He'd known what he was doing, but that didn't make it better. "That's not the part that matters, though. Not really."

"Then what does?"

"You said those words, and then you went to the fucking Olympics, Bryce! You lived your dream, and I was left here, trying to figure out what to do with the pieces of mine that I'd just lost."

Shocked, Bryce murmurs my name so softly I almost don't hear it.

I'm not done, though. Angry tears burn the corners of my eyes, and I'm so tired of protecting him from himself. I don't want to pretend I just got over it or that I haven't let myself fall. I gave him all of me, every last goddamn piece, and it still hadn't been enough.

Those are the truths he needs to know, or we won't get anywhere.

"And there is a part of me that is scared I'll always hate you for it." My voice cracks against the tears blurring my vision. "And myself. Because I was in love with you, and I was stupid enough to think, eventually, you would love me back."

There, I said it.

The words I've been holding in since 2016 are out. They hang heavily in the space between us as a montage of emotions sweep across his features—shock, disbelief, uncertainty, sadness, and then it settles on anger. Whether it's directed at me or himself, I don't know, but it's unexpected. For the first time since we met, I had this unnerving need to fill the silence.

"I'm not trying to make a big deal out of this or hurt you; I need you to know my side of things. I'm happy you can talk to me about what happened, but it doesn't mean you get to ignore my side of it. You broke my heart, Bryce."

To my utter shock, he inhales a deep breath before walking around the counter, heading straight toward my front door.

I quickly follow. "Where are you going?"

"I'm leaving," he declares as he slips his shoes on. He won't look at me. "This was a mistake."

My heart plummets, but anger also surges. "Let me get this straight. I finally have the guts to open up to you and you leave?"

"Yeah, because I'm not giving myself the chance to do that to you again."

Then he's gone, the door swinging shut behind him. With my heart in my throat, I move to the living room window and watch as Bryce crosses the parking lot to his car. He slides behind the wheel and hesitates for a moment before starting the car and pulling away.

I'm speechless.

Chapter 24

NOW

May 2023
Omaha, NE

Early the next morning, the ringing of my phone startles from a restless sleep on the couch.

Reaching for it, I groggily overcompensate, and fall right of the couch. With a painful groan, I answer the phone without even looking at the screen, hoping it's Bryce. "Hello?"

"I was worried you weren't going to answer."

I deflate at the sound of Mia's voice. "Well, I did."

"I was thinking a dinner date might turn into a breakfast—"

"He didn't even make dinner." I lean back against the couch, using my free hand to rub the sleep from my eyes. "He left before we got that far."

"I . . . He . . . *What?*" she sputters out. "What do you mean, he didn't even make dinner? That's the whole point of a dinner date. What the fuck happened?"

I groan again. "So much happened, but I need coffee before I tell you that story. Hang on."

Mia knows how serious I am about needing coffee, so while I prep the pot, she talks about her day and about general things going on in her life. I ignore the remaining remnants of last night's disaster littering on my counter. While I'd put the food away, I didn't have the energy to deal with the dishes last night.

Once I have my coffee in hand, I move out to my balcony, sinking into one of the comfy chairs. I relax as I took the first sip.

"Okay, time to start talking, Josie," Mia declares after wrapping up one of her stories. "What happened?"

I tell her every single detail about the night before—from the moment Bryce called me to the second he pulled away. I don't leave a single detail out.

"And then he walked out, Mia," I wrap up. "The first time I allow myself to open and be vulnerable, he walks out. Just like I knew he would."

Surprisingly, I'm able to get through the story without breaking down. I'm mostly just pissed, and I'm fully expecting my best friend to feel the same way.

"I'm not sure you're being very fair here, Jos." I nearly choke on my coffee. "Sorry, but I'm being honest. I don't think he ran away. At least not the way you think he did."

I scowl. "You're supposed to be on my side about this. You're my best friend."

"I'm always on your side, you know that." My scowl stays in place. "But, as your best friend, I also have a duty to call you out when you're being ridiculous."

"Oh, so now I'm being ridiculous?"

"You unexpectedly confronted this man with a whole lot of shit. Not only did you make him realize how badly he hurt you, but you also told him you loved him."

My scowl drops. "I needed him to hear it."

"I think he already knows. You're one of the things he's fucked up in his life; he's made that clear, and you basically told him you can't get over it. I don't know, I think I'd walk away, too. Sometimes it's better to process things away from the other person than end up saying something you'll regret."

"I know," I groan, dropping my head back against the chair. "I fucked it up. I was too honest, too quick. It was all going so well. Why did I have to bring up the past?"

"Because it needs to be discussed. He knows what he did to you, so you need to stop pretending he doesn't, but he needs to let you talk about it. Actually talk about it."

"Every time I think we can bring it up in a healthy way, it backfires. And then I'm worried that forgiving him is going to be harder than letting him go."

"Good, that's how it should be. Forgiveness isn't meant to be easy.

I sigh because Mia has a point. Forgiveness takes a lot of effort and it's not something that anyone can hand out at the drop of a hat because someone said they were sorry.

But I can get there. I know deep within my heart that we can get there. We just have to keep working on it.

"But you think we can do it, right?" I ask. "We can work it out and move on?"

"I think there's a reason he's back in your life and you deserve to know what it is. Both of you."

I consider her words for a moment, sitting up straighter. "I think I should call him."

"I think that's a good idea. Let me know how it goes."

I promise I will before hanging up the phone. As I pull up his contact information, I take a deep, steadying breath, and dial the number. It rings a few times before cutting to voicemail.

"Hey, it's Bryce Clark. Sorry I missed your call. Just text me."

He isn't responding to text messages, which means I have to leave a voicemail.

With a sigh, I wait for the beep. "Hey, it's me . . . Josie, I mean. I think we need to talk. That didn't come out the way I wanted it to, you have to know that. Anyway, give me a call, or send me a text when you can. I'm not up to anything today. Yeah, okay, bye."

Groaning, I end the call, and set the phone face down on the chair beside me. He won't be calling me back anytime soon, especially after that voicemail.

This is why I don't date. This is why I'm probably going to be forever alone. I'm awkward as hell around men and hate confrontation.

My phone starts ringing a second later, Bryce's name glaring back at me. I scramble to pick it up and don't even hesitate to accept the call. "Hello?"

"Hey." He sounds out of breath. "Sorry, I'm working out."

Oh. That is not a mental image I need right now, but all I can think about is sweaty, muscular Bryce. It's a little fantasy inducing. "Oh, sorry!" I swear my voice squeaks a bit. "I'll let you go; you can call me back later."

"No, it's fine," he replies before I can hang up. "What's going on?"

All I can think about was him standing there, shirtless, muscles flexing, as he tries to catch his breath. How am I supposed to convince him to give me another chance when my mind is in the gutter?

"Did you, uh . . . did you listen to my voicemail?"

"No, I called you right back as soon as I finished a set."

That had to mean something positive, right? "Oh, okay, you can delete it. I rambled a lot."

"Now I just want to listen to it more," he teases. For a split second, I pretend everything between us is normal. "What's up?"

I clear my throat. "I wanted to apologize for last night. I meant what I said. I was being honest with you, but I didn't mean to scream it at you. Also, I don't hate you."

"I'm glad you don't hate me, but I'm also glad you were honest with me. I'm sorry I left, but I needed to get out of there. Maybe you don't understand that, but I had to."

I understand it, more than he probably realizes. I know what it's like to want to run away from the pain. I've tried it several times. "I'm not mad at you for leaving, Bryce, but we need to talk about this."

He hesitates for a second too long. "I think that's a bad idea, Josie. We rushed into this, and I think we need to slow down. We both need to figure out how to move on from what happened. If you can't forgive me, I'll accept that. Just . . . I need you to think about it."

Before I can reply, the line goes dead.

As soon as I realize he hung up, I text Mia.

He said he wants space. Thinks both of us need it.

I think he's right. I just hope he doesn't give you too much space. There's giving people a chance to catch their breath, and then there's walking away.

And which choice do you think he'll make?

Her response doesn't come through for about twenty minutes, which has me going a bit crazy. When it finally does, it was rather cryptic.

Hopefully the right one.

What the fuck does that even mean?

My head and heart don't always work in tandem when it comes to Bryce Clark, a fact that's been true since the beginning. I thought this time it would be different. He walked out; he hung up on me; he decided he didn't want to try again. So why can't I get on board with it and start piecing myself back together? Again.

I've had the chance to see a glimpse into what it'd be like to be his, only to watch it disintegrate in front of me. Yet I feel like I have more questions than answers now.

A knock at my door jolts me from my thoughts. Frowning, I check my phone to see if I missed a text from one of my parents, but find nothing. No one else comes over unannounced.

The person knocks again as I stand from my couch.

"Josie?" a familiar voice calls from the other side of the door. "Hey, are you home?"

My heart thumps against my chest as I try to figure out what he's doing here. The other question racing through my mind is whether I want him to be here. Before I can think about it too much, I find myself walking to my door. As I reach for the nob, I realize I have two choices here: I can either double check the lock, or I can—

He's just turned to walk away when I open the door. When he faces me at the sound of the door, my breath catches in my throat. I've grown so used to seeing him in a suit, or some variation, every day at the office that I'd almost forgotten this version of him. The one that will live in sweatpants. The man standing before me is so close to the familiar that I can almost reach out and touch the memories.

"Hey," Bryce greets, stuffing his hands in his pockets as he approaches. All the handsome boyish charm I had fallen for at nineteen on full display. "I wasn't sure if you were home. I didn't see your car."

I lean against the door. "I moved it into my garage because it's supposed to storm tonight. Were you really looking for my car?"

The faintest tint coats his cheeks as he takes a step closer, shrugging. "I'm always looking for signs you're around, Josie. You know that."

Instantly, my mind flashes back to the first time he ever said something like that to me. Just like that moment, my heart stutters, and I lost the battle not to smile. "And you still don't have a medal to give me."

Recognition flashes in his eyes and he laughs. "Mom still doesn't trust me with them."

"I've seen you look for your phone for five minutes while it's in your hand," I point out. "I'm beginning to think she might be onto something."

He ducks his head, looking sheepish. "Yeah, you might be right. This . . . uh, this isn't a bad time, is it?"

The question brings back the reality of the situation. Bryce is on my doorstep after telling me he wanted space. That was only hours ago. "No, not at all, but you are the last person I expected to see, especially after our phone call earlier."

His bashful look remains. "That's actually why I'm here."

I cross my arms over my chest, shielding my heart the only way I can. "If you're here to make sure I understand it's a bad idea, you don't have to say anything. You got that message across, believe me."

"Um, no, I came to apologize for that. About the phone call, about the other night, about the last time we were together before all of this. Basically, I wanted to apologize for about a hundred fucked up things I've done or said to you since we met."

"Only a hundred?" I ask, making my tone obvious to let him know I'm teasing. More than anything, I want this tension to break. I know that if we can't get some of this tension off us, we won't have the chance to take things further.

Thankfully, the faintest grin appears on his handsome features and his gray eyes drift up to meet mine. "Give or take a few. It's a rough estimate."

"You don't have to apologize for what happened in the past, Bryce. All I wanted was acknowledgment of how it felt, for both of us."

"And I didn't give you that. Which is why I'm sorry, for every shitty thing I did, but I'm not sorry it got us here."

I stand a bit straighter. "And where is here, exactly?"

His blue eyes hold my gaze. "To start of something new, something different. If you still want to give us a chance, that is. If not, say the word, and I'll go."

"No, stay." I need him to know that more than anything, I want him to stay. "But you walked away, and I'm confused as to how we got here."

"Because I was scared." The confession is so quiet, I almost don't hear it. "I was scared I was going to do that to you again, but then I had a phone call this afternoon and was given some good advice."

"Yeah? What was that?"

"That sometimes walking away is the right answer because staying would mean saying something you couldn't come back from. The important thing is that you come back."

The advice is so familiar, I know exactly who he spoke with. "You talked to Mia."

"More like Mia yelled at me, but yeah." He grimaces. "You made me face the pain I'm capable of inflicting, Josie, and that scared the shit out of me. Knowing I could hurt someone like that is terrifying. I'm here now because I'm tired of not knowing what it's like to be with you."

God. The way I've gone from believing I never would hear those words, to longing to hear them, to finally hearing them when I least expect it felt like growth. They aren't words I need anymore. I will never again put another shred of my worth in the hands of a man, but there had been a time I did. And I'm suddenly grateful the timing had never been right until now.

"Being with you will mean facing some of my biggest fears," he admits. "Part of what I've been doing for the last few years is learning to face the things that scare me."

Biting my lip, I grip the door tighter. It's taking every bit of restraint I have not to launch myself at him. "You're at my front door, Bryce. Mia's not here, so there's nothing scary here except for some tarot decks and, potentially, a friendly ghost. The jury's still out on that last one, though."

Grinning, he takes a tentative step closer until he gives up and completely invades my space. My breath catches in my throat as he drops his gaze to my lips, where it lingers for a few charged seconds before flicking up to meet mine again. His eyes are dark, pupils dilating as he looks at me with an intensity I've never seen before. I don't even realize he's raised a hand until it's cupping my cheek, slowly moving to the back of my head. I could live in this moment forever, surrounded by him.

"That's where you're wrong," he murmurs, his low voice sending shivers down my spine. My eyes flutter closed for a second. "You scare the shit out of me, Joslyn."

In less than a tenth of a second, his lips are on mine and his hand finishes its path to the back of my head, tilting it for the best angle. There is nothing sweet, chaste, or innocent about this kiss. No, it's meant to consume. It's meant to make my knees buckle and fall deeper into him.

I fall willingly.

My arms wind around his neck as I stand on my toes to get closer to him. Groaning against my lips, he hooks his other hand around my waist, pulling me flush against him. There's no space between us as I melt against him, relishing in the feeling of him. The kisses we shared a week ago in the Old Market were nice, but they weren't what I wanted. We had too much history to be content with sweet, stolen moments.

When breathing becomes a necessity, I'm forced to pull my lips from his. He doesn't hesitate as his lips descend my jaw, trailing down to my neck. I moan as he places open-mouthed kisses along the column of my throat, sucking lightly so as to not leave a mark.

My fingers tangle in his hair as I tilt my head back, needing to give him as much access as possible.

Gripping his hair, I tug until his lips are back on mine, our tongues entwining almost instantly. I feel his hands drift further down my body until they graze across my ass and grip just below it. Shock startles through me as I realize what he wants. Tightening my arms around his neck, he lifts me, and my legs wind around his hips.

It shouldn't turn me on that he can lift me so effortlessly, but it does. I've always been too much for every other guy, but Bryce makes me feel perfect. For him, I am perfect.

I don't realize we're moving until I'm pressed against the wall just inside my apartment, feeling every inch of Bryce against me. The sound of the door shutting behind us echoes through the otherwise empty place. Needing to catch my breath, needing to know that this is happening, I pull back enough to rest my head against the wall, panting. Bryce seems to take the hint and drops his head against my shoulder to catch his own breath.

"You're in charge, Josie," he breathes, voice rough. "You tell me what you want."

Warmth spreads through me at the familiar words, having heard them more than a few times in the years I've known him. I smile as I looked up at the ceiling, deliriously happy that this is happening. Still, I can't shake the slight fear that this is going to happen, and we'd be done. "And if I say I want you?"

He lifts his head from my shoulder, and I look back at him. "You have me." His gaze is soft as he speaks, and his voice is so damn honest that it nearly makes me cry. "You've always had me."

That's what I need to hear. Not a promise of forever, but a promise that he'll be there in the morning. I lean in to kiss him once more before I push his shoulders until I can get on my feet.

He complies, stepping back enough to release me. As my feet hit the ground, I realize he thinks I'm rejecting him, which couldn't be further from the truth. Grinning shyly, I nod toward the hallway that led to my room. "Let's not do this against the wall? Maybe another time we can, but I've missed you."

Desire flashes through his eyes again, and he nods before pulling me back against him to reconnect our lips. From there, we stumble our way down the hall, only separating to rid each other of the clothes getting in the way—his shoes, my shirt, his shirt, my leggings. It resembles one of those cliché scenes in a movie where the camera follows the trail of clothes to find the couple. I love every bit of it.

In the blink of an eye, I'm laying back against my pillows, both of us down to our underwear as Bryce hovers over me. He's been retired for over a year now, but he's in the best shape I've ever seen. There's something comforting about having him on top of me, hands skimming down my sides, making me arch into him. I am more than familiar with this calm feeling, had felt every time we'd been in a similar situation, but this time I can put a name to it—Bryce feels like home. No matter how hard I try to ignore it, try to fight it, try to protect myself from the reality that I would lose it, Bryce Clark has always felt like home to me.

I groan, my head tilting back as he moves his hips, allowing me to feel everything, including his smirk against my collarbone. For the first time, I allow myself to believe I don't have to lose him, or this. That I can find my home in him.

"Please," I moan, heat coursing through my body. "Tell me you have a condom."

He stops, his smirk still against my skin. "Already grabbed it, babe."

I let out small whimpers as he glides down my body, lips ghosting against the top of my breasts and then down my stomach. I look at him with hooded eyes to find him staring back at me, gauging my reaction. His fingers hook against the corner of my boy shorts, hesitating as he waits for my consent. My only response is a happy sigh as I shift my hips, allowing him to pull them down, my legs opening to accommodate him as he moves lower.

From there, it's a haze of soft touches and warm kisses. Of his hard, muscular body moving against my soft, curvier one. Of whispered sweet nothings, and dirty thoughts accentuated with breathy sighs against my ear and filthy kisses. A lifetime could have passed, or a minute, but all I know is we are wrapped up in one another and I don't want it any other way.

When he finally pushes into me, my jaw drops open in a silent gasp, pulling him closer to me as his lips latch onto a spot below my ear. Bryce's arms are solid, holding him up as he moves in a slow, but deep, rhythm. The only sounds in the room are his labored breaths mingling with my soft whines and moans.

Fingers tangling in his hair, I pull until he gets the hint and moves from my neck to find my lips in a slow, languid kiss.

It's way too soon to know for sure if this thing with us will last, but I know in that moment—the same way I knew in the hotel in Omaha that first time—that I'm not going to let it go without trying. I want him; he wants me, and the rest of the details are things we can work out later. Including the realization that I never stopped loving him.

Chapter 25

THEN

April 2016

Mesa, AZ

I squinted up at the sun as it beat down on me, enjoying the warmth against my skin. Back home, the humidity on a warm day like this could choke the breath from people's lungs, and it wasn't something anyone wanted to bask in. Here in Arizona, though, the dry heat was tolerable, and I was more than content to feel it against my skin.

"You know, pale people like us shouldn't be basking in the sun." The deep voice came from my right. It was a voice I would recognize it anywhere. Beneath my sunglasses, I turned to squint at Bryce. "Didn't your high school show you terrifying skin cancer pictures, or are you clueless?"

"They did." I grinned up at him. "But I've always been one to disregard the rules."

He raised a brow. "You're caked in sunscreen right now, aren't you?"

"Oh, absolutely. I just reapplied about ten minutes ago, too; but I'm sure I'll have about a thousand new freckles when I get back to Omaha."

"I've always liked girls with freckles." The comment was so casual that it caught me off guard. Thankfully, any blush that coated my cheeks could be written off because of the sun. "Can I sit?"

Not trusting myself to speak, I nodded.

Bryce dropped his bag with a *thunk* and settled onto the bench beside me, our thighs, and knees pressing against each other due to the lack of space. My cheeks flushed hotter when I felt curious looks from around us, focusing more on Bryce than me. After four impressive collegiate seasons at Arizona, he was well-known, especially when he was only miles away from his school and with Olympic trials a couple of months away.

It wasn't lost on me that I was sitting beside the man everyone was paying attention to, expecting to be an Olympian soon—and they were noticing who he was associating with.

"I haven't seen your partner in crime so far this weekend," he commented, eyes trained on the pool as he fished a water bottle from his bag.

It was only a three-day meet, ending Saturday night, and they were about to wrap up prelims for the second morning.

"That's because she's not here." I could feel his gaze on the side of my head. When I turned to look at him, he was staring at me in surprise. "I'm doing this one all on my own."

"You came all the way out here to cover a meet by yourself?" The shock was more evident in his tone.

"Yeah," I laughed lightly, glancing back at the pool to make sure I wasn't missing anything important. "Mia's watching the livestream while she works, but she couldn't take the time off to come out with me. I needed a break before finals started."

"I forget you're in school," he admitted. "You're graduating this year, right?"

"Just one more month, thank God! You graduate and potentially go to the Olympics. I just become another college educated, unemployed millennial with no clue what she's doing."

He laughed. "You make it sound like a club."

It was so easy for me to relax around him, which I wasn't used to. "I'm sure it is. Also, I noticed you didn't argue about the part where I said you were going to the Olympics. Do you feel confident about your chances? Off the record, of course."

His relaxed state faltered ever so slightly. "I don't know how to answer that without sounding like an ass. You and I both know it doesn't matter how prepared I am—that meet has a way of surprising everyone."

"I'll take that as a yes," I teased, nudging him with my shoulder. "And you didn't sound like an ass."

"I'm not sure other people would agree with you. You know we're on our way out of one of the greatest generations this sport has ever seen, right?"

That was true, and it was all anyone could talk about. Mia and I had a running list of the big names we expected to retire at the end of the summer, most of which had already been confirmed. While it was sad to see, it also means the path would be clear for younger swimmers, like Bryce, to see what they were capable of outside of the shadows cast by other athletes. Goodbyes were always bittersweet like that.

"It's going to be interesting, that's for sure," I said. "I'm already predicting that none of my predictions for trials will pan out."

He nudged my shoulder back. "And what about you, Josie? What do you think my chances are of making the team? I'm confident you and Mia have talked about it."

I raised my eyebrows, ready to tease him. "You think we talk about you? I'm sorry to disappoint, dude, but—" I laughed when he let out an annoyed huff. "Honestly, we think you have a good shot. Your times are right in that range for all your events—obviously some seem more likely than others—but we're hopeful you'll punch a ticket to Rio."

"At least I know I have you two in my corner."

Although I thought he already knew the two of us have been Team Bryce for a while, I firmly replied, "Always."

While I was confident in my declaration, I wasn't quite ready to face his reaction to the unwavering support. The way his gray eyes widened, mouth opening a bit—as though he'd been splashed with cold water—before he turned back to the pool in front of us. Not needing to say anything more, I followed his lead, and did the same.

We both watched the next several heats in silence, but I could feel the way his gaze flicked from the pool to me. Each time his eyes landed on me, I felt my cheeks flush a little more.

"You're here for the whole meet, right?"

Not pulling my gaze from the pool, I nodded in confirmation. "Yeah, I leave Sunday night."

"We should hang out tomorrow night," he suggested. How he could be so casual when asking me something like that, I'd never understand. Clearly, he didn't realize the simple suggestion could almost short circuit my brain. "Just the two of us. We can go into Tempe, and I can show you around."

Bryce Clark—a man so far out of my league I didn't even day-dream about him being with me—had basically asked me out on a date. Of course, it wasn't a date—we lived with half the country between us; he was almost an Olympian, and he had made it clear that he didn't want a relationship. But it was as close to calling it a date as one could. Sure, we've chatted several times since we first met, sure it got flirty—but I thought it would stop there.

"If you don't have other plans, I mean," he went on to ramble. "I could pick you up or we can meet somewhere. I thought it'd be nice to hang out, since we never get to."

Even if it wasn't a date, it was the chance to get to know him in a way I haven't before. "Sure, I'd like that. I get shuttled to the pool from the hotel, but I don't think they'll take me into Tempe. Could you pick me up?"

When I looked over at him, I saw the briefest bit of surprise swipe over his features before the cool confidence I was used to came back. "Yeah, absolutely. I should head out, get some rest before tonight. I'll text you, and we can figure out a plan."

I agreed, and we exchanged goodbyes. Once he left, I couldn't focus on the pool anymore. My mind was racing a mile a minute as I tried to decipher what I'd just agreed to. He didn't call it a date, but it wasn't not a date either—I didn't know what to expect.

Hours later, I'm sitting across from Bryce in a crowded college bar in Tempe, wearing denim shorts, and a cute tank top. Loud voices, music, and laughter surrounded us as we drank shitty beers. Our focus was fully on each other.

For the most part, we'd spent the evening getting to know each other. We compared our college towns, his much larger than my small one back in Nebraska, our majors, and our plans after graduation. Talking to him was one of the easiest things I'd ever done. I even found myself leaning in closer.

The basic topics of conversation seemed to go deeper, getting more personal than two people hanging out alone for the first time should, but it was natural. Which also meant the conversation naturally returned to swimming.

"I noticed you were talking to Will Jacobson this morning," Bryce commented, effortlessly shifting the conversation from one topic to the next. "Are you going to interview him?"

I set down my beer, nodding. "Yeah, I'm supposed to reach out to him next week before we all get buried in finals. He's a little obsessed with his plans for his future, isn't he?"

"He's a pretentious dick," he replied, leaning back in his seat. "He'll go on a rant about how swimming is fleeting and anyone who decides to dedicate their time to it outside of college is an idiot. I want to prepare you for what you're in for."

While I got that vibe from Will, I never thought he would say something like that to another athlete. "Has he said that to you directly?"

"Oh, yeah, multiple times. My real question is, what is he going to do if he makes the team? He can't make a noble exit if he makes the team, and, although I hate to admit it, he has a chance of making it."

"Maybe he'll make an even nobler exit from the sport at the Olympics? Bigger stage for a bigger ego."

He shook his head. "No way. I said he might make the team—that doesn't mean he'll do anything worth noting at the games. I'm not sure he'd make semifinal, let alone the podium."

"Which means he'd exit while the world's focus is on everyone but him. He wouldn't be the first swimmer to do it."

"Yeah, but he's a pretentious dick. Something tells me he won't be happy fading into the background; it's not his style. Honestly, you should just skip the interview, save yourself the headache."

"I can't do that." I frowned. "He was one of the first athletes to follow us on social media, he's been supportive of us."

"I've been supportive of you guys!"

Which wasn't a lie. Since meeting almost a year ago, Bryce had actively shared our articles on his own social media; both of us having interviewed him several times. He'd even offered commentary on what was happening. In all reality, no one was as supportive of us as Bryce. Still, I couldn't ignore the other athletes.

"I know," I said. "And you know how much we appreciate you—so many of our followers are thanks to you. You've helped us make connections we could only dream about."

"But . . ." he pressed, looking slightly impatient.

"But Will came within the first fifty followers and people are interested in what he has to say. Unfortunately, doing something like this means sometimes interacting with people I might not like. It's the same as doing a group project."

Bryce pointed the neck of his beer bottle at me, his face twisted into a grimace. "See, now you've got me picturing what it'd be like to do a group project with him, which is a whole other kind of hell. So, thanks for that."

I couldn't stop myself from picturing it, too, and made a face of my own. Bryce laughed harder, and I realized I needed to change the subject before he talked me out of doing the interview.

"Will you let us interview you about the shift in dynamics swimming will see after this summer?"

An easy grin brightens his features, flashing the boyish charm that made my stomach twist. "You know I'll let you interview me whenever you want."

I rolled my eyes. "Yes, I know, but we need to interview more than just you, Bryce."

He let out a dramatic sigh. "All right, fine, I'll let the Jacobson thing go as long as I continue to be one of the people you turn to the most."

My laugh grew louder. "Oh, my God, Bryce, let it go. You're our favorite. Is that what you wanted to hear?"

"Always." He hid his smirk by taking a drag of his beer.

I couldn't focus on what that smirk did to my insides; it was dangerous territory. We needed a change of subject, now. "So, I have a question for you."

His eyes sparkled with amusement. "Ask away."

"Let's say you make the team," I began, grinning despite myself. "Are you getting the Olympic rings tattoo? If so, where?"

His amusement grew as his grin shifted into that smirk that never failed to make me feel things. "Why? You got a thing for dudes with the Olympic rings tattooed on them or something?"

I had no idea where this coy flirtation was coming from. It was the last thing I should be doing. Still, I smiled back. "I mean, it's a plus side, right? Besides, I like tattoos in general."

His eyebrows shot up as he took a drink. "Well, that's good to know."

"And yet you haven't answered my question."

"Hell yeah, I'll get it. I already have the artist picked out. I'm thinking about the side of my ribs or my shoulder."

The idea of the rings tattooed across the side of his ribs conjured thoughts that were anything but safe. While that tattoo was a rite of passage for the athletes, it was also something fans looked forward to seeing—literal, lasting proof of what hard work could do. "I like the ribs."

"Yeah, me too," he agreed, before glancing down at his phone. "Uh, what time did you want to head out? It's nearing one."

I didn't want to leave, ever, was the answer that came to mind, but I couldn't say that. When we had decided to get drinks, Bryce decided that it was best to get a ride. So, he met me at my hotel, and we got a ride into Tempe. Still, he needed to drive back once we returned to my hotel.

"I don't leave until tomorrow evening, checkout's not until eleven. I can stay out for a bit longer," I told him. "Unless you need to head back."

"Nah, I'm all yours tonight." He grinned. "I have tomorrow off, with no plans. One more round?"

I was definitely blushing now. "Sure, that sounds good."

With a nod, he disappeared into the crowd to get our drinks. I took the chance to check over our Adair Swim Blog accounts and text messages. I glanced over at the reply Mia had sent when I told her where we were and typed a quick message to let her know I was okay. I knew she was asleep by now, but we liked to check in with each other and I knew she'd panic if she woke up without hearing anything from me.

"Letting Mia know I haven't killed you?" Bryce's voice pulled my attention from my phone as he sat back down, sliding my beer over to me.

I nodded as I reached for it and took a drink. "Obviously, wouldn't want the police to show up at your door in the morning."

"I appreciate it. So, what are your plans for tomorrow?"

"Honestly, I don't know. I don't want to carry my stuff around all day, so I'll probably get a lift to the airport after checkout and find a quiet place to start working on articles."

He grimaced like that was the worst idea in the world. I didn't want to spend that much time at an airport, either. "Or I could pick you up and we could hang out again. Go into Phoenix early, grab some lunch—whatever."

"Oh, I don't want to put you out. I'm sure you have other things to do."

"I literally just told you that I didn't." He leaned against the able to look at me. "I want to spend time with you, Josie."

What the hell was I supposed to do with that? "I would appreciate it. Thank you. But please don't feel like you have to."

"I want to," he corrected. "Trust me."

We didn't get back to my hotel until after two, and Bryce insisted he walk me up to my room before heading out with a promise to be back by eleven. In turn, I made him promise to text me when he got back home, telling him I wouldn't be able to sleep if I didn't know he made it home safe.

I got little sleep that night, even after he told me he was home. I was too busy thinking back on the night we shared and what it all meant. It was proving much harder to let go of the fantasy now that I'd had a glimpse of what it was like.

⸺ oℓℓ ⸺

As promised, Bryce was back at my hotel by eleven the next morning, laughing and joking as he loaded my bags into the back of his SUV before driving us to Phoenix. Just like the night before, the drive was comfortable, filled with silence except for his playlist in the background.

We were both content with the silence; him focusing on the road and me looking out the window at everything we passed. There were a few instances where I noticed the way his hand would linger over the middle console, like he didn't know what to do with it. It made me wonder what it'd be like to reach over and tangle our fingers together.

But that's not what he's looking for.

Once in Phoenix, we grabbed lunch, and then walked around downtown for a bit. The conversation continued to flow as I relaxed even more around him. His personality managed to pull me in, even from the very beginning. Sure, he's attractive, but he was also incredibly sarcastic, funny, and so genuinely kind that it was hard not to be drawn to him.

And I could see myself falling head over heels for him if ever given the chance.

Before I knew it, Bryce was pulling up to the curb at the end of the terminal, away from the crowd. Glancing at the time, I realized my flight would be boarding in about an hour. I hadn't realized how quickly the time had flown by.

He was out of the car before me, heading to the back to unload my bags, and I scrambled to follow him. I stood beside the curb, not knowing what to do or say, as he set my bags beside me. He closed the tailgate, moving toward me until he was standing before me, a little closer than necessary. We stood staring at each other for several long seconds.

"Thank you for this," I said, breaking the silence. "I had a lot of fun hanging out with you."

He stared down at me, his six-foot-one frame making it so I had to tilt my head. There was a gentleness to the way he looked at me, but there was something else that I couldn't put my finger on. "Yeah, me too."

I didn't know what else to say. There was nothing else to say, but I also wasn't ready to leave this little bubble that we had created. I just kept reminding myself that he wasn't looking for a relationship, and that reminder was enough for me to reach out for the handle of my suitcase.

To my utter surprise, his hand reached out and grasped mine. Both of us stared down at our joined hands. I expected him to pull away, but watched as he interlocked our fingers instead.

His gray eyes flickered to meet mine, holding my gaze for a heartbeat. My breath caught in my throat as his eyes drifted to my lips. Then he closed the last bit of distance between us, his free hand cupping my cheek.

Before I knew it, his lips were on mine, warm and soft. As cliché as it sounded, it was like fireworks went off in the pit of my stomach. Gripping his hand tighter, I kissed back. His hand moved from my cheek to my neck, changing the angle to deepen the kiss. My free hand moved to rest against his chest, trying not to melt into him.

I wanted to savor every second he was willing to give me.

Eventually, we reluctantly pulled away. Both of us smiling. I stayed on that cloud for a couple more seconds before his eyes widened and he stepped back. He didn't let go of my hand, though.

"Shit," he cursed, panic clear in the way his shoulders tensed. "I shouldn't have done that."

The confidence and adrenaline the kiss had given me evaporated as soon as the words left his mouth. I tried to keep the disappointment from my features, but I knew I wasn't successful. "Oh, it's okay. We can just forget—"

"No." He tugged me closer to him, his free hand moving to my hip, and I couldn't be more confused. "I wanted to do that, Josie. I just shouldn't have."

"Is this because you don't want a relationship?"

He swallowed. "Yeah. At least, not right now."

Well, that re-inflated the little balloon of hope I probably could've done without. Where there was hope, my imagination ran wild.

"That's fine, Bryce." I stepped back and released his hand. "We can just be friends." He almost looked like he didn't believe me, so I stood on my tiptoes and pressed a quick kiss to his cheek. He relaxed. "I'll see you in a couple of months?"

"Yeah. I'll see you in a couple months, Josie."

Grinning, I grabbed my bag, and turned to head for the door. I'd only taken a couple steps when I turned to look back at him. He hadn't moved. "You said not right now."

Stuffing his hands in the pocket of his sweatshirt and nodded. "Yeah, I did."

"But . . . maybe one day?"

The faintest of grins pulled across his lips. "Yeah, Josie. Maybe one day."

I knew that I had just made everything ten times worse for myself, but it was what I needed to hear. Blushing, I ducked my head. "See you in June, Bryce."

He nodded. "See you in June, Josie."

With nothing left to say, I grabbed my bag, and made my way through the sliding glass doors into the airport. When I glanced back over my shoulder, my heartbeat skipped a little when I saw he was still there, waiting until I was out of view. I forced myself to keep moving, the possibility of one day making it easier.

Chapter 26

NOW

May 2023
Omaha, NE

For three weeks, Bryce and I experience utter bliss as spring starts to creep into early summer. We never broadcast our relationship to anyone at work, but anyone who pays attention likely noticed. Which, luckily for me, meant that Sarah had. Not wanting to talk to her about the shift in my relationship status, I do my best to avoid her.

Except for one Friday afternoon in May, where Hunt & Sloan hires an ice cream truck to give us a little break. I'm waiting in line, she sidles up to me.

"I'm not at all surprised to see you here," she teases, but there was a biting undertone to the comment. I bristle. "What are you getting?"

"I'm not sure yet," I admit. "I can't see the menu yet."

"I'll be getting a small dish of vanilla."

I hum, checking my phone. "Sounds good."

We stand in silence for several seconds. I'm nowhere in the mood to carry on a conversation with her, and she doesn't seem to know where to go with it. I'm trying to peek around people's shoulders to see the menu, pointedly ignoring my friend, when I spot Bryce heading toward me, two dishes of ice cream in his hands. Instantly, I realize what's happening, and grin, stepping out of line to meet him. I ignore every one of Sarah's protests.

"They had your favorite," Bryce tells me, holding out a dish filled with dark chocolate. "I figured I'd bring it up to your desk since you have that huge release you need to finish editing."

"Just sent it back to the team." I dig into the ice cream. "I am all caught up on work. Funnily enough, I sent you a message to see if you wanted ice cream."

"You probably sent it right when I headed down." Then he glances over at Sarah, giving her a stiff nod. "She's glaring at you. It's probably not my place to say this, but I don't think I like her."

"Have you met her besides the first few times?" I ask, rather than voicing my agreement. I'm not sure I like her anymore either. He shakes his head. "Then how do you know what you really think about her?"

"Vibes," he answers, like it solves all the big questions. "Trust me, I was right about Will Jacobson, and I'm right about her."

I roll my eyes. "You can't keep bragging about that."

"I will until I die. You've told me enough stories, and I've seen it with my own eyes; I don't like the way she treats you. She's not a good friend."

Sarah isn't really a friend, at least not the way Mia is. Or even Carter. Before I can say that, though, his phone rings. I watch as he fishes it out of his pocket, frowning at it. "I have to take this; I'll be right back."

Since I have no other work to do and I've taken lunch at my desk, I decide to relax outside, enjoying the sunshine. I lean against a nearby wall, enjoying my ice cream for a few moments before Sarah comes sauntering over, empty-handed.

"Where's your ice cream?"

"They didn't have vanilla." I raise an eyebrow as someone walks past with a dish of vanilla ice cream. I point it out with my spoon, which makes her quick to defend herself. "It just didn't sound good anymore."

"It's your choice, Sarah. I don't get why you had to lie about it, though."

She rolls her eyes as I take a bite of my ice cream. "So, what's happening with the two of you? Seems like you're back to being best friends."

The last thing I want to do is tell her Bryce and I are together, but I also don't like bold-face lying to anyone. Including her. "We're working it out."

She gives me a skeptical look. "I kind of got the impression he broke your heart. I don't want to see him do it again."

I feel the need to defend Bryce, myself, and the past we shared. "Yeah, he did break my heart, but I've realized that I wasn't that fair to him at the time, either. He had a lot of stuff going on, things I will never understand, and I could—"

"What, like depression?"

I don't respond, more annoyed at her disbelieving tone. Apparently, my silence is the only answer she needs because she scoffs. "Oh, please. How ridiculous is that?"

"Excuse me?" My heart drops to the pit of my stomach. "What do you mean?

"I heard he went to the Olympics," she says, like it somehow makes him immune to mental health struggles. "Like, multiple times, apparently."

"I'm aware of his career highlights," I reply dryly. "But I'm not sure what your point is here."

"Don't tell me you're going to defend him? You just said it yourself—he's an Olympian. What could he possibly be depressed about?"

"And you're clueless about what you're talking about, Sarah," I snap. "You have no idea the mental and emotional burden athletes carry, on top of all the physical requirements. They spend their entire lives training for something that is over in seconds. If they're lucky enough to get to the Olympics, like Bryce, then everyone is watching them.

"And once everyone is watching you, you can't mess it up. An entire country is literally cheering you on, hoping you'll bring home the gold medal. If you are lucky enough to get on the podium, what happens then? You've worked your ass off for this one moment, and suddenly you're there. Where the hell do you go after that? What do you do?"

Stunned by my reaction, Sarah blinks at me. Behind her, I can see Bryce wrapping up his conversation. Just as she opens her mouth to respond, I realize I'm not quite done. "I don't owe you an explanation, Sarah. No one owes you an explanation as to why they struggle with their mental health. Ignorance is a choice, and you chose to speak on something you're clueless about, so don't act offended when I call you out."

She crosses her arms over her chest. "The way you just jumped to his defense makes it sound like you're more than friends."

I want to scream. Is that really the only thing she got out of this? "That's none of your business, either."

"I introduced you, Joslyn, and you told me you wanted nothing to do with him! I think it's my business a little bit."

"As you might remember, Josie and I have known one another for several years." Sarah stands up straighter as Bryce approaches. "You didn't introduce us; you just assisted with the inevitable."

Inevitable. It's a word I'd once used in relation to him breaking my heart. To hear him use it to explain what's happening between us now causes me to smile despite the situation. Perhaps our reunion, and whatever follows, is as inevitable as the pain that led us here. Maybe the word doesn't always have to be linked to such a horrible moment in my life.

"I'm just trying to be a good friend here." Sarah's whiny voice pulls me back to the moment. "I don't know what happened between the two—"

"And you never will."

Her mouth snaps shut at my firm declaration, and she narrows her eyes into a slight glare. "Excuse me?"

"You have no business knowing about the past. It doesn't involve you, and it doesn't matter anymore. And you're not trying to be a good friend, Sarah—you're fishing for information and I'm not giving you anymore."

"You realize he's playing you, right? He's not depressed or whatever else you claim. He's an Olympian."

I glance at Bryce, worried about his reaction. He looks annoyed, but not at me.

"Does that give me some kind of magical immunity I didn't know about?" He raises an eyebrow. "Because it's fucked if it does, and no one told me."

His biting, sarcastic humor only comes out when he's feeling defensive. It's a coping mechanism, a way to make himself feel less vulnerable, but it also tended to make me smile.

"That's obviously not what I meant," she huffs out. "I just—"

"No, that's exactly what you meant. You're not in a position to judge my choices or hers."

I manage to contain my laugh as Sarah rolls her eyes.

"I don't want to see her get hurt."

"Says the woman who has attempted to set her up with every man who's walked through Hunt & Sloan's doors like she's on some kind of reality show. Do you actually have any idea what she was looking for in a partner?"

Sarah has always been clueless about what I want. Sure, some had traits that met my ideals, but overall, there were always red flags. Red flags I found myself looking past because the person I wanted was not coming back, or so I thought. Now she's looking to ruin things with the only person I want it to work with.

Bryce shoots me a look that is equal parts apologetic and panicked. "I'm sorry, Jos, that was out of line. I was—"

"Right," I finish for him, flashing a timid smile. "You were right." I turn my attention to Sarah. "Look, if this is your idea of being a good friend, we have vastly different opinions on what that means. Bryce and I have a history, and we're trying to figure out what we have. This is our business, and ours alone. You can either support us or leave us alone."

She opens and closes her mouth several times. We'd crossed the line of professionalism ages ago and had gathered some unwanted attention from people who were still in line to get ice cream, but this needed to end.

"Well, I never thought I would be treated like this," she finally says, exasperated. "Especially after I helped you find one another—"

Bryce cut her off with a loud, humorless laugh. "You're delusional if you think you had any part in this."

We need to get out of this situation before one, or both of us, says something that'd get us in trouble. Placing my hand flat against Bryce's chest, I turn to look at him until his glare moves from Sarah to meet my gaze. His stormy eyes soften immediately. I give a small nod toward the entrance to the building.

He holds my gaze for a moment longer before giving in. Without another word, I step past Sarah to head back into the building. I don't have to look back to know Bryce is right behind me. A lot of the tables in the lobby and cafeteria area are filled with people working or eating ice cream. I spot some members of my team, and some of Bryce's, but the confrontation with Sarah has me feeling anything but social.

Bryce's hand suddenly closes around my free one, tugging me toward the back of the lobby. As I follow his lead, I realize there is a small, two-seat table left unoccupied. Neither one of us speaks until we're settled in. Even then, we take several bites of our slightly melted ice cream before Bryce breaks the silence.

"I told you I didn't like her."

I choke on a laugh, shaking my head. "I'll never live this down."

He grins around a bite of ice cream. "Never."

Chapter 27

NOW

Omaha, NE

With a deep breath, I look at myself in the mirror to take in all my hard work. At the last minute, Bryce had asked me to go to a work party with him at one of the nice downtown hotels. His team is celebrating closing a major deal, and my boyfriend had been an integral part of it.

Although the invite came last minute, I didn't hesitate to pull out my hunter green, faux wrap chiffon dress. I save it for moments like this, after all; no matter how rare they are. It hugs my curves, the fabric airy enough for the spring weather while the bell sleeves keep me from needing a jacket as the evening cooled.

"Okay, I'm ready," I declare, stepping out of my bedroom. "This isn't too formal, is it?"

Bryce glances up from his phone, his eyes widening as they scan over my outfit, taking in every detail. I shift, uncomfortable under the scrutiny of his appreciating gaze.

He stands from the couch with a grin. "You look beautiful. I never get to see you dress up like this."

I don't have a lot of reason to dress up like this, especially in the time we've known one another. Even at work, I tend to take advantage of the casual side of business casual. On the rare days I wear sundresses, I usually pair them with a denim jacket. I never feel the need to dedicate an hour to my hair or makeup just to go to work, even though I enjoy it.

"You said it was cocktail, right?" I fidget with the hem of my skirt. "This is the nicest thing I have for spring."

Bryce closes the distance between us, pulling me closer by curling a hand around my hip. "I promise, you look stunning."

Before I have the time to react to his words at all, he leans down to connect our lips in a soft, lingering kiss. Though I know it isn't the wisest decision, I allow myself to melt against him as he deepens the kiss, reveling in the feel of our tongues tangling together in a dance that will always send shivers down my spine.

As I pull away, he releases a groan and attempts to chase after my lips. Smiling, I step back. "I know you don't want to go tonight, but you have to. Let's get there and then we can get out."

Slumping, he steps back to retrieve his phone from the coffee table. "Thanks for coming with me. I would literally rather be doing anything else."

"Including swimming the 1500?"

He makes a face, but still nods after a bit of consideration. "Yeah, including that." My look of surprise earns a laugh. "Both of those options suck. I hate doing things that suck."

I pat his cheek. "Welcome to adulthood."

He rolls his eyes as he steps back to grab his keys. It's no secret he hates doing stuff like this. He hates being put in the spotlight for anything other than standing on a podium. Back when he was swimming, his least favorite day of the year was when the sport hosted their annual award show, made even worse when he was nominated for something. I recall spending those nights in my pajamas obsessively checking social media for photos of him in a suit. Which is something I now see more regularly than not.

"It's exciting, though," I say, snapping my bag closed after making sure I have everything. "You've barely been here two months and you've already helped land one of the biggest clients we'll get this year. That's a good reason to celebrate!"

"Yeah, of course." He glances up from his phone. "At least they have an open bar, right? We should go."

He waits beside me as I lock the door, and then a comfortable silence settles between us as we make our way to his car to head downtown.

"Here's my plan: we get in, say hello to everyone we need to, mingle for an hour, and then we get the hell out. We'll grab food and spend the rest of the weekend in bed, pretending work doesn't exist."

"It sounds perfect." When I glance at his handsome profile, I realize how tense he is—his strong jaw is set, and he's gripping the steering wheel like it's the only thing anchoring him to earth. "My place or yours?"

"I think it should be yours. It's closer to the breakfast place we've been wanting to try."□

"So nice of you to decide you'll stay." I relax into my seat when I notice some of the tension leaves his shoulders. "I don't recall asking you to."

The corner of his lips turns up, his grip on the steering wheel slacking. "I could go home, just say the words."

"No, no, I didn't say that. I kind of like having you around." I pause. "I always want you around."

When he glances over at me, there's amazement in his eyes. Like he's been waiting to hear me say something like that for so long that he cannot believe he's hearing it now.

His right hand leaves the wheel to rest on my thigh, squeezing gently. "Me too. Everything is better when you're around."

"That's such a sappy thing to say," I tease, but I can't ignore the way my heart flutters. "And that's coming from a romance writer. We love sappy."

"Nothing wrong with a little bit of sap," he says. "Thanks for coming with me tonight, Josie. You really do look beautiful."

A blush coats my cheeks. "You're the only person I would do something like this for."

Not an ounce of dishonesty exists in my statement, which he must know, because he raises our joint hands to press a kiss against my knuckles.

***

What we hoped would be only an hour ended up being three.

The party isn't as bad as we'd dreaded, but it's a lot of kissing ass and commenting on the strength of our company's sales team. I meet some of Bryce's colleagues, which further confirms how different he is from all of them—none of them can hold a conversation without bringing up capital, expense accounts, the state of the company, or the inaccessible jargon that even I, an employee of the company, couldn't understand. Then there were the significant others of those involved who stayed glued by their side, fluffing their egos.

Bryce does his best to stay by my side, but someone would whisk him away every so often. Which is how I make friends among a small gathering of about five other significant others. That's where Bryce finds me every time he makes it back around to check on me.

As the night wears on, my eyes drift around the room to find him as I chat with the others. Every time I spot him, I fight back a frown. Bryce looks uncomfortable, always gripping his drink a little too tight or fidgeting. Though he towers over several of the people in the room, he ducks his head, and avoids eye contact. I know he's good at his job; he just doesn't look comfortable basking in the glory of it.

By the time Bryce finds me to leave, my social battery is drained, and all I can think about is getting out of my heels and dress. I almost cry when his hand presses against the small of my back, lips brushing against the top of my head as he asks if I'm ready to leave.

I exchange numbers with a few people before bidding them all goodnight and let Bryce lead me from the hotel. His car is already waiting for us at the entrance.

"God, that was exhausting," he groans as soon as the door shuts behind him. He loosens the tie around his neck. I watch as he flings it into the backseat. "I hate wearing this thing."

"You wear a full suit to work at least half the week."

He pulls away from the curb with a roll of his eyes. "And I hate it every single time."

The admission isn't at all shocking. Bryce has always preferred sweatpants. Up until recently, any time I thought of Bryce, I pictured him in casual clothes or in one of his swimsuits; it took weeks for me to get used to seeing him in business attire. Part of his hatred for this party is a consequence of having to spend the night dressed up.

"What's up with the face?"

"No face." I quickly relax my features.

He glances at me before pulling onto the congested downtown street. "Don't get shy on me now, Josie. I know what that face means."

"What does it mean, then?" I challenge.

"It means you have something you want to tell me, but you're not going to tell me."

"And why wouldn't I tell you?"

"Because you think I won't like what you have to say."

How easily Bryce can read me freaks me out sometimes. Our instantaneous connection is another thing I can't let myself think too hard about.

It's too dangerous, too much of a sign that I was with someone I'm not sure I can hold on to. I already know what he can do to me, and I can't stomach it again. It's safer to draw the line between us where I can.

As I sit with my thoughts, I find myself torn between being honest with him and pretending everything is okay—at least until I'm certain of what's going on.

"I'm worried about you," I admit. "I'm worried you're keeping things bottled up again, even though you know you can talk to me."

"What do you think I'm keeping from you? I feel like I've been pretty open since we got together."

In terms of talking about us, he openly talks about the past, present, and about the future. But when I try to talk to him about the here and now, or even the future in terms of himself, he's a little cagey. "You have been, but not about everything."

"All right. Then what's my current big secret?"

I sigh, reminding myself that we'd made a promise to be honest with one another. I can't go back on that now.

"I don't know if you're happy, Bryce." His grip tightens on the steering wheel. "To be honest, I'm not exactly sure what happy Bryce Clark looks like. I've only seen glimpses, usually when it's just us, so I know it's not this. Happy Bryce is not what I saw tonight."

He keeps his gaze locked on the road ahead, even when he stops at a red light. "And how do you know that?"

"Are you aware you turn parts of yourself on and off?" I ask, and he scoffs like it's the most ridiculous thing he's ever heard me say. "No—you do. The Bryce who showed up tonight is the same Bryce I see during work Monday through Friday. He's not the person who exists the rest of the time. He's not the person I know."

"You're being ridiculous, Josie." His tone isn't harsh or defensive. It's almost adoring. Like he thinks I'm being cute.

"I'm not," I insist. "And I have to say, I don't always like that version of you. He's cold, distant, and a little unapproachable. Even to me."

He frowns. "I didn't realize I was doing that."

I shrug, trying to keep the conversation from drifting into the overly serious territory. "It's okay. I wanted to check in on you—make sure you're good."

"I am," he says, a little too quickly. "I am. I've only been here for two months; I'm still getting my footing, getting used to things."

I know that isn't all there is to it, but I also don't want to push the subject. We're still getting our footing, as friends, and as a couple—I'm in unchartered territory. I know he'll have a breaking point when it comes to this conversation, but I don't know what it will be like.

"All I'm saying is that it's okay if this isn't what you to want to do with your life, Bryce," I say, keeping my tone even. If he takes nothing else from this conversation, let it be that. "It's okay if you don't have it all figured out."

"And what would I do if it's not this?"

"I don't know. But it should be a good thing, because it means you get to figure out a new dream."

"You sound like a Disney movie."

I study him for a second, looking for cracks in the façade he's putting forth. "Maybe, but it doesn't make it any less true."

His gray eyes flick in my direction for the briefest second before focusing back on the road. "I'm fine where I'm at, Josie. I promise."

I wonder if he's aware his words are a lie. If given the choice, neither one of us would be in this career right now. We'd be together, but we'd be doing it almost anywhere else.

Chapter 28

NOW

June 2023

Omaha, NE

Over the next two weeks, it becomes more, and more apparent Bryce isn't being honest with me. With his recent work success, his managers trust him with more clients. With his workload stacking up, I watch the corporate lifestyle start to get to him.

Though he still refuses to download the messaging app our company uses, his phone is never far from reach. Date nights get interrupted by phone calls, his alarm cuts Saturday mornings short, and his laptop is either open on my kitchen table or his. There is no avoiding work.

For the first time in the six years I've known him, he looks haggard, and the goofy, laid-back personality beneath his serious façade is almost nonexistent. His temper is shorter, too. He struggles to focus on one thing at a time, and we've stopped talking about anything more than the basic rundown of our days.

As mid-June neared, Omaha livens up with festivals and sporting events I want to share with Bryce, but he's too caught up with work to notice. After seeing how great things can be between us, our relationship is now reminiscent of what it had been years ago. I'm feeling like an afterthought, and each day makes my heart sink a little further.

Apparently, I'm not the only one to notice our lack of time, though, as he approaches my desk one Friday afternoon, looking more relaxed than I'd seen him in days.

I can't help but match his grin, my heart feeling lighter. "Hey, what's got you in such a good mood?"

He looks around to make sure no one is watching before leaning in to kiss me. When we part, he leans against back against my filing cabinet. "I'm all caught up on work."

"Good job," I praise with a laugh. "I'm happy you can do your job."

"I'm not going to start working on anything else today, which means I am yours for the whole weekend. No work interruptions this time, I promise."

"Really?" My eyebrows raise, not quite being able to believe we can have a weekend to ourselves without Hunt & Sloan interrupting us.

His grin broadens as he nods once. "Absolutely. I was thinking we could hang out around downtown this weekend. After work, we can drop your car off at my place, grab dinner in the Old Market. Then tomorrow morning we can go to the farmers' market you wanted to walk around and spend the day together, maybe go to a museum or something."

I slump a bit, realizing he's feeling guilty about how absent he's been.

"Do you really want to go to the farmers' market?"

"Of course, I love overpriced honey!" I raise an eyebrow at him. He sighs. "Honestly, I want to spend time with you. I miss you, and I want to do whatever you want to do."

Paired with his earnest expression, his words are almost enough to make me melt into a puddle right then and there. "All right, deal. But you get to decide where we eat tonight, and we'll decide together what we do after the farmers' market."

"Sounds like a plan to me. I do have a meeting in ten minutes, though, so I should get going. I'll be out of here by five. Meet me by the elevators?"

"Absolutely." As he leans in to kiss my forehead, my smile grows, and the butterflies in my stomach erupt. I've always been a sucker for a forehead kiss. "Have a good rest of the day!"

"You, too, beautiful," he calls over his shoulder.

As I watch him retreat, giddiness bubbles in the pit of my stomach and I picture what is going to be the perfect weekend. This is exactly what we need to make sure we are on the same page and heading in the right direction. I vow to do everything in my power to make sure it's as perfect as it can be.

I should have known better than to wish for a perfect weekend.

Friday night was great, for the most part. Bryce ended up staying at work until almost six to wrap things up, so I ran home to pack an overnight bag before meeting him at his place. We went to dinner at the brewery we had our first date at, needing something familiar, and dependable. Afterward, we walked back to his place, talking about the night this all started back in 2016.

With the night ending similar to the one forever etched in my memory.

This time, though, we don't stumble through the door of a hotel room, and I know where I stand in Bryce's life, and I don't have to question what would happen when he woke up.

But when I wake up Saturday morning, it's to an empty bed. The time nearing ten in the morning, I get up in search of Bryce, figuring he's working on breakfast before we head out. Instead, I find him clad in sweatpants, no shirt, and sitting at the table with his laptop open and phone pressed to his ear.

Sighing to myself, I decide not to make a huge deal out of it as I pad across the kitchen to get coffee. At least there's coffee.

When his eyes land on me, he offers an apologetic smile. Which I return before focusing on fixing coffee. Knowing he'll likely need some more, I bring the pot over and fill his mug. The black abyss in his mug tells me how stressed he is.

"Hey, man, hang on for a second," he tells whoever he's talking to. He moves the phone away to mute the call before speaking to me. "Give me ten minutes, then we can go. I figured we could get something to eat down there."

"Sure," I say, knowing it won't take much for me to be ready. "I'll go get dressed."

As I pass, he grabs my hand, and pulls me into a short kiss. Both of us are grinning when we part, a sign the day is still salvageable.

Only it isn't.

Ten minutes turns into forty-five. Once we are finally at the farmers' market, Bryce's phone rings three times over the three hours we're there. Each call takes approximately twenty minutes, and his resolve crumbles by the time we make it back to his apartment. The phone rings again as we're putting away everything we bought. With a loud groan, he leaves me to finish up.

From across the room, I watch as the last of his resolve breaks. He's arguing about negotiations and numbers he's already discussed. When he finally hangs up, he drops his head in his hands with a tired sigh.

I take the moment being offered to me.

"I wish you'd be honest with me, Bryce." His head snaps up in surprise, like he'd forgotten I was there. To be honest, that's how it's felt all day. "You keep telling me about all the hard work you did, and continue to do, but you can't even tell me the truth. I can see it, plain as day, and you still refuse to say it."

"There's nothing to say, Josie," he snaps, standing, and heading to the refrigerator for a bottle of water. He leans against it once it's shut. "You just want me to tell you I hate my job. You want me to tell you that you're right, and I don't know what I'm doing."

I press my lips into a thin line. "That's not true. I'm worried. You were excited about this weekend and your job keeps getting in the way. You're exhausted and agitated. We promised we'd be honest with one another."

"You keep saying the same thing—telling me I'm not happy. You don't offer any advice on how to fix it! I don't know what you want from me. I'm not swimming anymore, and this is what I do now. I'm trying to move on."

His expression shutters, and the way his shoulders tense lets me know we are barreling toward a fight. Bryce never took being called out very well.

"And I'm ready to be so supportive of you, but I don't understand why you seem to think this is the only answer. Is this what you want, Bryce? I mean, honestly, is this something that makes you excited to wake up in the morning?"

He snorts. "That's a childhood fantasy, Josie."

"No, it's not," I stress. "You dread getting up in the morning, you dread doing this job. I know because I've spent enough nights with you to know. You start counting down the hours until you have to go back. That's not how you should live!"

"All right, fine!" The way he raises his voice, the way he tosses the empty water bottle onto the counter, causes me to flinch. I've never seen Bryce lose it, not really. "You're right. I hate my job! Is that what you wanted to hear?"

The wounded look on his face broke my heart. "No," I admit, tone soft. "God, no. I don't want to hear that. I want you to be happy. I want you to find something that makes you happy."

"What, like you did?" he shoots back without missing a beat. It never ceased to amaze me how easily people could deliver hurtful words without even flinching. "I'm doing exactly what you did—I'm working a stable job with a good company and I'm making it work. I'm doing what adults do. It can't always be perfect!"

"What does that mean? That you're doing with what I did?"

His brow arches. "What do you think it means?"

It's more than enough of an answer.

"I haven't given up on my dreams, Bryce. I've put them on hold, but they're still there. I haven't accepted my current situation as my forever. I'm not pretending like this job is my future. Everyone knows I'll be moving on. Meanwhile, it took you months to admit you're not happy!"

"When?" he demands, ignoring the last sentence, anger radiating off him.

"When, what?"

"When are you moving on? When are you going to write something you want to publish? When are you going to do any of things you brag about one day doing? Because, I got to admit, you look like a hypocrite from here."

In the blink of an eye, I'm twenty-six, and getting my heart broken by this man. This time, though, I hadn't seen it coming. This time, I'm far from prepared, and it hurts so much more.

"You're telling me how miserable this job is making me when you can't even admit what your own is doing to you," Bryce continues, hitting me where it hurts the most. "You act like you've got it all figured out, but can't even leave your own hometown. Maybe I don't have a clue what I want next, but at least I've done *something* with my life!"

I take a step back, unable to break his stare as the words that left his mouth hang between us. I don't know what to make of them; I don't know how to move past them; I don't know how to keep them from breaking us.

The sting of his words slowly activates new fears within me as they echo through my mind. *You look like a hypocrite.*

"Well," I breathe out, stepping around the island to put as much distance between us as possible. Tears sting the corners of my eyes. "I guess it's true what they say about not asking questions you don't want to hear the answers to."

His anger dissipates before my eyes, panic overtaking his features. "What are you talking about, Josie? I asked the question; you never asked me anything."

I shake my head, tears trailing down my cheeks. I'd never let myself cry in front him, and his eyes are locked on the tears. "Oh, but I did. I asked you to be honest with me, and you finally were."

"That's—*fuck*! That's not what I meant."

"It is, and if it's what you truly think of me, then so be it. It's just proof you never actually knew me. I might not be living an exciting life as a famous author, but that doesn't mean I'm not working toward my goal. Dreams change, Bryce. They shift and they bend, their brightness fades and, sometimes, it feels like they vanish altogether. But there's always something nagging at you, reminding you it matters, and you should still chase it. I haven't stopped listening to that voice, even if you don't hear it."

My voice rose as my rant continues, a slight quiver to it, but I refuse to back down from him. Not this time. "Maybe one day I'll find the story I'm meant to write. Maybe I won't. I won't ever stop picking up a pen and trying. I think it's pretty shitty of you to pass judgment on an aspect of my life you chose not to be part of."

His eyes are so wide, like the world he had been building was crumbling down around him. Like he was watching me slip away. I knew that look; I knew that feeling. Mine is doing the same thing, again.

This time, it's my turn to walk out, but I know there is no coming back.

"I'm gonna go," I declare, staring him in the eyes. "I'm not doing this again, Bryce. I won't let you push me to the side while you refuse to acknowledge the shit you have going on."

His eyes flash with anger, jaw clenching. "We agreed we'd work on this, that we'd do this together."

The fight leaves me, exhaustion seeping into my bones. I'm so tired of doing this with him. "I know, but I can't be the only one holding up that side of the deal. This isn't productive, Bryce. We're where we've always been; you refusing to let me in and be honest, then reacting by saying the exact thing you know will break me. I'm not doing this to myself anymore."

He takes a tentative step toward me, but stops when I shake my head.

I make my way back to his room to gather my stuff, and he doesn't follow me. With each item I shove into my overnight bag, my heart fractures a bit more. On the bed sits a sweatshirt I "stole" one of the first nights I stayed over. It isn't oversized on me, but it's soft, smells like him, and makes me feel like I'm wrapped in his arms. My hand hesitates over it for a moment before I turn to gather my things from the bathroom, leaving it behind.

Bryce is standing exactly where I left him when I return to the living room, my bag slung over my shoulder.

His distant gray eyes meet mine across the room. "So, this is really how it ends?" His deep voice cracks around the words. "We're really leaving it like this?"

I smile, though it's forced and sad. "Yeah, before one of us ends up hating the other."

He let me go. He doesn't call after me; he doesn't reach for me. No—he watches as I walk out of his apartment, the door swinging closed behind me.

Part of me aches for him to chase after me, plead for forgiveness, but I acknowledge it won't change anything.

We both have things we needed to work on, and right now, we need space to do it. He's right about a lot of things, which makes the words sting more, but they also wake me up. All this time, I've been worried he isn't ready for a second chance, but maybe I'm not either.

I hadn't woken up this morning knowing my heart would shatter, but I've been preparing for this moment since I saw him at his desk all those months ago. Still, the impact hurts worse than anything I could have prepared for.

Chapter 29

THen

April 2015

Charlotte, NC

There was so much to look at.

This was the first swim meet I'd been to with so many famous faces. Adair Swimming had only been up for a little under a year and while our traffic was good, having the chance to interview a well-known name would only aid in boosting us to another level.

That was our goal this weekend.

"Was that . . ." Mia trailed off beside me. I turned to see her gaze following someone who had just walked past us. "Holy shit, that was Michael Phelps!"

Getting an interview with him would be impossible.

"Remind me again why we decided to do this?" I found myself wondering out loud, watching as he stopped to sign a couple of caps for kids.

"Because we're completely unrealistic?"

She wasn't wrong; I'd never felt more out of my element. What kind of college kid and recent grad decided to use their hard-earned money to fly to a different state to cover a swim meet, not get paid for it, and post about it to a couple hundred followers? Sounds like code for "unrealistic" to me.

"We're trying to make this work," I reasoned out loud. "If we want to make this work, this is where we need to be."

"Right," Mia agreed, determination crossing her features. "We just need to get comfortable. We deserve to be here; we worked hard to be here, even if no one else cares."

I wished my confidence and determination would bubble to the surface the way hers had.

Mia declared it was time to find seats before navigating us through the crowd. I sort of trailed behind her, trying to take it all in as chlorine assaulted my senses. Once we got to the starting blocks, she spotted a couple of empty seats, and started climbing toward them.

Once we were settled, my gaze swept the length of the pool. Warm-ups were well underway, so the pool was jam-packed and the deck was a chaotic mess. Coaches were whistling and calling out to their athletes, swimmers from all over the country were navigating the crowded deck with an ease that only came from experience.

My gaze didn't stay locked in one place for very long. Then I felt the prickling sensation of being watched. Just near the starting blocks, my gaze locked with a pair of eyes that were so gray, I could see the hue of them from here. Or maybe I just somehow already knew those eyes. My breath caught in my throat as our gazes remained locked on one another.

Unattainable was an understatement when it came to Bryce Clark, especially for someone like me. Although we didn't know one another, a gut feeling told me he was trouble and, if I got too close, I'd be the one who got hurt. Even before meeting his stare, I knew if I let myself get too caught up in him, my stupid little heart would form a stupid little crush and I'd be fucked.

The boy came with a whole mess of caution tape. Rumor was, he'd just gotten out of a long-term relationship. Most people thought he'd be engaged by the time he graduated next year. Mia and I did our best to avoid gossip within the swim community, but when it's swirling everywhere, it's hard to ignore.

It's even harder to ignore when the rumors turn out to be true, and everyone loses their minds over it. As far as we knew, he'd been single for most of the year, and he'd made it clear his focus was on finishing school and making the Olympic team next summer. Despite that, he'd become known as a flirt.

The exact kind of guy I should avoid at all costs.

The flip-flop sensation that occurred in the pit of my stomach when he grinned at me solidified the fact that I was making the right decision. Still, I offered a shy smile in return.

"What are you staring—Oh, hello, Bryce Clark," Mia cooed. "He's hardcore staring at you, Jos."

A blush coated my cheeks as I pulled my gaze from him. Well, he was an up-and-coming name in the sport; it didn't do any good to avoid someone like him. "No, he's not. Guys like him don't look at girls like me."

Clearly not in the mood to let me get away with hating myself, Mia rolled her eyes. "That's bullshit, and obviously not true, because he's still staring at you."

"What?" My gaze snapped back to his, and my heart whirled when our eyes locked again.

This time, I didn't break eye contact. I let myself get swept up in the fantasy that he could be looking at me. That someone who looked like they belonged in a rom-com would look twice at me. We held each other's gazes again until his coach said something, forcing him to look away.

Which was probably for the best.

Nothing else eventful happened during prelims, but Adair Swimming got a good amount of attention on social media. People seemed excited to know we were covering the meet in person. Once the session was over, we asked a volunteer for a recommendation for lunch and she pointed us in the direction of a local café.

As soon as we exited the stadium, a lot of things happened at once—Mia turned to ask me something, but then she kicked something in her path, stumbled, and she barreled toward the ground too fast for me to get a grip on her.

"Shit!" The deep voice seemed to come out of nowhere, followed by a strong, tanned arm catching Mia just before she hit the ground.

She let out a gasp as she came to a halt mid-fall. My eyes drifted to the arm, taking in the vibrant colors of the Olympic rings permanently etched into his skin.

"Are you okay?" the voice asked, helping her to stand. "I'm sorry, I thought my bag was out of the way."

My heart leaped into my throat at the recognition. I should've picked up on that voice as soon as I heard it.

As Ronan O'Brien helped Mia regain her footing, the sight of him snatched the air from my lungs.

Ronan was by far one of the most beautiful human beings I had ever seen. He was tall, with a lean, muscular build, sharp jaw, and bright green eyes. Where Bryce had a boyish charm to him, Ronan looked like he belonged on a red carpet.

And now he was holding my best friend in his arms.

She looked just as stunned as I felt, barely able to tear her eyes from his arm to focus on his face. My best friend did not fangirl, but I could see the internal battle raging within her.

"Seriously, are you okay?" Pulling her gaze from the tattoo on his arm, she nodded. "I am sorry; I set my bag down because some kids wanted pictures—"

"It happens," Mia cut him off, finally finding her voice. He backed off once he was sure she was standing on solid ground. "Thank you for helping me."

With a smile that could send anyone's knees buckling, he said, "Ronan O'Brien."

Mia quirked up an eyebrow as his gaze returned to her. "Seriously? You think we don't know who you are?"

Holding onto the confidence he exuded like it was a lifeline, he gave a shrug. "I figured you did, but I like to keep people on their toes."

If Bryce was covered in caution tape, Ronan came with lights and sirens. At twenty-five, he was known for partying and never having a serious relationship. His popularity grew after a successful 2012 Olympics, where he brought home a handful of gold medals. He was one hell of a swimmer and was likely heading to Rio next year. On top of that, he was charismatic, aiding in a growing reputation as being the golden boy with an edge.

"It's nice to meet you," Mia replied, her own confidence chasing away her earlier unease. "I'm Mia Sheridan, this is Josie Martin. We own and run Adair Swimming."

"Wait, really?" He glanced between us. "I've seen some of your stuff floating around. I read your article on all the craziness that's been going on the last few months. It was really good."

A flustered look appeared on Mia's face once more, a soft blush coating her cheeks this time. She had written about him in the article, deep diving into a seemingly rash decision he made to leave his longtime coach for another one halfway across the country. "Um, thank you."

"We've gotten a lot of positive reactions with that article," I said. "We also have a lot of really cool stuff planned for the lead up to the Olympics."

He slid his phone from his pocket. "Then I should make sure I'm following you, so I don't miss anything."

Both Mia and I stared at him, our jaws nearly on the floor. I hadn't been angling for a follow at all, but my phone buzzes in my pocket a couple of seconds later. I didn't need to look at it to know he'd made good on his promise.

"I need to get going." He slid his phone back into his pocket, barely glancing at me as he looked toward Mia. "It was nice meeting you both. Mia, I'm sorry I almost killed you."

As quickly as he appeared, he was walking away, leaving us dumbfounded. It wasn't until he rounded the corner that I realized something important.

"We forgot to get a picture with him."

Mia turned to look at me. "I can't even be mad about that. We were both fangirling a little too hard over him. If we want to be taken seriously, we need to not let it affect us."

"We will." We have to. "I just . . . I knew he was hot, right? I just didn't—"

"Expect him to be quite that pretty in real life?" Mia finished, and I nodded. "Girl, I get it. Come on, we can talk about hot people over lunch."

Less than twenty minutes later, we had placed our orders at the crowded café and were searching for an empty table.

Once we settled in, I took the first sip of my iced mocha and let out a sigh.

Mia raised a brow at me. "You have a real problem, you know that, right?"

"Obviously." I grinned around my straw. "But let's not talk about how I'd die without coffee. Let's talk about what just happened with Ronan O'Brien!"

She waved me off, barely glancing up from her phone. "There's nothing else to talk about—he's hot, we met him, we forgot to get a picture, he's following us on social media. We did what we were supposed to do, time to move on."

"Whatever, Mia, he was totally into you," I replied.

"No, he wasn't." She set her phone down, looking across the table at me. "However, Bryce Clark was sure interested in you. Tell me, what's your opinion of him?"

My eyes narrowed, knowing she was well-aware of what my opinion was. "That I should stay as far away from him as possible."

She genuinely looked confused. "I don't get that. I thought he was your kind of cute, plus he seems interested!"

"Both of which are part of the problem."

I didn't know how to explain that getting to know him would be a big mistake. He was my kind of cute. Having only ever researched him for the blog and never met him meant I could live in this little fantasy bubble. He was like a celebrity crush that was out of reach.

Meeting him would pop that bubble and I'd be so screwed.

"Oh my God, you think he's cute! You avoid talking about him because you have a crush on him."

"I don't know him," I argued. "I can't have a real crush on someone I don't know. Do I think he's dangerous? Yes, I—"

"The fact you neither confirmed nor denied your crush just told me everything I needed to know." She looked positively gleeful. "You like Bryce Clark. Now, what will we do with this information?"

Everything inside me sank. "We're not doing anything with that information. Nothing."

"Why not? You're both young and single. He's hot, Josie."

"And I'm not the kind of girl he would go for, Mia. Have you seen his ex? She's gorgeous."

"You mean thin," she corrected, scowling at me. "As your best friend, I will not condone self-hate. We will not diminish our own worth by comparing ourselves to someone else. Any man who can't see that you're gorgeous can just fuck all the way off."

Having a best friend who had a similar body type to my own and understood the struggles I faced with body image was still new to me. Shortly after meeting, we'd made a pact to help one another learn to love ourselves.

"He also has more important things to focus on than his love life," I pointed out. "He's said so in many interviews.

"If you want me to leave it alone, I will, but you can't deny that you caught his eye."

I couldn't let myself get caught up in whatever daydream my overactive imagination concocted, but I wasn't about to tell her that. Ignoring the second half of her statement, I said, "I think it's for the best."

Before either one of us could say anything else, my phone vibrated with a notification for a new follower.

Mia let out a gasp, snatching the phone up before I could and practically shoving it in my face. "I told you!"

Bryce Clark has followed you back!

I stared at the notification, my jaw nearly hitting the table. That was the last thing I would have expected, especially unprompted. □

"It probably has nothing to do with me," I argued. "Ronan probably told him to follow us."

Mia sighed, setting the phone down as a waiter approached with our food. "You're hopeless."

Chapter 30

NOW

June 2023
Omaha, NE

Seeing Bryce at work is hell.

In the week since we split, we've avoided one another at all costs. The few times we have crossed paths at company-wide meetings, in the crowded cafeteria, or in the silent halls, we dance around one another, saying nothing.

There will be a split second where we look at each other, a moment where I think one of us will give in and speak. But both of us will go our own way, pretending it never happened.

"I'm always looking for you, Josie." Bryce's words echo in my mind, like a song on repeat. A reminder of how we will always be connected, even if we can't make a relationship work.

A week and a half after the breakup, Sarah comes sauntering up to my desk, her dark red lips twisted into a smirk. "I take it you heard the news?"

She looks too pleased with herself to be here to share anything good. "I don't have a clue what you're talking about."

She braces against the desk across from me, the personification of smug. "Your boyfriend quit."

I barely stop my jaw from dropping open. "What do you mean, Sarah?"

Her eyes flash with glee. "Oh, you really didn't know! I knew you two wouldn't last."

Heart pounding against my chest, I grit my teeth, unwilling to give into whatever she wants. "You need to stop being so invested in other people's lives."

She shrugs. "I like seeing how things pan out, and I'm usually right. Look at what happened with you and Bryce."

"I never said anything happened between us," I snap. "It's none of your business, Sarah."

"Something obviously happened, otherwise you would know he's leaving."

"Did he tell you that or one of your little gossips?"

"I can't believe you haven't heard when it's all anyone is talking about right now, Joslyn! He quit last week and is moving." My heart drops to the pit of my stomach. "Apparently, he found something else, and is going to one of the Carolinas."

"W-what?" The stuttered word seemed to entertain her even more.

"Or maybe he found someone else." She smirks. "I can't say I'd be too surprised."

Something in me snaps at the mirth in her words. Bryce had been right about Sarah from the beginning. "Shallow" was too kind a word for her, and I refused to let her get away with her snide comments a moment longer.

"Maybe he did," I shoot back, startling her. "It would just make your day if he did, wouldn't it? From the moment you realized we knew each other, you wanted all the details, and you wanted me to stay far away from him."

"Oh, please," she scoffs. "I didn't want to see you get hurt."

I narrow my eyes at her. "Is that it? See, I'm beginning to think you don't want me to actually end up with any of the guys you introduce to me. Maybe it's a sick game to you, being able to talk a guy into asking me out before he's met me, wondering if you can make me desirable."

Her eyes widen at my accusation. The reality washes over me like a bucket of ice water—I'm nothing but a joke to her.

"You stopped pushing me toward Bryce because we already knew each other, and you couldn't claim anything that happened next as a victory," I go on. "His opinion was already formed, and you couldn't influence it."

She stands straighter, lips forming a thin line. "Now you're really being ridiculous! Listen to yourself. I knew how it was going to end. I was protecting you."

"And how was it going to end?"

"Not the way you wanted, not with a guy like that!" Her eyes widen as the words tumble out of her mouth. "Joslyn—"

I stop her with a shake of my head and a bitter laugh. "Jokes on you, Sarah. I had him years ago, I had him a week ago, and the only reason I don't have him now is because we needed a reality check. I have never once questioned whether he was attracted to me."

"You're lying. There's no way—"

"Because I'm not a size two?" I snap. "That doesn't matter. It's never mattered to anyone but you. You see me as a project, something you need to fix, but there's nothing wrong with me. I like the way I look; I'm happy in my own skin, and there's nothing I want to change. So, get over whatever fatphobic shit this is and leave me the hell alone!"

Not giving her a chance to respond, I push back from my desk and walk right past her. Stunned, she said nothing as I passed, and I couldn't care less right now. I was done with her.

I had someone more important to talk to right now.

By the time I reach Bryce's side of the building, I've calmed down enough to have a civil conversation. But of course, he isn't at his desk.

Instead, Bill, one of Bryce's team members, looks up when I approach. "Hey, are you looking for Bryce?"

"Yeah, is he in the office today?"

He points at the corner behind me. "You probably passed him on your way over. He's in one of the breakout rooms right around the corner."

"I don't want to interrupt a meeting, I just had—"

"He's not in a meeting," Bill cuts me off. "He wanted some extra space to get things sorted. He doesn't mind being interrupted."

I have a feeling that won't be true once I walk up to him. "Is he leaving?"

Bill hesitates at my question. "I think the two of you need to talk."

It isn't that simple; it never has been. "Thanks, Bill."

When I find the room Bill directed me to, Bryce is hunched over the desk, work surrounding him. When I pull the glass door open, his gaze snaps up from the paperwork.

"Hey," I greet with an awkward wave, the door closing behind me as I step into the room.

Looking surprised and confused, he pulls his earbuds out with a frown. "What are you doing here?"

It's the first exchange we've had in over a week.

"I heard you were leaving." I shrug. "I was hoping you could clear the rumor up for me."

He swallows thickly. "I thought you knew."

"Nope." I pop the "p" at the end. "But I think that's great! I just wish you would have told me yourself, instead of planning to sneak off and hope I didn't notice."

"That's not what I was going to do. Give me more credit than that; I was going to talk to you about it."

"I really hate that I don't believe you. I found out from Sarah, which was fun. She came over to rub it in my face, so I finally told her to fuck off."

Bowing his head, he says, "I wish I could have been there for that. I always told you I didn't trust her."

"You're deflecting from the real issue again."

"What do you want me to say, Josie? You already know the truth."

Knowing he's leaving the company floods me with relief. What I hadn't been expecting was him leaving Omaha, even though I don't know what else there is for him here.

But I wish I was reason enough for him to stay.

I plaster on my fake enthusiasm again. "I'm so happy for you, Bryce. Really. I just wish I heard it from you."

He blinks at me. "You're . . . you're not mad at me?"

"Are you kidding me?" I laugh. "Of course, I'm not mad! You've got it all figured out, right? That's why you're leaving?"

He stands, turning to face me fully. "No, it's not—"

I take a step back, toward the door. I don't want to hear the reason. I don't think I could hear the reason. "That's not important, Bryce. I'm glad I found out before you left."

"I was going to tell—"

"No, you weren't, Bryce." I want to believe that he would've told me goodbye before he left more than anything, but history told me otherwise. No one likes confrontation, but Bryce Clark has a habit of running from it. "I think I found out exactly how you wanted me to."

Deep down, I know Sarah is the last person he'd want me to hear it from, but I can't help but wonder if he's okay with it because he didn't have to be the one.

Instead of arguing with me, he deflates; shoulders sagging, arms hanging at his sides, wearing a frown. He still looks tired, but there's a lightness about him that I haven't seen since 2015. He seems excited to see what comes next.

Suddenly, the small room feels like it's shrinking. With my heart pounding against my chest and my vision blurring, I realize I need to leave, now. I can't see him be so excited about something I don't get to be a part of.

Once again, we have reached the end.

This time, though, we are ending it my way.

"I hope life finally gives you whatever it is you're looking for."

"Josie, please—"

"No, Bryce." I shake my head. "This was our last chance."

I don't give him the chance to say anything as I turn for the door. As I scurry back to my desk, I fight not to let my tears fall.

All this time, I've been pushing him to figure out what he wanted, and now he's doing just that. He's doing the very thing I want him to, yet I'm consumed with two thoughts: first, he's leaving again; and second, why is everyone able to move on but me?

In a matter of weeks, Bryce Clark came and went from my life once more. He advanced in a job he hates and left without so much as a second thought. Yet I'm still in the same job I've hated for years, too afraid to go after what I truly want.

Too afraid of failure. Too scared to get out of my own way.

Bryce has proven he's grown up, that he's changed, but I never got the chance. Instead, I'd waited for him to hurt me, never wanting to own up to the fact I was still stuck. I'm the one who hasn't changed, and he'd pointed that out to me.

"Joslyn? Are you all right?"

I don't know when it happened, but I'd stopped on my path to lean against the wall, my breath coming out in shudders. My manager is beside me, concern etched on her features.

Something in me snaps.

The idea of forcing a smile on my face and going back to work, pretending nothing is wrong, makes me feel ill.

Suddenly, weeks and months of rational thought culminate into this one exhausting moment. With a deep breath, I remind myself I can do this. It's time to do this. I need to do this. Or I'll forever be stuck.

Not for him, but for me.

"I think we need to talk."

Chapter 31

NOW

June 2023
Omaha, NE

"I'm unemployed."

My mom's spoon clatters against her plate, her head snapping up. "Since when?"

I glance down at the time on my phone. "Two hours ago, I'd say."

She takes a sip of her coffee, like she's bracing herself for whatever she's about to hear. I turn to my dad, expecting him to still be reading the paper, but he's looking right at me. "I'm proud of you, kiddo."

Five simple words from my dad dissipates the rest of my fear. He understands what it's like to be screwed over by a company that doesn't care about their employees, and he knows what it's like to miss out on something he loves because of work.

"I am, too," Mom interjects. "I just want to make sure this doesn't have anything to do with Bryce."

"It doesn't," I promise, shaking my head. "We, uh, we broke up, and he's moving to one of the Carolinas. I'm not really sure of the details."

"I didn't know Hunt & Sloan had an office out there," Dad muses.

"They don't, he quit too. However, his boss actually let him finish his two weeks."

Mine had been so stunned that she told me to pack my things and go. The first place I went after calling Mia from my car was my parents' house, hoping they would be supportive, even if they didn't get it.

"Sounds like it's not a company worth hanging around if they've lost both of you so close together."

"What are you going to do now?" Mom asks, ever the practical one.

That's the big question, isn't it?

"I'm going to go after what I want," I admit, choosing my words carefully. "I'm going to write. I have some savings, and I can take on freelance jobs if I need to, but my priority right now is finally making a choice for me."

Mom's eyes glint with tears as she reaches for my hand. "And you have our full support, sweetheart. You've given up more than enough. Don't let yourself get held back anymore."

"You make it sound like I'm leaving Omaha," I choke out with a laugh. "That's not the plan."

"I know, but if you're given the chance to go somewhere else, you should take it."

"We're always looking for new places to visit," Dad adds. "And you won't even have to put us in the spare room."

Mom rolls her eyes while I laugh; the prized RV parked in the driveway is visible through the window. When they leave, there wouldn't be anything for me here. I've always talked about leaving one day, but one day is scary.

"Bryce was good for you," Mom continues, "but maybe you need to be good for yourself. Maybe that needs to be your priority right now."

"I'm finally realizing that," I sigh. "Part of me wishes I had the chance to say that to him, you know? I've realized I wasn't fair to him. I tried to fix his problems instead of my own."

"We all do that, sweetheart. It's human to protect those we care about. I think he'll understand that if you ever get the chance to tell him."

"I will probably never see him again."

"You don't know that. You've already been proven wrong about that with how many times you seem to run into one another."

"Please don't give me some cliché about how those who are meant to be together always find a way." I laugh with an eye roll.

"You're a writer. You should know better than anyone that most clichés are based in truth."

Not for me, not this time. I'm not sure Bryce and I can move past this, even if given the chance. "I hate to get your hopes up, Mom, but I think we're really done this time."

"Oh, fine," she sighs. "You know, I always liked that boy."

"Me too, Mom," I murmur, hundreds of memories coming to mind. His eyes, his smile, his laugh, the way it feels to be held in his arms. "Me too."

I spend most of the day with my parents, going over the itinerary for their trip and helping them pack. When I finally make it back to my apartment, the sun is casting a hazy pink through the apartment.

Dropping my stuff by the door, I make my way over to my desk, snatching up a notebook, and pen before heading to the chair by the window.

Writing has always been there to help me sort through things, help me figure out what I want and what's worth my time. If I'm going to pursue writing, I need to write, and I'm far from short on ideas.

I'd told Bryce I was waiting for the perfect story, but forgot it's already within me. I don't have to write a perfect romance; I can write a real one. I can write characters who are flawed, who don't have their whole lives tied up in a pretty bow.

Despite everything, my relationship with Bryce was real. Real was better than perfect.

Staring at the blank page before me, I begin something new. There are no expectations, nothing to ebb the flow of my creativity. Whatever I put down in black ink can be complete shit, or it can be something amazing.

I've never given myself the chance to close the chapter he first sauntered into. The reality of a blog I poured my heart, time, and money into failing, and getting my heart broken by a young man who didn't know what he wanted—it had been a taboo subject for too long.

Back in 2021, when it was all over, I never wallowed over what it could have been and what it never had the chance to be. I never said goodbye to that part of my life.

That version of Josie was strong, confident, and she believed she could do anything, even if others doubted her. I want to find her again, even if none of the other stuff came with her.

I'm finally in a place where I need to reflect on the past to move forward, so I write it all down. It's messy, but full of love, laughter, and the overwhelming scent of chlorine. While I don't want to go back there, I'm grateful for every memory.

Chapter 32

NOW

June 2023
Omaha, NE

There are moments in a writer's life when the story flows naturally. When the characters take your little idea and run with it, weaving a wonderful story. Those moments are rare, but I have one of those amazing nights. I write until my hand cramps, and the exhaustion is too much to ignore.

When I wake up the next morning, I feel lighter. It still hurt. I'm still sad. I also feel like I'm standing on the edge of something great. I feel like the possibilities of this story are endless.

I'm about halfway through my first cup of coffee and glancing over the words I'd written last night when there was a knock at my front door.

Setting my mug on the counter, I make my way to the front door. Figuring it's a delivery or the nice lady next door who shares her baked cookies with me, I don't even glance in a mirror before I open the door. Then let out a gasp when I reveal Bryce. "Holy shit."

The hint of a smile twitches at the corners of his lips as he looks me up and down. I'm suddenly very aware of the bralette and pajama shorts I wore to bed last night. "Good morning."

My grip tightens on the door, resisting the urge to slam it in his face. "What are you doing here?"

"I didn't expect you to answer the door, honestly."

"Yeah, well, I failed to look through the peephole, otherwise I wouldn't have."

We both know my words are a lie, but he doesn't call me out on it. Instead, we just stare at each other in the doorway. I've never felt self-conscious in his presence before, but I feel the need to cross my arms over my chest now. I feel like I dove into the deep end without knowing how to swim. I don't know what I was supposed to do or say.

"I should have been the one to tell you I was leaving," he finally says. "It shouldn't have come from anyone else, especially Sarah. I'm sorry, Josie. God, I'm so sorry."

"That doesn't matter." In the grand scheme of things, it would have made no difference to hear it from him. "You're still leaving."

He ducks his head, briefly looking down at his shoes. "When I put in my notice, I wasn't planning on leaving Omaha. I realized you were right, so I decided to leave. I was going to talk to you about it, see if we could fix things between us. I wanted to tell you've always been right about me, about my fears, but I'm here because I don't want to lose you."

My heart stuttered, hope bubbling up. I swallow, knowing I need to get a grip on it. "You're moving away, Bryce."

His gray eyes meet mine again. "Carter bought a pool in South Carolina."

"What?" I gasp. "Why would he do that? He's training for the Olympics in Georgia!"

Bryce chuckles. It's such a Carter thing to do; I can't fault Bryce for his amusement. "It's his last one. He was panicking over what he would do next, and bought a rundown pool. He's going to open a club."

"There are so many steps between panicking and buying a pool. How's this even going to happen?"

"He talked himself into it and then panicked more once he had the keys," Bryce explains. "He called me and asked me to do it with him. It'll need some work, but there is a small pool I can run private trainings or small clinics out of for a while. It won't be fully operational until Carter's there, then I'll only coach part-time and deal with the business side of things from there."

"And is this what you want?" I ask, worried he'll hate me for asking the question. I don't want him to jump in to save his best friend without thinking about it.

"Honestly, I didn't know I wanted this until he basically threw it in my lap, but, yeah, I want this. My coaches changed my life, and I want the chance to do the same for another kid. Just because I'm done swimming doesn't mean I'm done with swimming."

He's smiling, and it's far from forced. He looks healthy and . . . happy. It's startling to finally see what happy Bryce looks like. I don't want to look away.

Even if it means losing him, I'll do whatever I need to keep him this happy.

"You did it." Tears sting the corner of my eyes. "You found what comes next."

He grins back at me, so content with the direction of his life. "I have you to thank for that. You made me see what I refused to see; I wouldn't have said yes to Carter two weeks ago. I owe you more than you could ever know, Josie, and I'm sorry it's taken me so long to say that. I just wish it wasn't the result of a fight that ended us."

But it isn't enough to make him stay.

"You would have figured it out. I know you would have. I'm so happy for you."

"Thank you."

There is so much unsaid in those two little words. I can feel the weight of them, the way they cover years of things he never had the guts to say.

"I, um, I wanted to talk to you about something else."

The shift in his demeanor makes me look up at him again. He looks a little less sure of himself, more nervous, like he's about to . . .

"Oh, my God," I breathe out, my palms sweating. He looks panicked. "Is this our grand gesture moment?"

It's either that, or goodbye. For real this time.

He raises a brow, looking a little amused. "Should I know what that means?"

I roll my eyes. "Men, honestly! It's a moment in a romance novel where all hope is lost, but then the hero, or heroine, comes sweeping in to fix all the wrongs. It's the moment the story starts all over again."

His smile could fix every crack in my heart. "Yeah, Jos," he murmurs, taking a step closer. "This is that moment."

I clear my throat around the tears. "You better impress me. I've waited my whole life for this."

"Well, it's pretty simple, babe." We don't break eye contact; I couldn't even if I wanted to. "I don't deserve another chance. I've fucked it up so many times, but I'm ready this time. I'm ready and I'm so goddamn in love with you, Joslyn."

His eyes follow my tears as they make their way down my cheeks before he brushes it away. "I wasn't perfect, but I love you, too. I have for a long time."

He leans into me, pressing his forehead against mine, swiping his thumb across my cheek. "Me too. Josie . . . come with me."

My mom's words come flooding back, reminding me it's time to go. Here is my chance. We have a lot to work out, but I want to see where this could go, and I want us to have a fair shot at it.

I'm tired of saying one day; I'm ready for it to be today.

He presses a soft kiss to my lips before standing to his full height, hand dropping to entangle with mine. He doesn't move away, but gives me enough room to breathe.

"You asked me what I wanted, Josie, and I want the same thing I've wanted since the first time I saw you in Charlotte—you. I'm tired of making myself believe I can't have you, or that I don't deserve happiness. Everything else we can figure out later, but I want you. I want us. I know you said I wouldn't get another chance, but I'm hoping this is still part of my second one. I didn't leave you; I wasn't going to leave you. Not without this moment."

His emotions are as clear as day to me. He wants this—us—just as badly as I do, but he's giving me the final say. If I say no, he'll leave, and never look back. If I say yes, we'd have everything we ever wanted.

"South Carolina has nothing to do with us," he points out. "This is our chance to really start over, without memories beating down on us everywhere we turn."

There's no reason I shouldn't say yes. "I quit."

Hands gripped my hips, shock washing over his features before it's replaced with a grin. A grin he presses against my lips in an overjoyed kiss. "Fuck yeah," he murmurs against my lips. "I'm so proud of you."

Laughing, my arms weave around his neck as I pull him in for another kiss. "I love you, Bryce."

It's the first time I've said those words to him, and it feels like a weight lifts off my chest. Our smiles are blinding as we stare at one another, basking in the moment.

"Seriously, Jos, come with me. You'll be closer to Mia, you can write—"

My eyes widen, and I tug on his sleeve. "Come inside."

I barely have the chance to take in his confused look before I pull him through my apartment to where I left the open notebook on the counter. I hand the notebook to him before I reach for my coffee as he reads.

His gray eyes scan the page before he smiles, focusing on reading what I'd written. Mia's the only other person who's seen this kind of writing from me, but this time it's different. In the form of words on a page, I'm handing a piece of myself to Bryce, trusting he won't break it.

"I found the story I want to tell," I tell him, setting the empty mug down and leaning against the counter. "The funny thing is, I had it in me all along."

He sets the notebook aside, his voice barely above a whisper. "Is there a happy ending?"

I shrug, biting my lip to keep my own smile from taking over. "I hope so."

Arms caging me in, he kisses me deeply, brushing his tongue against my bottom lip. Every ounce of love we share pours into the kiss. There isn't a shred of doubt between us in that moment.

When he pulls away, he rests his forehead against mine, not moving far, as though he intends to pull me in for another kiss.

"Yes," I breathe.

My eyes flutter closed as his lips seek mine again. This kiss isn't as deep—we are too busy smiling against each other's lips, excited for the chances we're taking.

Chapter 33

THEN

April 2015
Charlotte, NC

On the second day of the meet, I took some time to call my mom before heading to the pool to watch the finals start. Mia headed in before me, deciding to scope out some seats for us. As soon as I got my mom on the phone, I regretted calling when there were so many people around.

"Mom," I groaned, closing my eyes as I pressed my phone tighter against my ear, looking around to make sure no one was standing close enough to hear me. Athletes were scattered all around me, talking to each other or their coaches, or simply making their way into the pool. "You know that's not why Mia and I are here. Please stop."

"All I'm saying is that it wouldn't be the worst thing if you came back with a nice young man," she replied. I knew she was teasing, but I also knew she wasn't lying. "I've been watching the meet, you know. That Bryce Cla—"

"Mom, no," I stressed, mainly because I could literally see him standing less than twenty feet away, talking to Ronan. They both looked directly at me when my voice rose. I turned my back to them. Looking at them while my mom was talking about Bryce was out of the question. "Please, stop. I'm not trying to get a boyfriend here; I'm just trying to get people to let me write articles about them."

"Well, that's no fun," she teased. "I'll let you go, sweetheart. Have fun!"

"Bye, Mom. I love you," I replied, which she echoed before I ended the call.

With a sigh, I checked a couple of notifications before I stuck my phone in my pocket. As soon as I turned to head inside, I realized Bryce was leaning against the metal barricade meant to keep fans away from the athletes. He was smiling playfully at me, Ronan nowhere to be seen. My knees locked and I could do nothing but stare back at him.

"I promise I wasn't trying to listen," he said. "I also couldn't help it."

A blush coated my cheeks and dread filled the pit of my stomach. I had tried to keep my voice down. I probably should have moved somewhere else when Ronan waved at me. "How much of that did you hear?"

His grin dropped into a smirk that caused a flip-flop sensation in my chest. I couldn't look away. "Long enough to know that I can't help with the 'getting a boyfriend' part. Nothing against you. I just got out of a very serious relationship, and I'd rather not jump into something yet."

"Oh, my God," I groaned out.

"Nah, I'm fine. I was just naïve enough to think I found the one at eighteen." I almost laughed at the face he made. "So, I'm just going to be single for a while. Plus, it sounds like you were okay without the boyfriend, am I right?"

"Can the earth please open up and swallow me whole?" I pleaded under my breath, but he heard me.

"If it did, that would mean I couldn't help you with the second part. You said you needed people to write articles about, right?"

"Oh, no." I shook my head. "Please don't feel like—"

His smirk dropped back into a boyish grin that did something else entirely to me. Then he held out his hand. "I'm Bryce Clark, and I'm trying to make the Olympic team. I'm not sure how many people would care, but I'd be happy to let you write an article about me. If, you know, you want to."

It amazed me how a person could be both confident and full of self-doubt at the same time. "Not care? Bryce, literally everyone is holding their breath to see what you do in the next year."

To my utter surprise, a blush coated his cheeks, and he ducked his chin, avoiding eye contact. "Wow, uh, okay. Most people would just respond with their name, but telling me every eye in the swimming world is on me is cool, too. No pressure."

My eyes widened, and I took his hand. His hand was large and warm, fully encompassing mine. "Oh, God, I'm so sorry! I didn't mean it like that. Hi, I'm Josie."

And just like that, the bashfulness was gone, and he met my eyes again. "I know. Ronan told me who you were."

"Which would explain why you followed us. Carter followed us not too long after you."

"He felt bad for almost killing your friend."

"Mia," I supplied. "Her name is Mia."

"Right." He nodded, but I had the distinct impression he couldn't care less what her name was. At least not right now. "So, Josie, are you going to take me up on my offer?"

I frowned, but then remembered what he was talking about. I should decline interviewing him, or suggest I hand it over to Mia, because this boy was trouble. I knew it in the way my heart thundered against my chest; I knew it in the way I found myself staring into his gray eyes; I knew it in the way my eyes raked over his body. Keeping my distance would be wise, but I really didn't want to be wise.

"Yeah." I grinned with a nod. "If you're up for it, I'd appreciate the opportunity."

An easy grin stretched across his features as he stuffed his hands in the pockets of his white hoodie. "Absolutely." He nodded toward the building behind me. "I need to head in, get warmed up, but we'll talk, yeah?"

"Yeah. Just message me."

"Of course," he said, already taking a couple of steps backward. "It was, uh . . . It was nice meeting you, Josie."

I kept my grin in place even as my cheeks flushed. "You too, Bryce. Swim fast."

He ducked his chin again, looking the tiniest bit bashful. I stood frozen for another second, watching as he caught up with Ronan, who was waiting beside the door. Both of them looked back at me, making my heart leap into my throat. Bryce's eyes widened a bit before he headed in. Ronan gave me a knowing smile before following his friend.

In that moment, I knew that whatever else followed between Bryce and me, I wouldn't trade this moment for anything. Maybe he'd break my heart, maybe we'd find something more, or maybe we'd just be friends—it didn't matter. Bryce Clark came with a lot of caution tape, but he was also the kind of person I wanted to know.

Epilogue

July 2023

Omaha, NE

Everything happens quick after that.

Bryce finishes the rest of his two weeks out without incident. On his last day, he happened to be leaving at the same time as Sarah, who stared on stunned as he slid into the passenger seat of my car, greeting me with a kiss. Neither one of us said anything, but it felt monumental to pull out of the parking lot for the last time with him beside me.

This is a chapter we are closing together.

My family took our news a lot better than I thought they would. They were overjoyed. My mother instantly bragged about her calling our relationship years ago. Bryce just laughed and kissed her cheek, thanking her for recommending that I get a boyfriend all those years ago.

It didn't matter how long it took us to get here.

Mia screamed in delight when we told her. Her voice crackling from the phone and through Bryce's nearly empty living room. Bryce cheekily declared he always knew she secretly liked him. She then washed away his comment by assuring him that he was the furthest thing from her favorite. She quickly followed it up with her infamous "if you hurt her again" speech. I grinned at how he tensed up.

Her excitement came more from the fact that, for the first time, she and I would be within driving distance of one another. Charlotte was only an hour and a half away from Columbia.

Carter had the same reaction when we called him next. It was even complete with his own threatening speech to his best friend.

With Bryce already having rented a place in Columbia, a two bedroom that Carter could crash at while he was in town—all we had to do was add me to the lease. We had to be down there in ten days, so we hastily finish his packing and clean out my place. We also spend as much time with my parents as possible.

In what feels like the blink of an eye, I'm walking out of the leasing office and heading toward my future.

Bryce looks completely at ease, shutting the tailgate of my SUV while chatting with my parents about our new place. My heart flutters at the realization of what I'm about to have. I don't have to think back on everything it took to get here.

When he notices me, his grin is as blinding as I know mine must be. "Ready to go?"

I stop beside him, melting against his side as he slings his arm around my shoulders. "Absolutely."

After one last round of hugs, I slide into the passenger seat. With tearful eyes, I watch out the window as Bryce wraps up his own goodbyes by pressing a kiss to my mom's cheek and promising we'd check in.

Before I know it, he's sliding into the driver's seat beside me and putting the car in drive, reaching for my hand, and entangling our fingers as he pulls out of the parking lot for the last time.

I don't know what the future holds for us. I don't know if we'll make it, but in that moment, I think back to the girl I was at twenty-two, who wondered what it would be like to have this. I wish I could go back to tell her how deserving she is of this. But that would just ruin the surprise.

I know how that story ends, and she'd find out for herself one day.

The End.

Did you love Bryce and Josie's story? If so, please be sure to leave a review! You can leave one at Goodreads, The StoryGraph, BookBub, or wherever you bought the book. Reviews help authors and readers get connected and are always appreciated!

Dying to know what happens with Carter after he panic buys a pool? Get the next book in the series, *Tell Me Tomorrow*, now.

LET'S STAY IN TOUCH

For updates on upcoming releases, be sure to follow me on social media and sign up for my newsletter. All new subscribers to my newsletter will get a BONUS scene from *Maybe One Day*.

Scan the code and come say hi!

Acknowledgements

Holy shit, I wrote a book. I never believed this day would come, but the fact that you're reading this means it has.

So, first and foremost, I would like to thank YOU, the reader, for giving this little story of mine a chance. Each book a writer pens takes a little piece of their soul with it, and I'm grateful you've decided to share this moment with me. And what a moment, and journey, it has been. I truly hope you were able to fall in love with something about this story the way I have. Bryce and Josie may not stay my all-time favorite characters, but they'll always be my babies.

Before I get a little personal, I want to give credit where credit is due. Enni, my amazing cover designer from Yummy Book Covers, took some vague ideas and mood boards and brought Bryce and Josie to life in a way I could never imagine. Everything about this cover design, and the whole process working with her, was truly incredible. My editor, Ashley at Earley Editing, LLC, went above and beyond to help tighten this story so I can share it with you. I cannot thank these two enough for their wisdom, guidance, and talents.

To Claire and Amanda, who have been my absolute *rocks* during this whole process. Thank you for putting up with me, thank you for reading every single message I sent, and thank you for sharing so many of the adventures that inspired this story with me. This decade long friendship started with a mutual love of all things swimming and has grown into something I cherish more than I could ever say, and I love you both.

To my family, who encouraged me to go for it when all else seemed lost. I'm grateful for all you've done for me, continue to do for me, and all the grumpy, stressed Ashlyn moments you had to put up with. I love you so much.

Lastly, to Aunt Kathy, who should have been here for this. It sucks that you're not. As I plotted and wrote this, I missed you every step of the way, but knew you were always there. I did it!

About the Author

Ashlyn Harmon writes books with a little bit of sass, a whole lot of swoon-worthy moments, and characters who are real and relatable. She loves writing the kinds of female leads she wishes she had more access to—unapologetically confident in their bodies and who they are. No character of hers will ever go through a major physical makeover for love. Her books are authentic in the way they depict people and their imperfections.

She was born and raised in Omaha, Nebraska, and is still daydreaming of getting out one day. When she's not writing her next book, she's working on growing her editing business. She thrives on helping her fellow indie authors tell their stories. On the days she's not working, you can usually find her watching ghost hunting shows, daydreaming about her next vacation, hanging out with her corgi, Berkeley, or with her nose buried in a book.

She is currently working on a bunch of new projects, including the next books in the Adair Swimming Series. To stay up to date on all that's happening, visit her website or follow along on social media. By joining her mailing list, you'll receive a free BONUS chapter of *Maybe One Day*, and a glimpse into the monthly happenings of an author and editor. There will probably even be adorable corgi pictures.

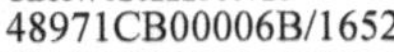

9 798990 011700